To Know Evil

To Know Evil

STEPHEN GASPAR

PEMBERLEY PRESS
CORONA DEL MAR

Published by
P E M B E R L E Y   P R E S S
P O Box 1027
Corona del Mar, CA 92625
www.pemberleypress.com

A member of The Authors Studio
www.theauthorsstudio.org

Cover design by Andrée Valley

ISBN13 978-0-9771913-9-0
LCCN 2009004858

Library of Congress Cataloging-in-Publication Data

Gaspar, Stephen.
  To know evil / Stephen Gaspar.
      p. cm.
  ISBN 978-0-9771913-9-0 (alk. paper)
  1. Monks--Italy--Fiction. 2. Italy--Fiction. I. Title.
  PR9199.4.G378T6 2009
  813'.6--dc22
                                          2009004858

This books is lovingly dedicated to
two of my favourite brothers,
Ryan and Tommy

A special thanks to my wife Susan,
the first reader of my work,
and to Aimee Parent,
my friend and fellow writer

Foreword

In northern Italy sits a small unassuming coastal town on the Ligurian Sea. Surrounding the town are low-lying hills that stand like silent sentinels, with heads bowed and hands folded in front of them in what would appear to be an almost pious posture. Leading northeast out of the town is an old dirt road that meanders into the hills. The road wanders almost aimlessly for sixty-six kilometres into the rugged countryside and comes to a sudden end at a river that flows past the base of a small mountain. The top of the mountain presents an excellent view of the entire area. Sitting atop the mountain is a partial wall of cut stone, rising above a mound of similar cut stone that has long since fallen into ruin. Aside from this account that follows, it is all that remains of a terrible tragedy brought on by an unspeakable evil.

The ruins date back to the second century B.C., and the Punic Wars. After Hannibal led his army in an unprecedented move over the Alps and invaded Rome from the north, the Roman Emperor commanded legionaries specially trained in engineering to erect a series of small outposts to help warn against any future invasion.

One such outpost was built atop a low mountain, referred to

in ancient Etruscan legend as Serpent's Mountain. The Romans knew little of the Etruscans and paid little heed to the reference, since no snakes were ever seen in the area, but those who knew the folklore about the site did not take the strange tales lightly. Stories of human sacrifice, sexual perversions, demon worship, and heinous tortures kept all but the very foolish—and the Romans—from treading in the shadow of the mountain.

Although the post witnessed Julius Caesar's troops as they passed it on their way to invade Gaul, this particular station experienced only minimal contact with the outside in two hundred fifty years. Indeed, assignment to this remote station was tantamount to being exiled into obscurity. A soldier sent there could consider his military career at an end. In the second century A.D., something strange overcame the men stationed at the outpost. In what can only be termed mass madness, the soldiers killed one another. This obscure fact has not made it into any history book, though the few who learned of it attempted, in vain, to explain the unusual event. Whether the madness was brought on by isolation or loneliness none could say, for there were no survivors to tell the tale.

It was not until the coming of the barbarians, more than three hundred years after this mysterious tragedy, that the distant outpost was used again, yet no army would dally there for long. Sometime before the fall of the Roman Empire, the station was found abandoned and claimed by an obscure order of Christian monks known as Gnostics. Over a period of two hundred years the Gnostic monks built an elaborate stone monastery atop the original outpost. These monks were renowned for their skills in masonry and carpentry, and other arts that are little known today. The monastery itself was a combination of Roman, Byzantine, and Gothic architecture. Its shape was basically square, with different buildings joined together, surrounding a spacious courtyard. The structure displayed an elegant simplicity, and was supported by tall columns and arches. In its day it could easily have been considered an architectural marvel.

It is worth noting that during the barbarian invasion in the third, fourth and fifth centuries, there is no record of the monastery ever being attacked by hostile forces. The Gnostic monks received few visitors from the secular world and were most particular about whom they allowed into their sect. It was this very particularity that condemned them to extinction. By the time the Benedictines discovered the monastery in the year 580, only one Gnostic remained, a Brother Alamar, who claimed to be 114 years old.

The Benedictine order was founded early in the sixth century by Benedict of Nursia, who established many monasteries in Italy, including the one at Monte Cassino. Benedict believed in a purposeful and ordered life, balanced by equal portions of prayer, work, and sleep. To guide monks in their search for salvation, Benedict penned a monastic legislative code. Known simply as the Rule, it spelled out in great detail the practices monks were to follow so they might earn a place in Christ's kingdom.

What follows is the story of what took place in that Benedictine monastery in the year 999 A.D., the incredible secrets buried there, and the terrible tragedy that brought an end to that fellowship of brothers.

One

Brother Thomas of Worms stood upright and pressed both hands to his lower back. He grimaced slightly as he raised his narrow eyes towards heaven. His thin lips moved in silent prayer, thanking God that his back could still bend. This northern climate was not good for his joints, and secretly he yearned for warmer countries. Brother Thomas looked over the garden. He was always sad when he harvested the last of his vegetables, for it heralded the beginning of winter and colder weather. He reached back and pulled his black hood over his tonsured head.

Down at the far end of the garden Thomas saw Brother Paolo's full form, standing over his basket. Brother Paolo did not move very fast, if he moved at all. He was sampling some of the vegetables he'd picked. Thomas wondered how many more full baskets there would be for the monastery if Brother Paolo did not help with the harvest. He eyed the other monk as he ate. May the Lord forgive him for such unkindly thoughts: the man even chewed slowly.

Brother Paolo turned and saw Thomas watching him. He bent over—though they were not standing close, Thomas could imagine the groan that accompanied the movement—and he picked up his baskets of bounty and headed in Thomas's direction. Thomas went back to his harvest. He knew it would be some time before the other man reached him.

"It was a very good harvest this year, Brother Thomas," Brother Paolo said convivially as he stopped nearby.

"Do you think?" Thomas responded, still bent over. There was some doubt in his words, but Brother Paolo seemed not to notice.

"The beans are quite exceptional and sweet."

"There is something about this soil . . ." Thomas scooped up some in his hand, straightened, and proceeded to examine it. "Even the rainfall is insufficient, which is strange for this climate. I do not know what it is, but . . ."

"These are the last two baskets," Brother Paolo said. "I could take them now . . . or do you wish for me to wait so we may go up together?" He added the last part with visible reluctance.

"No, go up now, Brother Paolo," Thomas said, "and I will follow in time."

Thomas watched the other walk away, waddling slightly as he went. It was better to let Brother Paolo go sooner. If they walked together Thomas would have to slow his pace considerably to match the slow gate of his rotund brother.

Thomas filled his two large baskets and straightened, wincing at the strain on his back. As he did, he spied two more filled baskets at the end of the garden where Paolo had been working. Thomas shook his head. Brother Paolo had obviously seen these two baskets, but had not wished to make another trip. That was why he had said his were the last two, and why he had not wished to wait for Thomas. He had feared Thomas would see the other baskets and suggest he come back for them. Of all the brothers in the monastery, Brother Paolo had the greatest aptness for getting out of any extra work.

Beyond the baskets Thomas saw the west road that led to the sea and the Frankish Kingdoms. Thomas turned east and to the fields where a score or more of the brothers were working. One of them saw Thomas and raised an arm in greeting. Thomas responded in kind. Like the garden, field work would soon be coming to an end.

Thomas of Worms bent down and picked up two of the four large baskets of freshly picked vegetables. He knew he would have to come back for the two remaining baskets. Under the weight of the baskets it was a slow plodding walk up the mountain path, so Brother Thomas recited the beatitudes as he walked.

Blessed are the poor in spirit: for theirs is the kingdom of heaven.
Blessed are they that mourn: for they will be comforted.
Blessed are the meek: for they shall inherit the earth.
Blessed are they who do hunger and thirst for righteousness:
for they shall be filled.
Blessed are the merciful: for they shall obtain mercy.
Blessed are the pure in heart: for they shall see God.
Blessed are the peacemakers: for they shall be called
the children of God.
Blessed are they who are persecuted for righteousness' sake:
for theirs is the kingdom of heaven.

Brother Thomas of Worms was dressed in the Benedictine habit, a tunic and scapular worn underneath a long full gown of heavy coarse wool tied at the waist with a cord. Attached to the gown was a cowl to cover his head. The early Benedictines had worn a habit of white, the colour of undyed wool, but some time ago the colour had been changed to black, which had garnered the Benedictine brothers the name "black monks."

He was about half way up the mountain trail when he passed two other brothers coming down the path. Though they acknowledged one another, they did not stop to speak, as all had duties to carry out. Many saw superfluous talk as a luxury, which went against their vows.

As he approached the monastery, Brother Thomas looked up at the structure. It was solidly built, practically a fortress. The outside of the monastery was rectangular, with high walls as if built to keep the divinity inside. Or were they to keep something else out? The monastery appeared more dismal and brooding today. Thomas could not quite rationalize his feelings towards the structure, yet he felt something was not quite right. He had been to other holy places in Christendom, some not as large and grand as this, while others had been truly awe-inspiring. But this one was different. He had known it when he had come here two years ago.

Thomas gazed about the surrounding countryside. The hills stood almost sullen, like a group of cowled monks with heads bowed and shoulders stooped as if prepared to receive a rebuke. A dull sun lay hidden behind layers of grey clouds lending the landscape an unsettling air. Though birds were seen to fly overhead, none ever nested in the vicinity. Little wildlife scampered through the woods, as if their instincts foretold of an unnatural danger. Was it this moody setting that gave the monastery its gloomy appearance, or was it the other way around? At times, Brother Thomas felt as if the monastery possessed an evil unto itself.

Was it evil, he wondered? Brother Domitian had often spoken of evil. Though he would never admit it, Thomas did not believe in evil as a tangible force, an independent thing. He believed the writings of St. Paul implied that evil existed in man's heart, forever locked in a constant struggle with goodness, and it was up to man to guard against it, to see that the evil did not win. Thomas could not share these thoughts with his brothers, of course—they could be grounds for heresy. He shook off his musings as he entered the monastery through the main gate on the western wall.

Brother Thomas passed through a pair of large oak double doors that hung on heavy ornate iron hinges. Though the two baskets were a burden, they did not slow him down. Unlike most of the monks, who took slow contemplative steps, Thomas walked with long determined strides as if he were constantly late for something. He strode across the wide spacious open courtyard, surrounded by a pillared and arched cloister, to the kitchen directly opposite the main gate. He entered the kitchen and was met by a melding of odours. In a large open hearth that could easily accommodate a grown man, coals burned, and over the coals hung a black iron cauldron, suspended in a hinged stand, in which brewed what some in the monastery referred to as soup. Standing by the pot and stirring it with a large wooden spoon stood Brother Bernard, with his sad, petulant face, tired eyes, and crooked nose.

Wordlessly Brother Thomas approached the cook and proudly displayed his baskets of bounty. Brother Bernard regarded the food almost contemptuously and motioned for Thomas to place the baskets on the table. Leaning sideways over the soup, Brother Thomas took in a long audible breath through his nostrils and smiled approvingly at the cook who stared blankly back. Thomas gave a slight shrug of his shoulders and put the baskets down on the table. He exited the kitchen, dreading whatever unpalatable concoction Bernard would make out of his vegetables.

Thomas walked through the western gate and stood for a moment before heading down the mountain to fetch the last two baskets of vegetables from his garden. From atop the mountain he could see the surrounding countryside. The mountain dwarfed the surrounding hills. It was a lonely, desolate spot, just the kind of place a man might come to find God and salvation. As his gaze shifted to the west, Thomas saw the approach of a lone traveler. Even from far off, Thomas could see the grey habit of a fellow ascetic, and he hastened down the mountain to meet him.

Thomas stood waiting on the edge of the garden with his laden baskets at his feet for the stranger to approach. The monk was perhaps several years older than Thomas, was heavily bearded, and carried a small travelling pack. The features on his sober face were dark, and from what Thomas could observe, he deduced the man was from the East.

"Greetings," Thomas called out in a friendly fashion. He did not forget his Hebrews: *Be not forgetful to entertain strangers: for thereby some have entertained angels unawares.* The stranger's appearance and manner were anything but angelic, yet if the devil could assume an appealing disguise, then why not angels the reverse? Whether the stranger be angel, demon, or man, Brother Thomas met him openly.

The stranger did not answer or acknowledge Thomas in any way until he approached and stood close. Since the Rule called for every guest to the monastery to be treated as Christ himself, Thomas waited to greet the man with a holy kiss or a brotherly embrace. But the man made no attempt at even the slightest contact, except to ask curtly, "This is the monastery of St. Benedict?"

Thomas was taken aback at the man's brusque manner.

"Yes," he replied, "this is the monastery of St. Benedict. Welcome."

Without a word or gesture the man turned and began his ascent of the mountain. Thomas snatched up his vegetables and escorted him matching the stranger stride for stride.

"I am Brother Thomas of Worms," he said, and waited for a reply.

After a moment, it was reluctantly given. "Brother Lazarus." The man's voice was low and coarse, and Thomas detected an eastern accent.

"You have come a far way, I see, Brother Lazarus," Thomas said as they plodded up the mountain path. The man did not speak, but this did not daunt Thomas in any way. "I trust you had a safe and comfortable sea voyage."

The man stopped and regarded Thomas suspiciously. "How do you know I came by sea?"

"Though you came by the western road I see by your manner of speech and dress that you are from the East, for I have travelled to the East myself," Thomas said. "I would conclude that you are from Constantinople. Therefore, undoubtedly, you travelled by ship and were put ashore at the coastal village of Lerici, or perhaps La Spezia, and from there came on by foot."

"I may have been journeying eastward by land from a country west of here," the stranger proposed. "How do you know I arrived by ship?"

"You have the smell of the sea on you," Thomas said simply. "I find it interesting, though, that you have come so far expressly to visit our monastery."

The man regarded Thomas with hostility. He clearly did not appreciate the black monk's ability to divine so much of his affairs.

"Who said I came here for such a purpose?" Brother Lazarus demanded, his dark, deep-set eyes narrowing.

"When we met, you inquired about the monastery, and you referred to it by name as if it were your destination. It would be remarkable if you had heard of this monastery from such a distance. You have not come across us by chance, but for a singular purpose."

Brother Lazarus stared at Thomas openmouthed. He studied the black monk's light green eyes as if searching for a hint of intent.

"Your order does not call for a vow of silence, I see," Brother Lazarus observed.

Thomas could not help but grin at the man's insinuation, and neither spoke another word until they were inside the walls of the monastery.

Brother Thomas directed Brother Lazarus to the abbot's chamber, and the two parted company. Thomas then delivered the remaining vegetables to the kitchen. He left the kitchen and was in hopes of visiting the library, when he heard the bell toll for *tierce*—the midmorning work of God. *Tierce* was only one of eight communal prayers of the Divine Office, which began long before dawn and ended at nightfall. When the Divine Office was signaled, every monk of the monastery stopped whatever he was doing to congregate in the church. Once everyone was inside, the *opus Dei* began with a psalm, silent prayer, a hymn, and readings from the Bible and the Church Fathers.

One hundred fifty psalms were sung each week—or more accurately, the psalms were chanted in a low melodious tone. Most everyone enjoyed the chants, mainly because of Brother Nicholas, a fresh-faced youth whose beautiful soprano voice filled the church to overflowing. As the soloist, Brother Nicholas would sing a line that was repeated by the other monks, or sometimes the order was reversed. The daily chanting dated back to Jewish tradition of worship, and for the Benedictine monks the chant was spiritually connected to every aspect of their lives. The chants radiated through their entire beings, uniting them and bringing them into contact with God. It was truly *musica mundana*— music of the spheres—and the very sound could conjure up images of celestial choirs. Not all the brothers had fine voices, but the soloist, Brother Nicholas, was extraordinary.

Nicholas had been in the monastery since he was a very young man, and he was not yet twenty years old. Brother Nicholas had been chosen as soloist for his exceptional singing voice which, when raised in the great echoing walls of the church, sounded more like the voice of an angel. When the other brothers joined in, it was the closest thing to a heavenly choir the monastery had ever witnessed. Though none of the monks in the monastery would admit it—even to themselves—some of them felt their eyes drawn to Brother Nicholas as he sang. Nicholas possessed an enchanting quality. Perhaps it was his voice, or perhaps his youthful, gentle, comely face and wide blue-green eyes that made some regard him as a precious cherub. Whatever the attraction, regarding Nicholas in that manner was not at all holy, and most of the monks endeavoured to drive such thoughts from their heads.

Most, but not all.

While in his choir stall, Brother Thomas looked over at Brother Nicholas who was attempting to catch his attention. Nicholas's anxious demeanour told Thomas the young monk wished to speak with him. The two were good friends and often talked in private, away from the watchful eye of the prior, Brother Vittorio. Though speaking was not forbidden in the monastery, supererogatory talking was frowned upon.

After *tierce* Thomas and Nicholas left the church separately. They would rendezvous in a small alcove in the library, but Thomas thought it best to take a long and circuitous route to the tryst. He was cutting across the courtyard when Brother Ferrutio caught his attention.

"Brother Thomas," Ferrutio spoke in the same low tone all the brothers used. Thomas of Worms pretended he did not hear, and walked on. "Brother Thomas!" Ferrutio spoke louder, though it almost pained him to do so. Thomas did not wish to cause Brother Ferrutio any more discomfort, so he stopped and turned towards him.

"Ah, Brother Ferrutio, good day," Thomas said.

"Thank God I found you, Brother Thomas."

"Why? What is wrong, Brother?"

"The prior, Brother Vittorio, is looking for you."

"Oh, is it serious?"

"With Brother Vittorio, everything is serious," Ferrutio said, not trying to make Thomas smile, but he did.

"Thank you, Brother," Thomas said and turned to leave.

"Are you going to Brother Vittorio now?" Ferrutio asked, concerned.

"Where would you suggest I find him?" Thomas asked, though he truly did not wish to know.

Brother Ferrutio assumed a sober expression and said, "I do not know, but I believe you should find him. Perhaps you should remain here, and I will find Brother Vittorio and bring him to you. Or perhaps we should—"

"Brother Ferrutio, do not trouble yourself," Thomas said, hoping to calm the man. "I shall find Brother Vittorio, or he shall find me. Do not fear. All will transpire the way it should."

"I certainly pray so," Brother Ferrutio called after Thomas as the German monk walked away, then called out, "If I see Brother Vittorio, where should I say you will be?"

"I was out in the garden, and I should get back to it," Thomas called back.

"But shouldn't you remain about the monastery?"

Thomas walked off, not bothering to respond.

Thomas did not like to speak in a deceiving manner, and he trusted God would forgive him. He was careful as he made his way to the library, hoping he would not run into anyone else, especially the prior. Fortunately for Thomas and Nicholas, however, the chancellor was not in the room and they could converse in some privacy. Whenever the two met they spoke in low hushed tones, which caused them to stand very close to each other when they conversed.

Brother Nicholas was the chancellor's assistant. He was also shorter and slimmer than Thomas, and had more hair on his head despite his tonsure.

"Did you harvest the last of your vegetables?" Nicholas asked, in a voice barely above a whisper.

Thomas nodded. He would not speak if a gesture sufficed, yet he did not mind speaking. In fact, he suspected he would have made an accomplished orator. "We should be feasting on fresh vegetables for a few weeks. After that . . ."

Nicolas smiled knowingly at this veiled commentary on Brother Bernard's culinary skills—or lack thereof.

"We received a visitor this morning," Thomas said, as he stroked his beard contemplatively. "Brother Lazarus from Constantinople. One has to wonder why he is here. I hesitate to say it, but he appeared very suspicious."

"I hesitate to say it, Brother Thomas, but you find most people very suspicious."

Thomas regarded Nicholas with a look of mock indignation and asked, "Was there a specific reason you wished to speak with me?"

"I asked you here, Brother Thomas, because I found something very exciting—a remarkable find!" Nicholas said, with his usual youthful enthusiasm.

"What is it?"

"In the library I came across what looks like an old, common psalter."

"And what is so exciting about an old book of psalms?" Thomas asked.

"It is not the psalms that are the find, but what was written beneath them."

"Are you saying the book contains palimpsests?"

"Yes!" Nicholas said, grinning. "You can still see the writing beneath the psalms, but it is faint."

"And what is so fascinating about what is written underneath?"

"Though the writing has practically all been scraped away, I was able to decipher some of the words," Nicholas said proudly. "They allude to the first Benedictines who came to this monastery."

"That is amazing!" Thomas exclaimed. "Just how—"

Brother Thomas stopped as he heard a door open to the library. Thomas and Nicholas eased into the shadow of the alcove. They stood side by side as they listened to the soft, slow tread of sandaled feet entering the library and coming closer and closer. Though he could not see clearly from his position, Brother Thomas suspected the person to be very close now. He did not wish to be found with Brother Nicholas in this way, so placing a restraining hand upon the shoulder of his companion, Thomas stepped rather quickly out of the shadows of the alcove.

"Ah, Brother Vittorio!" Thomas half shouted so as to startle the monk.

His sudden appearance and exclamation had the desired effect, for Brother Vittorio jumped back in surprise and fear.

"Oh, my apologies, Brother," said Thomas, laying a hand upon the other's arm. "Did I frighten you?"

Vittorio pulled back from Thomas's touch. His face and manner displayed both suspicion and trepidation—as they often did—and his close-set eyes darted from Brother Thomas to the alcove. "Why were you not in the garden, Brother Thomas?" he asked accusingly. "You told Brother Ferrutio you were going to the garden."

"Brother Ferrutio must have misunderstood," Thomas said. "I told him that I *had* been in the garden picking vegetables."

Brother Vittorio regarded Thomas suspiciously and asked, "What were you doing in there?" He had to look up at Thomas, for he was a small man with quick, nervous gestures.

"I came to the library looking for a book."

"What book?" Vittorio asked, and his flat pugnacious nose twitched ferret-like as if trying to sniff out deception.

"I came looking for one of the many Latin works of Jerome. Perhaps you know the work, Brother. Jerome explains how our distrust and suspicions are only reflections of our own sinful nature."

"No, I do not know it," Brother Vittorio uttered, ignorant of the other's meaning.

"Was there something you required, Brother?" Thomas asked in his typical friendly fashion.

Vittorio stared into the alcove as he spoke. "The abbot wishes to see you. He sent me to bring you to him."

Thomas took two steps towards the library door. Vittorio remained rooted staring into the alcove. The monk took a hesitant step towards it.

"Should we not hasten to the abbot?" Thomas said, turning to the other and gesturing towards the door.

Brother Vittorio turned from the alcove. With a self-righteous look, he brushed past Thomas and out of the library.

Like every room in the monastery, the abbot's chamber, which was separate from the other monks', was simple and austere. The room was furnished with a small crude table and two uncomfortable chairs. A large closed Bible stood upon a tall stand, and beyond that a plain curtain hung dividing the room. Two small, high windows lit the otherwise gloomy space. Brother Michael had been chosen abbot of the monastery by its members twelve years ago and would remain abbot until the day he died, which at his present age of fifty-one could be in a day, a year, or—God willing—even a decade. As was with many of the brothers in the monastery, the abbot's face was solemn, but also weary, as if the weight of responsibility for the salvation of all the souls committed to his care rested entirely upon his shoulders. Every time he spoke it was with a heaviness, as if those very words would be his last.

Brother Vittorio escorted Thomas into the abbot's chamber and stood sentry by the door.

The abbot stood at his desk, studying a document written upon a large sheet of parchment. The abbot himself was a large man whose heavy breathing was audible and regular. His small pea-like eyes looked even smaller set deep into his fat round face.

"You may leave us, Brother Vittorio," the abbot said not looking up.

Vittorio hesitated. "Are . . . are you certain?" he stammered. Brother Vittorio knew what was to come, and he eagerly desired to witness it.

The abbot looked up and met the other's eyes briefly. The look alone was an answer. Brother Vittorio promptly left the room.

Thomas turned and watched the prior leave. His head twisted back at the mention of his name.

"So, Brother Thomas, how long have you been with us now?" the abbot asked, sitting down behind his desk. His eyes seldom looked directly at the person to whom he spoke, almost as if the person were beneath his notice.

"Two years, Abbot," replied Thomas.

"And before you came to us, you were in . . . ?"

"Lyons," Thomas responded.

"And prior to that?"

"Britain."

"And prior to that?"

Thomas took a breath and said: "Cordoba, Cyrene, Alexandria, Jerusalem, Damascus, Constantinople, and Athens."

"You are quite well travelled," the abbot remarked casually.

"I believe a man should not let much grass grow beneath his sandals," Thomas said, just as casually. "I was fortunate as a very young man that my father's position allowed me to travel and to see some of the world. When I took up the Order, I retained the desire to travel. Do my past travels have anything to do with Brother Lazarus of Constantinople?"

The abbot started. "What do you mean?" he asked. His fat face shook slightly as he spoke. "How do you know of Brother Lazarus? He arrived only this morning."

"Yes, I know," Thomas said. "I met him at the foot of the mountain as I was returning from the garden. I thought it strange that an Orthodox monk would come all this way to visit our monastery."

"Brother Thomas, this has nothing to do with Brother Lazarus, and I wish you not to mention him again," the abbot admonished, showing more perturbation than Thomas thought was warranted.

"As to your travels, Brother Thomas, do you plan to leave us one day?" the abbot asked, regaining his composure.

Thomas hesitated, then slowly said: "I did have hopes of seeing Rome one day."

"Brother Thomas, you are originally from . . . ?"

"I am from Worms, Abbot."

"Ah, yes, Worms. That is in Germany."

"Yes, Abbot."

"Perhaps that is where the problem lies."

"What problem is that?" Thomas asked. "And what has it to do with my coming from Germany?"

"Brother Thomas, as members of the Benedictine order we took a vow of chastity, poverty, and obedience to the abbot. We live a communal life of working together, eating together, praying together . . . and we are expected to live in this monastery forever. Though we do open our doors to anyone, we do expect some sense of loyalty, and you have just admitted that you plan to leave us. You are what our patron, Benedict of Nursia, referred to as a *gyrovague*, one of those who spend a good deal of their lives drifting from region to region in different monasteries."

"Is that all?" Thomas asked.

"No, that is not all," the abbot said truculently. "Though we do not expect a vow of silence from our brothers, unnecessary conversation is avoided. You have been known to speak excessively, more than any other brother in the monastery."

"I see. And what does my coming from Germany have to do with it?"

"I am certain you will not take this the wrong way, Brother Thomas. My intent is not to besmirch our Emperor, Otto III, but as northerners, you are relatively new to our ways. It was not long ago that your Germanic tribes were converted."

"I am not certain what you are trying to say, Lord Abbot."

"Just why are you here, Brother?" the abbot asked.

"I am here for the same reason we all are here," Thomas stated. "To strive for the goal of personal salvation."

"And you believe educating yourself in the secular world will help you do that?" Thomas showed a hint of surprise, and the abbot added: "Yes, I am well aware of your personal studies. What do you have to say about them?"

"Only that, if we are to become wise, then surely knowledge is the path to wisdom," Brother Thomas said.

To which the abbot quoted, "*Let the wise display his wisdom not in words but in good works.* St. Clement I, late first century."

"My personal studies, as you call them, may be secular, but they are not ungodly. Our patron, Benedict of Nursia, himself, was an educated man."

"Benedict of Nursia renounced his earthly studies in favour of spiritual pursuits," said the abbot. "You would do well to remember the words of Augustine of Hippo from the early fifth century: *I desire to know God and my own soul. Nothing else; nothing whatever.*"

"I believe any enlightenment of this world is worthwhile," Thomas countered. "*For we must first understand ourselves before we can begin to understand God.*"

"I am afraid I am not familiar with that passage," the abbot said.

"Thomas of Worms, late tenth century."

The abbot let out a long, laboured breath and regarded Thomas impatiently. He said, "If you must study, Brother Thomas, remember First Thessalonians: *Study to be quiet.*" He waited for Thomas to respond, but the German monk used good sense and remained silent. "Perhaps you are not clear on your vocation," the abbot said. "Perhaps you have not thought through what this manner of life entails. Perhaps the Benedictine order is not the one for you."

Thomas nodded his head slowly. "Abbot, I will leave your monastery if you so desire. I would never stay anywhere I am not wanted or welcomed."

The abbot did not respond immediately. The two men stood silently in the room, each trying to determine the true character of the other. They were both strong men in their own right, and neither sought a battle of wills.

"I am not asking you to leave the monastery, Brother Thomas," the abbot began. "That is a decision you must come to on your own. I am telling you this as a means to help you find your way, to aid you in your spiritual pursuits."

"For that, my Lord Abbot, I am humbly grateful."

"And to aid you further in this worthwhile endeavour, I am commissioning you, purely as an act of devotion and penance of labour, to copy out a New Testament book."

Brother Thomas stared mutely at the abbot. After a moment, he found his voice.

"Are you certain this is the right devotion for me?" Thomas spoke. "My abilities as a scribe are not the finest."

"All the more reason to practice."

"Abbot, please—"

"Brother Thomas, it is done," the abbot said with finality, and their eyes met briefly.

Thomas knew that tone and that look. He decided not to pursue the matter. The German monk bowed briefly, then turned to leave the abbot's quarters, but stopped at the door and asked, "What book would you wish me to copy?"

The abbot paused for a moment with his eyes turned up towards the ceiling as if waiting for divine inspiration. "I believe The Revelation to John would benefit you considerably. Brother Gedeon will supply you with parchment."

Thomas of Worms bowed to the abbot again and left the chamber. He walked down the corridor with decisiveness and purpose. He had not foreseen this latest outcome, and there was little he could do but follow the abbot's direction. He had, on rare occasions, gone against the abbot's will, but never without a very good reason and never in a way that it would be obvious. He would have to carry out the duties of a scribe.

Brother Thomas went in search of Brother Gedeon who was the monastery's *percamenarius*—its parchment maker. Brother Gedeon was a very ordinary, nondescript man of middle age and medium height, with a very forgettable face. His only distinction was that he smelled bad. It was not an odour that could easily be identified. It was not quite like rotting flesh, not quite mould-covered vegetables, but it was a thick stench, a sickening putridity that once experienced could never be forgotten. It was a smell that was exclusive, thank God, to Brother Gedeon.

Since parchment was made from animal skin, Brother Gedeon followed the process from start to finish, beginning with raising the animals himself. Though parchment could be made from virtually any skin, the monastery kept pens of goat and sheep for just such purpose. Though Gedeon had learned long ago that the finest parchment was made from calfskin, the monastery was, alas, a poor one and could not afford cattle.

To make parchment Brother Gedeon carefully washed the flayed skin of the sheep or goat and then let it soak in a vat of clean water for a day and a night. It was then placed in another vat containing a solution of lime and water for eight to sixteen days, depending on the weather. Several times a day the vat was stirred with a large wooden paddle to help loosen the hair on the hide. The skins were then removed from the vat and laid over a log where Gedeon would scrape off the hair using a blunt, curved blade. Opposite the grain side, any remaining flesh was removed. The skin was then soaked in fresh water for two more days. Brother Gedeon would then take the skin and stretch it on a wooden frame and while the skin was still wet, he would carefully scrape both sides of the skin with a curved blade. The skin was then allowed to dry in the sun. By then, the skin was tight and was again scraped to a desired thinness. Finally, the parchment could be removed and rolled up until needed. This long, smelly process lent Brother Gedeon his very distinct odour.

Thomas knew he would find Brother Gedeon behind the monastery among the animal pens. It was well known by most of the brothers that Gedeon was usually the first to wake and liked to inspect the pens early in the morning. Aside from sheep and goats, the monastery also raised geese, pigs, and chickens. To Brother Thomas it appeared that Brother Gedeon was more at ease with his animals than he was with people.

"Good day, Brother Gedeon," Thomas greeted him, careful to stay upwind of the *percamenarius*.

Gedeon glanced in the other monk's direction and grunted a greeting.

"All the animals are looking well today," Thomas commented.

Gedeon again grunted in reply. It occurred to Thomas that perhaps Brother Gedeon spent a trifle too much time with his animals.

"You certainly do excellent work raising these beasts. It shows in the parchment you produce."

Brother Gedeon grunted again and said, "You obviously want something, Brother Thomas. Best tell me what it is now, and forgo all the pleasantries."

"I require parchment, Brother."

Gedeon grunted a burst of surprise. "I did not know you listed scribe among your many talents."

"Neither did I, but the abbot has commissioned me to copy a book."

"So it is not for anyone in particular?"

Thomas shrugged his uncertainty. "It is for the abbot. It will most likely be put away in the library, and perhaps one day find its way to some poor church or wayward monastery."

"Would you be willing to use palimpsests?"

Brother Thomas winced. He did not relish the idea of rubbing down parchment that had already been written upon to use over again.

"I would prefer new parchment, Brother *Percamenarius*."

Just then the bell tolled for *sext*, the noontime prayer.

"Whatever you prefer, Brother Thomas," Gedeon said, "will have to wait."

After *sext* the monks gathered in the refectory for dinner, the main meal of the day. The meal, eaten in silence, usually consisted of soup, bread, fruit with cheese or eggs, along with Brother Thomas's fresh vegetables. Meat or fish during a meal was rare, and would only be served on special occasions, but never on a fast day. Today was a day of fast.

After lunch, Thomas met Gedeon in the scriptorium, a room on the second floor and next to the library. Inside, away from the fresh air, the *percamenarius's* odour was even more offensive.

The scriptorium was smaller than the library, with several slanted tables the monks used for copying out sacred texts and other works pertaining to the Faith. The tables were set up in individual cloisters so the scribes might have some privacy to concentrate on their work. No candles were allowed in the scriptorium for fear of fire, so all work was done during the daytime when sunlight shone in through high windows. Only one other monk was in the scriptorium when Thomas and Gedeon entered, Brother Bartholomew, the master scribe and *armarius*. He sat hunched over his table, his once sharp, penetrating eyes squinting at the words he endeavoured to copy. Thomas had observed Brother Bartholomew's scripting, which was, of course, letter perfect and very neat. This surprised Thomas of Worms since the master scribe's hands shook considerably. Thomas wondered how the *armarius* could maintain such fine and detailed work, and concluded that the ways of God were awesome and wondrous. Though Thomas and Gedeon spoke little, and very softly when they did, Brother Bartholomew would occasionally stop his work to glare intolerantly at them for their distracting behaviour.

Gedeon led Thomas to the back of the room where rolled up pieces of parchment lay neatly tucked away in numerous wooden cubical compartments. They began to select parchments, not the very best parchments, or even fine pieces, for Brother Gedeon could not see wasting his best and finest on Brother Thomas and some minor work. With a sufficient bundle gathered, Thomas brought his parchments to a table in the scriptorium and, with a knife called a *lunellum*, he began to trim his parchments to be the exact same size. He then folded each parchment in half, which would make up four pages. Since parchment was actually assignments. Though it was at the discretion of the abbot to assign work to scribes, Bartholomew resented it, as he felt it was an infringement upon his role as *armarius*.

To match the ruled lines from sheet to sheet, Brother Thomas had to perforate several sheets at once with a sharp instrument, and then score lines upon the pages using a dull knife, being careful not to cut through the parchment. Thomas had just finished this when the bell sounded for *none*, the mid-afternoon prayer.

After *none*, Thomas approached Brother Domitian, the chancellor. He was the keeper of the monastery's books, its most valuable treasures, and Brother Domitian guarded them jealously. His job was to catalogue the books as well as keep a close eye on any that were being used. Like many of the monks who held a prominent position in the monastery, Brother Domitian was elderly as well as crotchety, and he resented any distraction that disturbed his daily routine. His face and hands were wrinkled, and his skin was deathly pale from spending the majority of his life in the library, seldom venturing out into the daylight. Thomas could not help observing that the chancellor's insalubrious pallor resembled the colour of aged parchment.

"Brother Domitian," Thomas began, "I find I am in need of a book."

Though Thomas had spoken in a mere whisper, Brother Domitian gave the German monk an indignant look and motioned for him to lower his voice.

"I have been commissioned to copy out The Revelation to John," Thomas informed him quietly.

"I am sorry, Brother Thomas, but I do not think we have an adequate copy," the chancellor responded. Though his pale lips moved, Thomas found he had to strain his ears to hear him.

"I am certain if you look hard enough you will find one," Thomas said mildly. "I would not wish to return to the abbot and report that in the entire library we do not have The Revelation to John. We most likely would have to borrow one from another monastery which means we would have to lend them one of our books."

Brother Domitian glared at Thomas with as much dislike as monks are allowed.

"Very well," Domitian spoke gruffly. "Come with me and we shall find the book you require."

Both the library and the scriptorium were on the second level of the monastery. The library was a modest-sized room, containing a few small desks and chairs. The books, which numbered eighty-three in all, were stored flat in wall cupboards that were tucked into cloisters identical to the ones found in the scriptorium. Thomas suspected the two spaces had once been one large room, but that at some time a wall had been raised between them. High atop some of the cupboards were elaborate shrines in which were stored the monastery's most precious and revered books.

Standing before a cupboard Brother Domitian began a systematic search as he ran his finger along the bindings of all the books upon the shelves. When Thomas reached up to touch a book, Domitian slapped his hand away. Rebuked, Thomas stepped back and allowed the chancellor to continue his search. Brother Nicholas entered the library and approached Thomas, but turned away when, with a silent gesture, Thomas indicated that now was not a good time to be seen together. After his meeting with the abbot, Thomas deemed it prudent not to be seen speaking with Brother Nicholas. Nicholas gave a knowing nod of his head, and walked away.

While perusing the lowest shelf of the fourth cupboard, Brother Domitian gave a low sound in his throat that Thomas took to be of a positive nature. From the shelf the chancellor drew out an old book. The cover of the book was dark with no design upon it, while the pages seemed uneven. The book was clearly not one of the library's treasures.

"Here it is," Brother Domitian announced without enthusiasm. "You may use this to copy from. It is an *editio vulgata*—a common edition. It was brought here by a monk from Spain many years ago. He died here and the book became the property of the library." The chancellor leafed casually through the pages, and Brother Thomas held out his hand for it. Though Domitian had little affection for the book, he still seemed reluctant to hand it over. "I expect this book to be returned to me personally when you have completed copying it," the chancellor said in a low voice, with a hint of a threat in his tone.

Brother Thomas took the book graciously but wordlessly and proceeded to the scriptorium. The book was indeed Spanish, though written in Latin, and contained not only The Revelation to John but also of Jude, and the three books of John. Brother Domitian's appraisal of the book had been quite correct; it was not a treasure. The script was very ordinary, the pages were unlined and trimmed unevenly. Indeed, the entire work was quite common, yet the monk who had scripted it must have thought highly of his work for at the end of the text he had written a warning to would-be thieves. It read:

IF ANYONE TAKE AWAY THIS BOOK, LET HIM DIE SUCH A DEATH THAT HIS BODY BE BROKEN, HIS MIND FEVERED, HIS SKIN FESTERED, SO THAT NO ONE WILL LOOK UPON HIM AND THE BIRDS WILL PICK AT HIS FLESH.

"Spaniards." Brother Thomas shook his head, and with half a grin, said to himself, "They have quite a mean streak."

Before he could begin his work, Brother Thomas needed instruments with which to write. In a cupboard in the scriptorium he snatched up a large selection of quills made from goose feathers that had already been dried and hardened. He laid them on his desk and looking over his supplies saw that he needed ink.

Thomas approached Brother Bartholomew's work station

and stood watching the *armarius* toil almost lovingly over his parchment. He dipped his quill ever so gently into the ink pot and withdrew it in one smooth flowing motion. Again and again he plunged his tip into the liquid with an experienced rhythm developed over years of practice. He scripted slowly, but with precision and grace. The quill barely seemed to touch the parchment, but left its black trail upon it. He performed it as a labour of deep love, done with pure affection.

So engrossed in his work, Brother Bartholomew did not even seem aware of Brother Thomas's presence until the latter quietly cleared his throat. The *armarius* looked up irritably with a start, and wordlessly inquired the reason for the interruption.

"I am in need of ink," Thomas whispered.

There were a few small inkpots upon the master scribe's desk. He picked up each, looking for one with ink, found one, and pushed it gruffly into Thomas's hand.

"The next time you are in need of ink you will have to make your own! And do not bother me again unless it is important!" He returned to his work.

Thomas examined the ink as he took it back to his desk. The black ink used by the monks was a carbon ink, made from charcoal or soot mixed with a variety of plant gums or sap.

Brother Thomas was almost ready to begin. With his knife, he sharpened the end of the feather shaft, and then slightly squared off the sharp tip. Carefully he put a fine slit up the centre of the shaft. Thomas would keep his knife handy while he worked for he knew he would need to sharpen his quill periodically. Now he was ready to begin.

Just then, the bell tolled to *vespers*, or evening prayers. After that, would be supper. Brother Thomas decided to wait until morning and begin fresh.

Two

As with the *opus Dei*, meals in the monastery were taken in common. The refectory was a large room containing two massive wooden tables with long heavy benches on either side. The black monks entered the refectory and paused to wash their hands in basins that sat by the door. After drying their hands each monk bowed to the high table and stood by his place until the prior and abbot arrived and took their places at the head of the table. As the youngest member of the monastery, Brother Nicholas was seated farthest from the head of the table. Brother Thomas's place was somewhere in the middle. The abbot rang a bell to signal grace. After grace all sat in silence while the food was brought from the kitchen and served first to the eldest brothers down to the youngest. Today's evening meal consisted of bread, wine, and soup that was simply the leftover stew served at midday to which Brother Bernard had merely added water. Brother Nicholas could never understand why Thomas always spoke in such a derogatory manner of Brother Bernard's cooking. They were not by any means bad meals, and as Nicholas would often hear spoken about the monastery, *fabas indulcet fames*—hunger sweetens beans.

During mealtime the brothers were particularly mindful of their manners, and were careful not to spill precious food or drink lest one be compelled to get up and do penance in the middle of the refectory. As prescribed in the Rule, there were readings during mealtime, and all meals were eaten in silence so as not to interrupt the monk who read from the Bible at a pulpit. Despite the silence that was observed during mealtime, the monks were able to communicate, very discreetly, albeit through a series of gestures. Moving the forefinger up and down the thumb at eye level simply meant, "Pass the wine, please."

Thomas and Nicholas did not sit close together, but they could still see each other from their seats. Through eye contact, they arranged to meet after supper in their usual nighttime rendezvous—outside the wall behind the monastery.

The night was cool, and a northern wind caused Brother Nicholas to turn his cowl up on his head, but he was reluctant to stand close to the wall of the monastery. The low clouds blocked out all moonlight, and the blackness lent Nicholas an eerie discomfort. All was quiet except for the sound of the wind. Nicholas did not know how long he waited for Thomas, but the brother's absence caused him further unease.

"Brother Nicholas!"

The sound of his own name caused Nicholas to jump.

"Why, Brother Nicholas, did I frighten you?" Thomas asked as he approached the other.

"What? No. Well . . . yes, a little," Nicholas said.

"I am sorry. I should not have crept up on you that way."

"What became of you, Brother?" Nicholas asked. "After this morning, I barely saw you again."

"The abbot has doubts as to my spiritual wellbeing," Thomas told him. "He quoted Augustine to me."

"A truly spiritual source," Nicholas commented.

"My dear Brother Nicholas, it was Augustine who said, 'Lord, give me chastity and continence, but not just now.'"

Nicholas suppressed a grin.

"Our abbot has banished me to the scriptorium to copy out a book as an act of devotion." Thomas spoke with disdain.

"Do you consider the task overly arduous?"

Thomas shrugged. "It is said that Origen of Alexandria castrated himself to prove his obedience to God. I suppose I should not consider my penance too severe."

Brother Nicholas smiled openly this time. "I do not believe it will hurt you," he said, then added, "The writing, I mean. After all, *qui scribit bis legit*—he who writes reads twice. Besides, with you in the scriptorium we will be working closer together, and it should make communication easier."

"Yes. The last time we spoke, you said something regarding a book and some early Benedictines."

"Yes," Nicholas uttered with suppressed excitement. "Yesterday Brother Gregori returned a book to the library. He said Brother Bartholomew had used it some time ago and had forgotten to return the book. Brother Gregori was afraid Brother Domitian would be upset with Brother Bartholomew for not returning the book sooner, so he asked if I could replace it for him. When I went to check on the book, I could not find it in Brother Domitian's catalogue."

"Did you question Brother Domitian regarding the book?"

Nicholas turned away abashed, not wishing to look the other monk in the face.

"Well . . . I . . . thought maybe I best not, because . . . I did not wish to get Brother Bartholomew into trouble. Besides, there was something about the book I wished you to see."

"Brother, what you are trying to say is that you did not ask Brother Domitian, but decided, rather, to make some mysterious episode out of all this."

"But it is a fantastic find, Brother Thomas! I am certain of it!"

"Then we are duty bound to inform the abbot and the

the skin of an animal, one side was the inner skin, and the other was the hide where the fur had been. Brother Thomas layered his parchment so that a skin side would touch a skin side of the next sheet, and the hair side of adjacent sheets would face each other. This method allowed facing pages to be similar, to give a more uniform appearance.

To prepare the pages prior to writing on them, Brother Thomas rubbed the sheets with pumice and smoothed it with chalk, to remove any oil and thus keep the ink from running.

"You are going to use ruled lines, are you not?" The question came from behind him, and though it was a mere whisper, Brother Thomas started, for the prolonged bout of silence had given him the impression that he was alone. He turned to see Brother Bartholomew. The *armarius* had trod noiselessly to Thomas's work station to observe his progress. Years of copying had given Brother Bartholomew a permanent squint. Even when he stood, his back and shoulders retained the exact stoop he had developed from years of sitting hunched over his table copying texts. His hair and beard were grey and bushy. Even his eyebrows were bushy. His old, wrinkled fingers were stained black with layers of ink from years of copying. Thomas had frequently heard the rumour about the monastery that whenever the *armarius* received a cut, he bled black, inasmuch as more ink ran through his veins than blood.

"I was not considering using lines," Thomas admitted.

"In this scriptorium only ruled manuscripts are produced," Brother Bartholomew stated with pride and finality. "Ruled pages are preferred. It will make your work neater and more uniform." Thomas nodded in agreement, and the master scribe asked, "What are you working on? I have not assigned you any work. What is it you are doing here?"

"The abbot has given me an assignment," Thomas responded.

At hearing this, Brother Bartholomew's face stiffened with suppressed rage. Thomas knew that the chief scribe coveted his position and believed that he should decide all the copying chancellor,"

"But once they get it we may never know what is in it," Nicholas argued. "We may have to wait years before the book comes down the line to us. Or perhaps we will never get a chance to examine it. If it is as important as I think, the abbot may send it to Rome, and we will never see it again."

"It is very rare that a book that momentous is discovered," Thomas said, with a hint of arrogance. "I, myself, have been extremely fortunate in the past to have made rather fantastic finds." When Thomas saw disappointment loom on the young monk's countenance, he thought better of it, and decided to lend Nicholas some encouragement.

"But perhaps you have a point," Thomas said. "There certainly would be no harm if we took a look."

Buoyed, Nicholas smiled broadly and said, "But as I told you, the pages of the book are palimpsests. Someone, who I am certain did not know what the original book contained, scraped the pages down and practically erased the text to write over it. Most of the original text is illegible."

"There is a way to bring the scraped-off text to light," Thomas said. "When I was in Alexandria, I learned how to bring out old writing by treating the pages with lime juice."

"Let us do that!" Nicholas exclaimed.

"Unfortunately northern Italy is the wrong climate for growing limes."

"Then all is lost," Nicholas said, his hopes dashed.

"You give up too easily, my young friend."

"What are we to do?" Nicholas asked.

"We may be able to bring up the writing by carefully passing a candle flame beneath the pages so the heat of the flame will darken the ink."

"Will that work?"

"We have but to try," Thomas said, then asked, "Where is the book now?"

"Well hidden in the library," Brother Nicholas said, with a conspiratorial look. "I thought we might visit the library late tonight after everyone has gone to sleep."

The monks of St. Benedict's monastery slept in a large dormitory on small simple cots lined with straw. After *compline*, the nighttime prayers, all the monks retired to their beds. Like every monk in the monastery, Brother Thomas went to bed in his robe, for as Brother Benedict had set down in the Rule centuries before, "Let the monks sleep clothed and girded with belts or cords but not with knives at their sides, lest they cut themselves in their sleep—and thus be always ready to rise without delay when the signal is given and hasten to be before one another at the Work of God, yet with all gravity and decorum."

As Brother Thomas lay in his cot, his biggest concern was Brother Vittorio. He knew the prior would not sleep until everyone else was asleep, so Thomas decided to feign slumber and wait. He did not remember falling asleep or even feeling that he was tired, but the next thing he knew Brother Nicholas was silently rousing him. Thomas looked up to see Nicholas standing over him with a wistful look tinged with anticipation. For an instant Thomas saw something in the young monk's face that he had never seen before. What was it? he wondered. Thomas sat up in his cot, disregarding the vision. He looked up and smiled at Nicholas. Borrowing one of the lit candles in the dormitory they carried their sandals and quietly crept out of the room and down the hall to the library. There, upon entering the room, they slipped on their sandals.

Though the monks of the monastery were not required to take a vow of silence, the Rule directed periods of quietude, such as meal time and during the Great Silence, which were observed and strictly enforced. The Great Silence began at the end of *compline* before retiring, and lasted until the end of *lauds* early in the morning. Since they were sworn to honour the Great Silence, neither Thomas nor Nicholas spoke a word, but communicated with the use of signs or simply a look or gesture.

In the library, Nicholas motioned for Thomas to take the candle from him.

Carrying the candle, Thomas followed Nicholas over to a book cupboard. Squatting down, the younger monk moved a few books on the bottom shelf and reached far to the back. He withdrew a book and held it out for Thomas to see. Nicholas then set the book upon a table, and they examined it by candlelight.

The cover of the book was hand-tooled leather with a cross in the centre of a circle, which was inside a rectangle that followed the edges of the cover.

Nicholas opened the book, and Thomas examined the palimpsest pages. He observed that the writing beneath the psalter was, indeed, all but illegible. Only parts of certain words could be read. Gingerly Thomas positioned the page over the candle flame carefully so as not to burn it. After a short moment, the writing underneath grew clearer.

Nicholas turned to Thomas with an expression that reflected his amazement. Thomas, on the other hand, only raised his eyebrows to show a modicum of surprise.

Everything seemed consistent with a book from the early seventh century—the style of the document and the uncial script which was characterized by a distinct separation of letters written with broad, single strokes. There seemed nothing extraordinary about it. It was not a book of a secular nature, but rather a history of the monastery and the first Benedictine monks who came here.

As he read the first line of the document, Nicholas heard something from out in the hallway, and quickly looked to his companion. Thomas heard it also. Both held their breaths as they strained to hear. The two monks exchanged questioning looks, and Thomas stepped rapidly towards the door. He reached the hallway with the lit candle held high. He saw nothing among the shadows, but he was certain someone had been there. Thomas suspected that it was the prior, Brother Vittorio, who was the abbot's eyes and ears in the monastery. Thomas returned to Nicholas and conveyed to him that considering the sudden appearance and disappearance of a second party, it would be prudent to secure the book and retire for the night.

The next morning after *prime*, the early morning communal prayer, Brother Thomas made his way to the scriptorium to begin copying The Revelation to John. Though he was most curious about the book on the early days of the monastery Brother Nicholas had discovered, Thomas knew he could not forsake his sacred task of copying Holy Scripture. Besides, he did not wish to arouse any suspicions regarding the book, or of Brother Nicholas and himself.

In the scriptorium he prepared his work station. Thomas opened the Spanish exemplar to The Revelation to John, and draped a weighted string to mark his place. Placing the text next to his parchments he began his first line. Thomas's artistic skills were even less developed than his scripting, so he decided to keep his work simple but neat. The title he wrote in script five times the size of his text. Writing was a two-handed task, his right hand holding his quill, and his left a *lunellum*—a scribe's knife, which he used to sharpen his pen, smooth out rough sections of parchment, and scrape away any errors that were made on the page.

A monk's work was never rushed. Though patience had never been one of his virtues, over the years Thomas had developed a degree of forbearance. That and pride for his work gave Thomas enough confidence to carry on at an unappealing task that held no allure for him. At the end of his first page he sat back to admire his work. From over his shoulder he heard an uncomplimentary groan.

Thomas turned to see Brother Bartholomew standing behind

him, observing his progress with some disdain.

"You have misplaced this word!" Brother Bartholomew said angrily to Thomas. "And here, you have left out a letter."

"Well, yes, but—"

"*Verbatim et litteratem et puntatim.*" Brother Bartholomew chastised him. "Word for word, letter for letter, and point for point."

"Yes, Brother, I understand," Thomas said meekly.

"You must never work *currente calamo*—with pen running on. You must stop and reflect on your work. This is God's word!" the *armarius* stated with reverence and vehemence. "It must show in your work. You must give each page, each line, each word, each letter its own might. The words must come alive. This work lives past you. In a thousand years men will look at your work, and they must see that you were moved by God's own word. Like our Creator, you must bring the word to life."

Thomas regarded his work. "I believe it looks rather good," he said defensively.

Brother Bartholomew gestured towards Thomas's page, and practically spat. "The words have no life! They lie flat upon the page! There is no fire in your work because there is no fire in your heart!" And he walked away shaking his head in disgust.

Brother Thomas turned back to his work and stared at it confused.

"Sometimes Brother Bartholomew can be quite harsh and critical of others' work."

The voice that spoke was low, but held assured strength. Thomas turned to see the *armarius's* assistant, Brother Gregori, standing over his right shoulder. Thomas had seen Brother Gregori around the monastery many times, but they had not taken the opportunity to speak to each other. Gregori was a sombre-looking man, whom no one in the monastery had ever seen smile. Thomas suspected Brother Gregori had experienced some great tragedy in his life, but was reluctant to ask him the details of his past. Gregori's high, broad forehead and long serious face bespoke intelligence, while his close-knit brow, tight-set jaw, and intense gaze lent him a commanding presence. He and Thomas were approximately the same age, about thirty-five. Both were tall, with dark features and trimmed beards, and both possessed a handsomeness that reflected the strength of their characters.

"Yes, so I observed," Thomas replied to the other's comment.

"I am Brother Gregori," the other monk said, with as much of a grin as he could muster.

He put out his hand, and Thomas shook it. Brother Gregori had a very powerful grip to his handshake, and Thomas suspected it was from years of working as a scribe.

"I am Brother Thomas of Worms," the German monk spoke.

"No need to introduce yourself, Brother Thomas. I have heard of you and of your accomplishments as well."

"Oh?" Thomas said modestly.

"Yes. You were the one who uncovered the *Didache* in a remote eastern monastery. A very remarkable find."

"I believe it was simply misplaced," Thomas said. "It was a very unorganized monastery, and I fear they may misplace it again."

"There is no need to be modest, Brother Thomas, it does not befit you," Brother Gregori said, and Thomas could see that the man did not believe in pretense, but rather respected total honesty. How much Brother Gregori was like himself, Thomas thought. Perhaps that was the reason the two monks had not spoken until now. Perhaps they were too much alike and instinctively saw each other as intellectual rivals set in a place where spiritual pursuits were the main goal.

"It was also you who discovered an original papyrus of Tatian's *Diatessaron*, and an unknown letter composed by Jerome," Gregori said, with an admiration tainted with envy. "Any man who is capable of uncovering treasures such as those is surely up to simple copying."

"Thank you, Brother Gregori. I am certain that was intended

to be a compliment on whatever meagre talents God has granted me. As for my abilities as a scribe, I do not believe my heart is in my work. What do you think?" Thomas asked, indicating the page he had completed.

Brother Gregori studied the work briefly. "It is . . . good," he said hesitantly.

"But . . . ?"

"But, take a look at this script," Brother Gregori said.

The assistant *armarius* went to his work station and brought over the exemplar he was copying. Gregori showed Brother Thomas a page from an eighth-century French manuscript.

"Do you see how each letter has an individuality of its own," Gregori put forth with admiration. "Observe the subtle detail, the sheer artistry."

"I am not at heart an artist," Thomas admitted. "I am afraid the best I might achieve is a work of symmetry and consistency."

"You are limiting yourself, Brother," Gregori stated. "Study the works of others. You need not try to duplicate their style, but rather use their work as inspiration."

"You have studied the great works, I assume, Brother Gregori."

"Like yourself, Brother Thomas, God has granted me the opportunity to travel, though not as extensively as you have. I have been to Alexandria, and on the Isles of Britain I had the opportunity and privilege to study the Lindisfarne Gospels," Gregori stated proudly. "I have even been so fortunate to have once seen the Book of Kells."

"I, too, have been to Britain, but have only heard tell of the Book of Kells," Thomas said enviously. He asked, "What is it like?"

"How can I describe it?" Gregori spoke thoughtfully, his eyes turned upward. "The text, unfortunately, is full of errors, yet the work itself looks as if it were done by angels. These are the works that inspire man to achieve greatness, Brother Thomas. If we study masterful works of great beauty, we are more apt to create it in our own work. It is man's work that inspires man."

"But does not God's word inspire us also?" Thomas asked, though it was more a statement than a question.

"Yes, of course, Brother," Gregori responded. "*Solo Deo gloria.*"

Thomas soon realized what both Bartholomew and Gregori were trying to tell him, and he began to see a marked improvement in his own work. Day after day he looked forward to his time in the scriptorium, and at night he would plan out his next page. As time passed, the discovery made by Brother Nicholas slipped from Thomas's mind as he became more and more consumed with his work.

One day Brother Thomas was in the scriptorium when Brother Nicholas arrived clearly agitated and breathless.

"Brother Thomas! Brother Thomas!" Nicholas began, calling from the doorway. In his haste, Nicholas was unaware that he was speaking loudly. The glares of disapproval from the occupants of the scriptorium quieted him.

Thomas sat at his desk, engrossed in his work. He was now enamoured with script and the art of copying, and could think of little else. So engrossed was he in his scripting that when Brother Nicholas arrived calling to him, he barely heard his name.

"Ah, Brother Nicholas," Thomas said, pausing long enough to look up from his desk. "What do you think?" he asked, regarding the scripting, while he rubbed the stiffness out of his right hand.

"Brother Thomas—"

"Who would have thought something that began as so much drudgery could turn into such joy," Thomas stated, barely noticing Nicholas, much less his disturbed state.

"Brother Thomas—"

"Do you see what I have done here? Observe how the top of this character forms the T of this line and how the lower portion of the character forms the L of the next line."

"Brother Thomas I must speak with you."

"I am not entirely satisfied with this page, though. It does not seem balanced. Perhaps if I make this—"

"Brother Thomas, will you listen to me!" Nicholas shouted.

All the monks in the room ceased what they were doing and stared in the direction of the distracting voice. It was enough to shake Thomas out of his work. He observed how Nicholas's usual calm face was filled with distress, and that his blue-green eyes were wide with horror.

"Why, Brother Nicholas, what troubles you so?" Thomas asked, concerned at his friend's anxiety.

"A terrible accident has claimed the life of Brother Ryan."

Thomas crossed himself, and his lips moved in silent prayer. He stood up and faced the young monk. "Tell me everything," he said earnestly.

Brother Nicolas related what he knew of the matter. Thomas's eyes locked onto those of his brother monk, while his lips pursed and he clasped his bearded chin between thumb and forefinger. All the thought and energy he had given his copying was now transferred to the matter of Brother Ryan's death. When Nicholas had related his tale, they both went immediately to the place where Brother Ryan had met his end.

The monastery was a collection of attached buildings surrounding a central courtyard. Most of the buildings were two-stories tall, except for the church whose high ceiling rose higher. Rising up higher than the rest of the structures was the tower, with its spacious flat roof that allowed the monks of the monastery an excellent view of the surrounding area, and gave them the impression of being closer to heaven. The tower dated back to the Roman post that had once sat on this very site. Here, centuries ago, atop the tower Roman soldiers had stood watch for invading hordes. A narrow spiral staircase led to the top of the tower, and it was at the bottom of this staircase where early that morning Brother Ryan's body had been found in an awful heap.

When Brother Thomas and Brother Nicholas arrived at the scene, many black-robed monks were standing about. With Nicholas close behind, Brother Thomas pushed his way through the group to get a close look at the dead body, which still lay at the foot of the stairs leading up the tower. The body rested in a twisted, unnatural, and grotesque position. Thomas studied the stairs and recalled the words of St. Gregory I: *We ascend to the heights of contemplation by the steps of the active life*. Better for Brother Ryan had he not been so active on these steps, Thomas of Worms thought to himself.

Brother Ryan was easily identified by his Celtic tonsure. The hair line was shaved in line from ear to ear, unlike the European tonsure where the top of the crown was shaved. Brother Ryan had been the only monk in the monastery with a Celtic tonsure. Despite his condition, the monk's face appeared calm and relaxed, almost pleasant—much the way Brother Ryan had looked in life. To Brother Nicholas, the image lent an unreal quality to the tragic scene, almost as if Brother Ryan were not truly dead, as if he might get up off the floor at any moment, dust himself off, and resume his work for the day.

Thomas knelt down beside the body to examine it more closely, then he silently uttered a blessing. As Thomas stood up he did not notice that he was standing next to the abbot who had arrived only a moment before. As usual, standing beside the abbot was Brother Vittorio, the prior.

"Did anyone see it happen?" the abbot asked those present. His question was answered with much shaking of heads and dumbfounded expressions. "Who found the body?"

"I did," Brother Felix spoke. He was a young, fair-haired monk from the French kingdom to the west. He had come to the monastery only six months ago. "I was on my way to the tower when I found the body lying there, just as it is."

"Why were you going to the tower?" Thomas asked bluntly.

"I go to the tower every day at this time."

"Why?" Thomas queried.

Brother Felix hesitated. He appeared unable to meet the eyes of his inquisitor. The abbot, who felt annoyed by Thomas's questions, still bade the young monk answer.

"I go atop the tower every day and look in the direction of my country," Felix admitted with shame. "I often imagine I can see it from there, and I imagine what it would be like to be home again."

"I will speak to you about this matter later, Brother Felix," the abbot said in admonishment.

"When was the last time anyone saw Brother Ryan?" Thomas asked the crowd at hand. "Does anyone remember seeing him at *tierce*? At *prime*?" Thomas scanned the faces in the group. All seemed reluctant to help. Thomas craned his neck and spied Brother Lazarus near the rear of the gathering. When their eyes met, Brother Lazarus turned and moved away.

"Brother Lazarus, wait!" Thomas shouted and moved after the monk, but he was restrained from following by a firm grip on his arm.

"That will be enough, Brother Thomas," the abbot said, casting him a rueful eye. The abbot did not release his hold on the German monk, even when he turned to look at the dead body and announced, "I would like Brother Ryan's body taken to the infirmary to be cleaned and prepared for burial. We will have services for him tonight."

Thomas moved towards the body but was restrained again by the abbot, who still had a hold on his sleeve.

"Not you, Brother Thomas," the abbot's voice spoke sternly. "I would like to see you in my chamber immediately."

In the abbot's chamber, Brother Thomas stood with his hands clasped in front of him beneath the large sleeves of his robe, and with his head lowered piously. This was the stance for receiving a rebuke.

The abbot paced silently about the room for a considerable length of time. He did this purposely to allow the monk to consider his inappropriate actions and how he might curb them in the future. Brother Thomas thought the entire pageant annoying and wished that the abbot would simply say something. After a long bout of silence Thomas got his wish.

"What am I to do with you, Brother Thomas?" the abbot asked.

"You might allow me to investigate Brother Ryan's murder," suggested Thomas.

"You will not investigate anything!" the abbot stated heatedly. "And who has spoken of murder? Brother Ryan, in all probability, slipped while on the steps of the tower and met his end in a terrible fall—regrettable but obvious."

"I find nothing obvious about it," Thomas said.

"I am certain we have all seen the walls of the stairwell sweat and the steps become slippery. It is not beyond reason to think that Brother Ryan slipped on the wet stone steps and fell."

"The walls of the monastery do not sweat at this time of year, my Lord Abbot. Also, I observed Brother Ryan's sandals and found them to show no trace of moisture."

The abbot's face turned a light shade of red as he took in a deep breath through his mouth and released it through flared nostrils. "Must you make everything a case of intrigue, Brother Thomas? Could not Brother Ryan have simply misplaced a foot and tripped?'

"That does not seem unreasonable," Thomas admitted, "except that Brother Ryan confessed to me some months ago that he had a fear of heights and could not bring himself to go up to the tower."

"Perhaps Brother Ryan was simply attempting to confront his fear, and when he made his fateful assent, he unfortunately met an untimely end."

Thomas endeavoured to look thoughtful at the abbot's explanation, then said: "I would be willing to believe that explanation if not for the tallow."

"The what?"

"The tallow," Thomas repeated. "There was a spattering of tallow upon Brother Ryan's robe, which leads me to suspect he was carrying a candle up the dark stairwell of the tower."

"Is that so unusual?" the abbot asked. "The stairwell is always dark, even during the day."

"That is true, but if Brother Ryan carried a candle, it is more difficult to believe he misplaced a foot."

"More difficult, perhaps, but not unreasonable."

"No," Thomas said, "not unreasonable."

"Then I do not understand why you would suspect that Brother Ryan's death was anything other than an accident."

"The tallow spattering on Brother Ryan's robe reveals that our Celtic brother was carrying the candle at chest-height. His murderer was presumably waiting for him silently on the stairs. Brother Ryan was most likely watching his feet as he ascended the stairs. The killer must have blown out the candle which caused it to spatter onto Brother Ryan, who was shaken at being thrown into complete darkness. Not forgetting he had a fear of high places, the killer used the opportunity to push Brother Ryan down the stairs to his death."

The abbot closed his eyes and slowly shook his head as he attempted to stifle his exasperation. "Did it not occur to you, Brother Thomas, that Brother Ryan, in his fall, spilled tallow upon himself?"

"In a slip a man would instinctively drop the candle in favour of gaining a purchase with his hands to help arrest the fall, and would not have carried a trace of tallow the way Brother Ryan did."

"I find my explanation the simplest and thus the best," the abbot said.

"I prefer my explanation," Thomas said.

The abbot let out an exasperated breath, and said, "Brother Thomas, when a monk enters a monastery he is asked to surrender all personal ambition, all self-assertiveness. We purge ourselves of the desire to be different, and we are loath to gain any personal notoriety or distinction. Despite this, I had heard of your so-called exploits before you arrived here; many of our brothers here have, also. *Ignoti nulla cupido*—no desire exists for things unknown. Yet, for some reason, you seem to desire the unknown. You constantly seek it out, and when you cannot find some mystery to occupy yourself, you create one. Six weeks after you arrived here you believed Brother Joseph was a Jewish infiltrator come to undermine the integrity of the monastery."

"Yes, but—"

"You reached this conclusion solely from observing him at mealtime, where you perceived that Brother Joseph did not eat pork and he made the sign-of-the-cross backward."

"He could have been a Jewish infiltrator," Thomas insisted.

"Or it could have been simply that Brother Joseph does not like to eat pork, and since childhood he performs many acts backward," the abbot said, as if tired. "A short time later you suspected Brother Bernard was trying slowly to poison you."

"Considering his cooking, I did not believe it was so unusual that—"

"Brother Thomas!"

"Abbot, if we are all blessed with God-given talents to use for the greater glory of God, then how am I not to use mine?" Thomas asked.

"If you must use them, Brother Thomas, confine yourself to discover who took the last slice of raisin bread from the kitchen, or attempt to ascertain who did not wipe his feet before entering the church. As for this latest incident, I do not want you to go about the monastery asking questions and accusing our brothers of murder."

"Perhaps there is only one brother in particular you do not wish me to question."

"Whatever do you mean?"

"Exactly what is it you do not wish me to know regarding Brother Lazarus?"

The abbot grew incensed at the question. He spoke slowly and firmly, but with suppressed rage. "Brother Thomas, you will confine yourself to the scriptorium, and put all your efforts into the penance you were given. You will not inquire into the death of Brother Ryan. You will not speak to Brother Lazarus. Is that clear? For if I learn that you are asking questions pertaining to this accident, I will take it as a flagrant act of disobedience, and you will be disciplined severely, up to and including being cast out of this monastery. Furthermore, I shall contact every Benedictine order and strongly recommend that you not be allowed within their walls. I trust I have made myself clear."

"Yes, Abbot," Thomas said meekly.

"Then you may go, Brother Thomas."

Thomas of Worms left the abbot's chamber and walked quickly down the corridor in the direction of the scriptorium. His jaw was set, and his eyes stared straight ahead as if he saw his true intent before him. Thomas did not wish to be disobedient to the abbot, but inherent in his German blood was a stubbornness that bordered on obstinacy. He could not let go of his conclusion that Brother Ryan had been murdered, even if he so wished. He felt compelled to pursue the matter regardless of the cost. His predicament led Thomas to recall one of the Doctors of the Church, Athenasius of Alexandria, and how he was exiled five times because he would not bend to the will of the Emperor. Athenasius had repeatedly risked exile because he knew his position was clear and his beliefs true. Yet Thomas of Worms realized he was not Athenasius. If he openly persisted in the matter of Brother Ryan's murder, Thomas knew the abbot would insist he leave the monastery, and where would he be then? How could Thomas possibly solve the murder if he was forced to leave the monastery?

Thomas entered the scriptorium. There he sat at his desk with pursed lips, and looked at his work. It now held little interest for him, but he was duty bound to carry on. He picked up his quill and saw that the tip was frayed. With his *lunellum* Thomas began to sharpen his quill. Try as he might, he could not stop thinking of the circumstances surrounding Brother Ryan's death. He could also not help thinking Brother Lazarus had something to do with it. And why did the abbot seem to be protecting him? Thomas desperately wished he could question his brothers regarding the dead monk, but he knew that would only bring the ire of the abbot upon him. Thomas began to make a mental list of questions he would ask if he had the chance. He was unaware of how much time had passed during his musings, for his quill had been trimmed down to almost nothing before he realized it.

Thomas picked up another quill and was in the midst of sharpening it when Brother Nicholas entered the scriptorium. He carried a book under his arm and came directly to Thomas's desk. No one else was in the room, but Brother Nicholas spoke loud enough to keep up appearances just in case anyone was within hearing distance.

"Here is the book you requested from the library, Brother Thomas," Nicholas said.

Thomas looked up and in an equally loud voice said, "Thank you, Brother Nicholas."

Both of them looked about the room and proceeded to speak in hushed tones.

"What did the abbot say to you?" Nicholas asked eagerly.

"Nothing of any consequence," Thomas replied. "There is something I need for you to do."

"You have only to ask."

Thomas smiled. "I knew I could depend on you. Now listen carefully, my friend, you must find out everything you can about Brother Ryan. See if he had anything on his person when he died.

Search his cot. Search the stairwell where he fell. Search the tower roof. Talk to everyone, and find out who saw Brother Ryan last and when. Ask if anyone knows anything about Brother Lazarus and why he is here."

Nicholas nodded his head as Thomas spoke, then asked: "What are you going to do?"

"I am going to stay here and work."

Brother Nicholas left the room, and Thomas remained seated at his desk. He stared down at the parchment before him, but did not see it. He was deep in thought. From within his sleeve he extracted a minute slip of parchment. He studied it for some time.

Thomas thought it best to remain in the scriptorium for the next two days, leaving the room only to join his brothers in Divine Office, meals, sleep, and, of course, the service and burial of Brother Ryan. Brother Ryan was buried out behind the monastery where all the Benedictine brothers were interred. Back in the scriptorium, Thomas tried to concentrate on his work, but the death of Brother Ryan vexed him. He consciously avoided Brother Nicholas lest he was being watched, but on the third day, he decided it was time for them to meet.

The scriptorium was quite busy that morning. Besides Thomas, there was also Brother Bartholomew the *armarius*, his assistant Brother Gregori, and two other monks copying texts. Everyone's attention was instantly caught by a rather loud thud that broke the silence. All eyes turned to see Brother Nicholas standing just outside the door picking up a book he had dropped. He was met with intolerant glares, but his gaze sought only Brother Thomas's. Clutching his book Nicholas proceeded down the hall. Thomas waited a sufficient length of time before he stood up and approached the master scribe.

"Brother Bartholomew," Thomas said in a hushed voice, "I seem to be out of ink, and I was wondering if I might have some of yours?"

The *armarius* looked up from his work and stared incredulously at Thomas with his brown eyes held in a squint and his face contorted as if he smelled rotten cabbages.

"Brother Thomas," he began, in a rebuking tone that was neither too loud nor too soft, "each scribe must see to his own tools. If you are in need of ink, I strongly suggest you mix up some yourself, and do not disturb anyone in the scriptorium."

"Yes, Brother," Thomas said meekly. "I completely understand, and I shall not bother you further."

Thomas walked quietly to his desk, picked up his ink pot and went over to a small cupboard that held a supply of plant gums and sap. With a stick he put a small amount of sap in his ink pot and left the scriptorium in search of the crushed charcoal and soot he would need to mix in with the sap to make ink. Thomas passed the library and lingered outside the door long enough for Nicholas to see him. The two monks met at the clay oven outside the kitchen.

"What have you learned?" Thomas asked, as he searched around the cold oven for a charred piece of wood.

Brother Nicholas cast furtive glances to insure they were indeed alone and out of sight.

"No one seems to have any idea who Brother Lazarus is or what he is doing here."

"The abbot knows," Thomas said, then asked, "What of Brother Ryan?"

"Brother Ryan was originally from Ireland and came here several years ago," Nicholas began. "Not much is known about him. He worked in the scriptorium for a time. I questioned Brother Bartholomew and he told me that he had Brother Ryan copy a book, and that he was an adequate scribe. I asked Brother Domitian about the book; he said it was a minor work that is in the library. After a bit of searching I found it. The book is a short treatise on early Christian writings. In hopes of finding some clue to his death I searched Brother Ryan's cot, the tower stairs, and the tower itself. All I found was a stub of a candle upon the steps."

Thomas nodded and said, "Evidently Brother Ryan dropped the candle when he was pushed down the stairs."

"Pushed down the stairs?" Nicholas repeated. "Brother Thomas, what are you saying?"

"I thought that would be obvious," the German monk said, but seeing Nicholas's confused expression, Thomas uttered: "I am afraid that Brother Ryan was murdered."

"Murdered!" Nicholas exclaimed. "What leads you to suspect that he was murdered?"

Thomas did not answer, but asked a question of his own.

"When was the last time Brother Ryan was seen?"

Nicholas thought a moment trying to recall.

"Some of the brothers were certain they saw him at *matins* and *lauds*, but no one can swear they saw him at *prime*."

"That means he was most likely murdered quite early in the morning while it was still dark," Thomas concluded.

"But why do you believe he was murdered?" Nicholas asked again.

"I will not lie to you, Brother, but confess it is mainly a suspicion that leads me to this conclusion. As I related to the abbot, Brother Ryan told me some time ago that he had a fear of heights and could not bring himself to go up the tower. Someone lured Brother Ryan to the tower with the express purpose of killing him."

"It could have been an accident," Nicholas suggested.

"That is the abbot's position," Thomas admitted. "But there is the fact that Brother Ryan had melted tallow drippings upon his robe which I believe he received when his killer blew out the candle prior to pushing him to his death."

Nicholas paused in thought, then said: "But if Brother Ryan had been carrying a lit candle when he slipped and fell, he would naturally have spilled the melted tallow upon himself."

"That is indeed a plausible theory, my young friend, one that is also shared by the abbot." Thomas reached into the fold of his sleeve and removed a small slip of parchment. "That is why I did not show him this. I am certain had he seen it, the abbot would have disregarded it, and relieved me of it before I could examine it more closely."

"What is it?"

Thomas carefully held the parchment for Nicholas to examine. There seemed to be some form of writing on the parchment in tiny letters Brother Nicholas could not identify.

"What does it say?"

"I do not know," Thomas replied. "The writing appears to be some form of ancient Celtic runes. Although I did spend a short time in the islands of Britain, unfortunately I cannot translate them. When I was examining Brother Ryan's body, I found this note clutched in his hand. I believe this note is what lured Brother Ryan to the stairs he would not normally climb, and he was most likely pushed down those very stairs to his death. All of which leads me to conclude we have a killer in our monastery."

Three

Thomas and Nicholas remained determined to find Brother Ryan's killer, but as days passed there was very little they could do in that regard. With no foreseeable avenues to pursue, Thomas returned to work copying The Revelation to John, and Nicholas, when he could, studied the book he had discovered on the early days of the monastery. He found the book fascinating. Nicholas did not consider how his obsession for the book resembled Thomas's newfound obsession as a scribe. Nicholas was aware, however, of just how Brother Thomas and he were alike, and that undoubtedly it was their similarities that made them fast friends. But they had differences, Nicholas knew—a world of differences. Perhaps in heaven there would be no need to worry about these differences—granted that heaven was Nicholas's intended destination—but he knew in this world there was.

Nicholas and Thomas came to the agreement that they would keep their interactions to a minimum, lest they become known to the abbot. Though the monastic life was one of communal living, close personal friendships were frowned upon. Nicholas did not like the idea of being unable to speak with Thomas daily, as he did so look forward to their conversations. For the time being, however, it was best the two of them stay apart.

Brother Nicholas could not risk being seen reading from the book, so it became his habit to rise in the middle of the night, remove the book from where he had hidden it, and read by candlelight. Nicholas soon found that reading of a bygone era late at night while the monastery was exceptionally quiet was rather disconcerting. A draft wafted through the building, making a sound like a lost soul whose cries whispered through the halls. The haunting sounds echoed eerily, deeply disturbing the young monk. The experience chilled him to his very soul. There were times Nicholas found he could not stop trembling with fright, yet he felt an almost uncontrollable compulsion to study the book. He was able to bolster his spirit, however, by reciting the Twenty-third Psalm.

The Lord is my shepherd; I shall not want.
He maketh me to lie down in green pastures:
he leadeth me beside the still waters.
He restoreth my soul: he leadeth me in the paths
of righteousness for his name's sake.
Yea, though I walk through the valley of the shadow of death,
I shall fear no evil
For thou art with me.

Sometimes, as he sat alone at a desk in the library, and the candlelight made strange unearthly shadows, Brother Nicholas imagined himself the last person on earth. As he read the centuries-old record that told of the first Benedictine monks who had founded this very monastery, his mind went back to what life must have been like in those days.

Greetings and blessing be upon you who reads this testimony. I write these pages so that a true account may be given of the year Anno Domini 580 during the reign of Pope

Pelagius II. It was a long journey from Monte Cassino in search of this monastery in which I now write these words. It was a pilgrimage on the 100ᵗʰ anniversary of the birth of our patron Benedict of Nursia that brought us in search of this place. We had often heard stories of our dearly departed patron, who being of noble birth, fled the immoral city of Rome to live a life of an anchorite, alone and away from corruption, much like the eastern desert hermits he so admired. As a truly pious man Benedict lived in a cave existing only on the bread brought to him by a kind monk. Brother Benedict garnered other ascetics who wished to learn from him, much in the way our Lord and Saviour Jesus Christ attracted disciples of his own.

There is a story of a group of monks from northern Italy who travelled south to find Brother Benedict and implore him to be their teacher. Brother Benedict journeyed with them to their monastery only to return and establish a number of other monasteries around Rome. Though he did not speak much of this northern monastery, I, Brother Antony, and several of my Benedictine Brothers have travelled far in search of that very monastery so that we might pay homage to our patron in an attempt to follow in his footsteps. It was only through the great love and admiration of our Patron that we have made this dangerous journey through hostile territory. By the Grace of God alone have we been able to pass safely through the land of the warlike Lombards to arrive at this remarkable and remote monastery.

We found the monastery inhabited by only one monk, Brother Alamar, who belonged to a vanishing order of Gnostic monks. We knew very little of Gnostics, but Brother Alamar, who invited us to stay in the monastery, was in no way reticent in telling us about his order.

The Gnostics, he related to us, were followers of Christ who believed sacred Scripture held a hidden meaning that could only be interpreted by the enlightened who possessed spiritual knowledge. Even their name — Gnostic — means knowledge, and they revere knowledge even more than love or goodness or faith. Brother Alamar told us that it is a Gnostic belief that this knowledge and only this knowledge will save them. Though none of us could acknowledge these beliefs, we did profess a certain veneration for Brother Alamar, as he claimed to be 114 years old. We asked him if he had ever heard of Benedict of Nursia so we might know for certain if this was indeed the monastery our patron visited in his youth. Brother Alamar said he could not verify this and would speak no more about it.

Little more was written about the Gnostics, but a later entry into the book described the monastery and the surrounding area.

It was agreed by all, and with Brother Alamar's permission that we would establish a Benedictine monastery here. The remote location offers a unique seclusion for a man to contemplate God. The soil is not overly fertile, but Brother Alamar has an adequate garden that can easily be enlarged in order to provide food for all. There is an endless supply of fresh water, and with hard work this monastery can be self-sufficient. From our position atop the mountain, we command an excellent view of the area, especially when one climbs to the top of the tower by way of a long, winding stair.

These buildings are exceptional in their construction and should last through the ages. We are fortunate to have come across such a fine structure surpassing anything we have ever seen. We are surprised to discover from Brother Alamar that the Lombards have not bothered to approach the monastery in any way. Brother Alamar has no recollection of any hostile forces ever attacking the monastery. It is surely the will of God to preserve this holy place and we will be safe here.

For several pages the document went on to describe rather mundane daily activities of the monastery. Nicholas's attention was arrested, however, when he read about the impending death of Brother Alamar.

We are all saddened that Brother Alamar has taken ill and is close to death. At his advanced years there is little we can do for him save to make him as comfortable as possible.

For the last few days Brother Alamar has been feverish and delirious. He has made strange remarks regarding "the end". We are at a loss for what that may mean. Surprisingly he has also admitted to knowing our patron, Benedict of Nursia, but he will not expound on it.

Since arriving here we have all thought it strange that there are no books in the monastery. Today Brother Alamar in his delirium has made reference to certain Gnostic books hidden somewhere in the monastery. He also mentioned a lost book of Jesus — a missing gospel. We could not get Brother Alamar to disclose where the books are located. He would only say the books were dead and buried beyond the library. After an extensive search of the library and every other room in the monastery we concluded that Brother Alamar was mistaken. Brother Alamar's delirium reached its crown when he referred to a key that is not a key to a door that is not a door. He would repeat this over and over sometimes laughing uncontrollably and sometimes in fear.

Late last evening Brother Alamar passed away, but he did not go peacefully. The closer he slipped towards death, the more agitated he became, as if he feared going.

Since the death of Brother Alamar many of the brothers have mentioned an uneasiness about the monastery, and we cannot seem to escape an unsettling sense of dark forebodings.

A recent tragedy has marred our new beginning here. Brother Dagan is the victim of a terrible accident. For reasons

*unknown, he fell down the stairs of the tower. The fall took his
life and we are saddened by his passing.*

*Dark rumours are spreading amongst the brothers regarding
our new home. God help us all.*

Reading this, Brother Nicholas felt the hair on the back of
his neck rise. He paused as he thought he heard someone call his
name.

Nicholas . . .

It was a little more than a whisper, yet he definitely heard it.

Nicholas . . .

The young monk could not determine where the voice
originated, but it seemed to echo in his ears.

"Brother Thomas?" his called out with a broken voice. There
was no answer. He swallowed hard, his mouth gone dry. "Brother
Thomas, is that you?"

Nicholas knew, of course, that it was not Brother Thomas who
was calling him, but he hoped against hope that it was. Unholy
terror began to take hold of Nicholas and he found he could not
move.

*Nicholas . . . I know your secret . . . Nicholas . . . I know what you
are . . .*

Brother Nicholas started. He felt himself grow sick with
dread, tinged with panic that anyone would discover his hidden
truth. His breathing grew more rapid. Panic loomed close, ready
to invade his sanity. He fought against the trembling sensation
that threatened to overpower him and send him running down
the hall, screaming at the top of his lungs. To counteract this
feeling, he decided to try something Brother Thomas had taught
him; he forced his mind to reason. Did this disembodied spirit
indeed know his secret? And if it did, how did it know? Surely
spirits knew everything that transpired in this world. But was it
an angel of God, or a demon of the devil? Despite his attempt
at reasoning, Nicholas was too agrieved, and to be truthful, too

frightened to continue studying the Benedictine journal any further. He trembled with terror as he put the book away and returned to the dormitory.

Tomorrow he would inform Brother Thomas of his findings from the book, but he would not mention his encounter with the spirit—to anyone. Communicating with Thomas would be difficult if they wished to remain discreet, but Nicholas believed he knew a way.

The next day, he tore off a small piece of parchment and secretly placed it on Brother Thomas's desk in the scriptorium before anyone arrived. When Brother Thomas went to his work that morning he found the parchment and read the tiny lettering written upon it. It was one word: berries.

The first time Nicholas and Thomas had met and spoken for any length of time was almost two years ago. They both had been out for a walk separately down in the valley. The river cut through the valley, and along it, among a grove of pine trees, grew bunches of wild blueberries. Thomas had run across Nicholas while the latter was picking a basket. The young monk was alternately placing berries in his basket and in his mouth. Never one to be timid, Thomas had introduced himself to the berry-stained youth and complimented Nicholas on his fine singing voice, which he had heard in the church. The two had talked and had become instant friends. Since then, whenever the pair wished to communicate in private, they met here among the pines and berry bushes.

They now sat upon a large rock while Nicholas related to Thomas all he had learned from the book. Thomas listened attentively with his lips pursed and his eyes locked onto those of his companion. When Nicholas finished relating his tale, Thomas stood up and interlocked his fingers in a prayerful gesture. The large sleeves of his black robe butted together, hiding his hands beneath them. He paced about the area with his head bent, as if watching the steps of his sandaled feet.

Nicholas, who knew this to be Thomas's way when in deepest contemplation, waited patiently as his friend silently paced back and forth. After a considerable amount of time Thomas stopped and stared at the other with his hand on his chin.

"Well?" Nicholas asked expectantly, "What do you think?"

"I think," Thomas began slowly, "that those Gnostics sound like a very interesting sort."

Nicholas was taken aback. "Is that all?" he asked.

"Well, consider," said Thomas. "The Gnostics, we are told, revered knowledge above all else. Such a culture would eventually acquire a vast and enlightened collection of works."

"Yes, but Brother Thomas—"

"They approach the wonders of God from a completely intellectual perspective."

"Yes, but Bother Thomas—"

"They have discovered a way for the heart and mind to combine in their worship and understanding of the mysteries of their Creator."

"Brother Thomas!" Nicholas exclaimed. "You cannot tell me you prefer the ways of the Gnostics to the ways of the Church, or as a Benedictine of this monastery!"

"My dear Brother Nicholas," Thomas spoke in a soothing tone. "Do not excite yourself. I am only trying to say that I find the ways of the Gnostics a fascinating study. I did not say I prefer their methods or wish to be one of them."

"But what of the rest?" Nicholas asked. "What of the incredible story of the last Gnostic monk, who, on his death bed, confessed to knowing Benedict of Nursia, and alluded to a lost gospel of Christ?"

"Yes," Thomas responded thoughtfully. "All of it very intriguing, to say the least. The Gnostics must have left some record of their existence here. If we are to pluck out the heart of these mysteries, we must find these books."

"We must tell the abbot."

"I believe that would be a mistake," Thomas said.

"But why?"

"I am afraid the abbot is not as open-minded as we. If he were to learn of the existence of this book, and that it possibly contains clues to the existence of Gnostic texts, he very likely would label them heretical, and we would never discover what they contain. No. For now we must keep the Benedictine text a secret, and endeavour to find some record the Gnostics left behind."

Nicholas shook his head. "I am not sure," he said doubtfully. "It seems very disobedient, and the Rule calls for prompt, cheerful and absolute obedience to the abbot in all things lawful."

Thomas of Worms sighed thoughtfully and regarded his companion. "Brother Nicholas, have I ever told you of my adventure in a certain eastern monastery, and how I uncovered the *Didache*?"

"Yes." Nicholas said. "Many times."

"Oh," Thomas said, crestfallen. "At any rate, there were some in that monastery who were opposed to my presence, and some vehemently averse to my prying, and some absolutely hostile when I began to search though the monastery. In the end I found the *Didache* and Christianity is greater for it. I take no credit for the discovery, for God surely guided my footsteps. Brother Nicholas, this could be a discovery of biblical proportions and could change the entire aspect of Christianity as we understand it. In several other instances I opposed authority to do what I believed was God's will. We are but servants of God. At your young age you must decide whom you wish to serve: God or man."

Brother Thomas could be extremely convincing in any discussion, and his argument in this case did sound meritorious. Truth be told, Brother Nicholas wanted to be convinced, so, as always, he would do as Brother Thomas asked. They would solve this mystery together, and each secretly hoped it would not be the end of them.

Later that night, the two brothers met in the cloister of the monastery. There, in the darkened archways, they walked and talked in whispers.

"Tell me, Brother Nicholas, was there anything in the Benedictine journal that you found of particular interest?" Thomas asked the young monk.

Nicholas concentrated and thought deeply, yet in the end shook his head.

"Perhaps in relation to a recent event in the monastery," Thomas prompted him.

Nicholas thought again. This time he did recall something. "Yes," he said slowly as comprehension dawned. "The Benedictine journal spoke of a monk being found dead on the stairs of the tower. It is the exact fate that befell poor Brother Ryan!"

"Very good," Thomas said. "Now what does that tell us?"

Nicholas felt a shudder come over him. He suspected it had nothing to do with the cool evening breeze that passed through the cloister.

"It bespeaks some horrible evil that pervades the monastery and transcends time!" Nicholas quivered with agitated dread. "Oh, Brother Thomas! It is evil! It is Satan! We must pray. We must flee."

"Now, now. Do not excite yourself unnecessarily," Thomas of Worms told him. "Though I believe the two tragedies are not a coincidence, we must not panic."

"We must, at the very least, tell the abbot."

"I am afraid we cannot," Thomas said.

"Why not?"

"I did not tell you before, but the abbot was opposed to my looking into the death of Brother Ryan. I can say with complete confidence that the abbot would not wish us to look into this matter any further. He might find it . . . heretical. No, as I stated previously, we must carry out whatever actions necessary in secret."

Nicholas thought on this for a moment. He was not sanguine

about deceiving the abbot, but he thoroughly trusted Brother Thomas, and let his faith rest in the German monk.

"So it would appear we now have two mysteries to solve," Brother Nicholas stated. "The death of Brother Ryan, and finding a record of the Gnostic monks."

"Yes, Brother," Thomas said, pleased. "For now we will put aside the former, and concentrate our efforts upon the latter. The psalter you discovered with the palimpsest pages was found in the library. Perhaps that is where we should begin our search."

As Brother Thomas said this, Nicholas instinctively looked up to the darkened windows that could be seen from the cloister. What he saw caused the young monk to stop in his tracks. As he gazed upward his mouth went slack and his heart seemed to lodge in his throat. He stood petrified.

Thomas had continued walking a few steps before he realized his companion had dropped behind him. Thomas looked back in the dark and called Nicholas by name. When the younger monk failed to answer or even move, Brother Thomas retraced his steps to where Nicholas stood. The German monk strained his eyes and regarded his companion. Nicholas stood staring with a look of shock and horror.

"What is it?" Thomas asked, anxious to discover what plagued the other.

When he did not respond, Thomas followed the young monk's gaze.

Nicholas continued to stare up at the upper floor of the monastery. Though the windows of the library were naturally dark, Nicholas was held in a grip of fear at what he saw coming from the scriptorium, which lay adjacent to the library. For there, coming from the windows in the scriptorium, was a ghostly light that seemed to float about, casting unearthly shadows. Nicholas had suspected that an evil presence permeated the monastery. Now this strange, spectral light appeared. He recalled the unearthly voice that had spoken to him the previous night and the whole affair held him in a grip of unholy terror.

"Someone is in the scriptorium!" Thomas almost shouted, and he started off in that direction. He had not got halfway across the courtyard before he realized Nicholas was not following. Thomas turned quickly about and strode back to where the younger monk still stood rooted, petrified with fear. Thomas had to shake Nicholas violently before he came out of whatever spell gripped him.

"Come!" Thomas spoke forcefully. "We must discover what that is."

Leading Brother Nicholas by the arm, Thomas hurriedly started off for the scriptorium.

They entered the monastery and bounded up the stairs. Thomas reached the scriptorium first and burst into the room. The ghostly light had disappeared. The room was dark save for the little starlight that filtered through the windows. He gave the room a cursory examination, and concluded that everything was as he had last seen it. Nicholas arrived at the doorway, but seemed reluctant to enter, fearing whatever demons might be within.

"Come in Brother Nicholas," Thomas urged him. "There is nothing here to vitiate you."

"Are you certain?" Nicholas said uneasily.

"Yes, yes, yes. You know I would not let you come to any harm. Please come in."

Only as a result of the reassuring words of Brother Thomas did Nicholas enter the scriptorium, and even then, he came warily.

"Whoever was in here is gone now," Thomas said with disappointment.

"Who or what do you think it was?" Nicholas asked hesitantly, as if not truly wishing to know.

"Whoever it was, he was here against the rules. No one should be in here at night prowling about with a lit candle."

"How do we know it was not some spirit casting a ghostly light?"

"Use your senses," Brother Thomas said, tapping his nose. "I definitely smell a lit tallow. No respectable spirit would use a candle," he said, with a hint of irony. "But regardless of who it was, how could he have got out of the scriptorium so quickly without passing us in the corridor?"

"Let us leave this place, Brother Thomas," Nicholas said nervously. "I sense something unholy and unnatural. I am sorely frightened."

"*Yet we do not despair or lose heart, because we put our trust not in ourselves but in Him who works in us*," Thomas said, quoting Saint Leo I, the Great. "Calm yourself, Brother. We will leave here shortly."

Thomas took a few minutes to examine the room more closely, paying specific attention to his own work station. Satisfied that nothing had been touched, he led Nicholas out of the scriptorium.

Just as they were leaving Brother Nicholas stopped and said, "Brother Thomas, it has occurred to me that only a few nights ago we were in the library prowling around late at night with a lit candle. That is also against the rules."

Thomas paused a moment, as if not certain how to respond, then said, "Brother Nicholas, that is totally different. Whoever was in here prior to our arrival was undoubtedly up to some roguery. We were prowling around late at night for a good and righteous cause."

Four

Thomas and Nicholas were certain that to find the hidden Gnostic texts, they would have to glean clues from the four hundred-year-old book Nicholas had discovered in the library. Whenever they could, the two monks poured over the text in an attempt to find a hint of the missing books.

"The old Gnostic, Brother Alamar, seemed reluctant to tell where the books were hidden," Nicholas observed. "Why do you think that was?"

"Perhaps sheer mulishness," Thomas replied distractedly while he read and reread a line from the book. "Brother Alamar might have been alone for many years and did not trust strangers with books that were precious and sacred to his sect."

"Perhaps he feared to give up the books for another reason," Nicholas theorised. "Perhaps he knew the works should stay buried, never to be read by men."

Thomas looked up slowly from his study. "Where do you get such fantastic ideas?" he asked.

Nicholas looked abashed. When he tried to respond he stammered, "It is just that . . . what I mean to say is that . . . perhaps men were not meant to know everything. There are secrets only the good Lord knows."

"Brother Nicholas," Thomas began in a Socratic manner, "would the good Lord put knowledge within man's grasp only to keep it from him? Or would God use that prize to allow man to grow beyond himself, to strive and use his mind to mature in knowledge and wisdom? I do not believe there is anything on this good earth that man is not meant to know."

"There is evil as surely as there is good," Nicholas almost whispered, as if afraid to speak it aloud. "Do you recall that the Benedictine, Brother Anthony, wrote that the monastery conveyed a sombre and foreboding atmosphere after the death of Brother Alamar?"

"I am afraid our early Benedictine brothers were highly superstitious and given to unsubstantiated flights of fancy."

"What about the remarkable similarities between the death of Brother Dagan four hundred years ago, and the recent death of Brother Ryan? Are you saying that is mere coincidence?"

"Coincidence yes, but most likely a deliberate coincidence," Thomas stated cryptically as he continued to study the book. "What do you think of this?" he asked aloud. "It says here that Brother Alamar mentioned the books were 'dead and buried beyond the library.' What do you believe he meant by that?"

Nicholas thought a moment. "Perhaps they buried the books with their dead Gnostics brothers," he said. "The old cemetery out behind the monastery can be seen from a window in the library, hence the term 'dead and buried beyond the library.'"

Nicholas was pleased with himself for this somewhat remarkable supposition, then thought it through with some distaste. "I do not relish the idea of digging up a graveyard in search of any books."

"Do not worry yourself with that," Thomas said. "That is the old Benedictine cemetery. Centuries ago graves were dug into the base of low, wide hills. If the Gnostics buried the books in Gnostic graves, that is where we must look."

"But it might take months to find the right location!" Nicholas exclaimed.

"We have little choice. Besides, it would have to be somewhere close, and most likely can be seen from the library."

For the next two weeks, Thomas and Nicholas searched the surrounding low-lying hills, sometimes together, sometimes alone. While on one such solitary expedition, Nicholas experienced one of the most terrible encounters of his life, one that would draw up painful memories from his past, memories that Nicholas would sooner have forgotten.

In his search for the old Gnostic burial place, Brother Nicholas allowed himself to wander off from the monastery and pause from his quest in the woods that lay in a nearby valley. He did not believe they would ever find the old burial ground, but he continued to look for the sake of Brother Thomas.

From overhead Nicholas heard the singing and chirping of birds that had not yet flown south for the impending winter. Nicholas looked up and about, and regarded his surroundings. It felt so different here in the middle of this natural setting. Here there were no massive stone walls, no rigid and set schedule that had to be kept. A person could be at peace here. A person could be himself and not have to pretend. Nicholas was certain God was as present here in the woods as He was in the monastery of St. Benedict. Here in the woods the trees were alive with colour, and he could smell autumn in the air, but soon the bright leaves would fall, and the death of winter would come and bury everything. Nicholas did not like the winter. He secretly wished for spring and rebirth, the time when nature would be resurrected as was his Lord and Saviour.

"So, young Nicholas!"

Nicholas started. Fear took over his body at the sound of the voice behind him. Nearly petrified, he had just enough will to force himself to turn and see Brother Sebastian standing close to him. He had not heard the monk's approach, for if he had,

Nicholas would have hastened away. Since his arrival at the monastery, Nicholas had always feared Brother Sebastian, a man both big and powerful. A heavy beard masked his face. His nose was crooked, as was his wicked smile, but his eyes told Nicholas of the man's true nature. They were dark brooding eyes, set so close together they sometimes seemed to penetrate the young monk's very soul. Nicholas's blood would chill when he felt those eyes trained upon him. Nicholas had read unholy intent in those eyes, and he had tried to avoid them whenever he could. Sometimes he could feel Brother Sebastian's gaze boring into him, either at mealtime in the refectory, or while he sang in the church. Brother Nicholas saw the devil himself behind those eyes. The young monk feared them, now more than ever. Nicholas started to tremble uncontrollably. He felt his legs give out from under him. Overcome by fear he stumbled backwards and fell against a tree.

Brother Sebastian was on him in an instant. He forced him to the ground. How could such a big man move so fast? But this thought was quickly driven out of Nicholas's mind to be replaced by horror and loathing. Sebastian brought his face close to the young monk's. Nicholas could smell the other's sweaty body, his unclean habit and fetid breath. Nicholas felt he might vomit.

"So, young Nicholas," Sebastian repeated. He did not call Nicholas "brother," for he did not intend this to be a brotherly act. "I finally find you alone." Sebastian roughly stroked Nicholas's hair and cheek.

Nicholas could not find his voice. The weight of the large man forced the air right out of him, and he found it difficult to breathe. Tears welled in his eyes and streamed down his face. Short shallow sobs escaped his lips. Nicholas closed his eyes tightly, dreading what was to come.

Nicholas heard a yell that did not come from Brother Sebastian. The oppressive weight and smell seemed to be lifted off him. Nicholas hesitantly opened his eyes. He saw Brother Sebastian rising off him as if by sorcery. Sebastian's face was engorged with rage. His beady eyes rolled back in his head, while his evil face grimaced. Nicholas then realized that someone was lifting Sebastian off him by violently pulling on the big monk's hood. This action strangled Sebastian, and his deep voice was reduced to gurgling and choking sounds. Brother Sebastian was thrown to the ground, where he landed with a grunt. He regained his voice, and with a loud bellow he half rose to face Brother Gregori.

Gregori stood over him, poised for an attack.

"Get out of here, Gregori!" Sebastian demanded.

"I cannot allow you to harm him," Gregori said gravely.

"This is none of your affair!"

"He is my brother, and I cannot permit this."

Sebastian rose slowly. He took a threatening step towards Gregori who deftly pulled his *lunellum* out of his sleeve and poised it threateningly.

"I will defend myself and Brother Nicholas to the death!" Gregori announced, and there was something in his manner that caused Sebastian to believe him and pause.

"You could not kill, Gregori," Sebastian said, then stated with an evil grin, "The Rule forbids you from defending him, and prohibits you from striking me."

"I would kill you, confess my sin, and God himself would forgive me," Brother Gregori said with absolute conviction.

The grin slipped from Sebastian's lips. Everything remained perfectly still for a moment. As Nicholas bemusedly looked on, he thought they might all be statues, but then Gregori spoke with a tangible certainty in his commanding voice.

"You will leave this monastery tonight, Sebastian," Gregori said. "You will leave, and never come back. If you leave peaceably, quietly, I will not have to report your actions to the abbot."

Slowly, the large monk turned his head and glared at Brother Nicholas who stared back, some of his fear having fled. Sebastian gave Gregori one last look, then turned his back on them both, and walked away hurriedly in the direction of the monastery.

Gregori put away his knife and approached Brother Nicholas who still lay upon the ground. Gregori put out his hand. "Are you injured?" he asked gravely.

Nicholas hesitantly grasped the offered hand, and allowed Brother Gregori to pull him to his feet. Nicholas shook his head in response. He had not yet found his voice.

"Fortunately, I was passing by in thoughtful prayer when I happened upon you," Gregori said. Nicholas could only nod.

"Surely God sent me here. Are you certain you are uninjured?"

Nicholas nodded again, then said, "Must we tell anyone of this?"

"It should be reported to the abbot."

"Please do not tell anyone, especially Brother Thomas."

"I will tell no one if that is what you wish."

Nicholas nodded his assent. He asked hesitantly; "Would you . . . would you have truly . . . killed Brother Sebastian?"

The other paused and looked about him. "We are all capable of killing," Gregori said in his usual sombre mode.

"But would you?"

"Sometimes, Brother Nicholas, we do not know what we will do until that instant, that very instant before we do it. I, for one, am pleased I did not have to find out today."

Nicholas smiled and said weakly, "I am pleased you did not have to find out either. I could not bear to have your soul placed in peril on my account."

As they walked side-by-side back in the direction of the monastery, Nicholas said, "Thank you, Brother Gregori."

"You are welcome, Brother Nicholas."

"If there is anything I can do for you, please do not hesitate to ask. I am in your debt."

"You do not need to feel obliged to me, Brother Nicholas. I could not have walked away from that incident, you see, for it would have damned my own salvation. You might say what I did was purely a selfish act."

Brother Nicholas did not totally understand or agree with what Brother Gregori had said. How could helping others be a selfish act? Brother Gregori had put himself in harm's way for his sake, yet he called it a selfish act. Nicholas was confused. Had not Christ Jesus said: *Greater love hath no man than this, that a man lay down his life for his friends?*

Nicholas did not tell anyone what had occurred in the woods, nor did he comment when rumours of Brother Sebastian's sudden disappearance from the monastery spread among the monks. Thomas speculated that Sebastian might have killed Brother Ryan and fled before he was found out, but still Nicholas said nothing.

After a few weeks Nicholas turned his attention once again to the problem of finding the old Gnostic cemetery. He seldom ventured out past the monastery walls, and when he did, he never went out alone. Nicholas began to stay inside in hopes he might learn more about the cemetery from some of the older monks. One day he decided to question Brother Domitian, the chancellor, regarding what he knew about early graves around the monastery.

"Why do you wish to know that?" Brother Domitian asked, not bothering looking up from his cataloguing.

"I simply wish to know."

"Do you not have enough work to keep your mind occupied, Brother Nicholas?"

Nicholas persisted, undaunted by the mild threat. "I can find nothing in the library that tells of early Christian graves. I suspect that if anyone knew, you would know, Brother Domitian."

The chancellor looked up from his work and fixed his grey eyes upon the ceiling.

"The ancient Egyptians buried their kings inside grand stone pyramids. Our Lord Jesus was buried inside a rock tomb, as was Hebrew custom. In and around Rome, our early Christian brothers were buried in catacombs beneath the city."

"Catacombs beneath the city?"

"Yes. Catacombs in Italy date back five hundred years before the birth of our Lord, but became most prevalent six hundred to seven hundred years ago, when land prices made burial costly. The rock around Rome made tunnelling easy, yet could still support multiple levels. Is there anything else you wish to know, Brother Nicholas? Brother Nicholas?"

The chancellor looked around, only to discover his assistant had left without a word.

Brother Nicholas searched excitedly for Thomas. He found him at his work station in the scriptorium. Nicholas rushed into the room and went directly to Thomas's desk.

"I know where the Gnostics are buried," Nicholas said in a suppressed hushed tone.

Thomas saw that his friend could barely contain himself and seemed unaware that the room was filled with scribes.

"Brother Nicholas," Thomas spoke loudly enough for almost all to hear, "Tell Brother Domitian I am not done with this book, and I will not be finished for some time. No, never mind. I will explain to Brother Domitian myself. Come with me."

Thomas led the agitated Brother Nicholas out of the scriptorium so they might speak in private. They found a secluded spot at the end of the hallway.

"Now, what were you saying?" Thomas whispered to his friend.

"I know where the Gnostics are buried," Nicholas replied.

"Where?"

"Beneath our feet," Nicholas said, grinning with pride. When Thomas failed to understand, Nicholas said one word: "Catacombs."

Thomas brought the flat of his hand to his forehead with a sharp, smacking sound. "Of course!" he exclaimed. "They would not have buried their brothers outside the walls, but beneath the monastery itself inside a crypt. Very good, Brother Nicholas. Very good."

Nicholas grinned even wider, but he was soon deflated. "Brother Thomas, I have never heard of a lower level of the monastery. How are we to find it?"

"What was it the old Gnostic said?" Thomas said, thinking aloud. "Dead and buried beyond the library."

"I know every text in the library," Nicholas proclaimed. "I can say with absolute certainty that the books we seek are not there."

"Of course not, my young friend. Our Benedictine brothers searched for them four hundred years ago and found nothing."

"Are you saying the books do not exist?" Nicholas asked confused.

"No, I believe they exist, but they are hidden. If you had paid more attention to your history lesson you might remember that during the barbarian invasions, many monasteries hid their most prized books in secret rooms so they would not fall into the hands of the invaders. If the Gnostics buried their books with their dead, I do not doubt that we will find a passage to the crypt somewhere inside the library—hence the old Gnostic's words 'beyond the library.'"

Later that evening, Thomas and Nicholas made yet another midnight tryst. As before, they spoke not a word and communicated only by looks and gestures. Together they searched the library. Thomas suspected that if there were a hidden passage to the crypt, it would have to be behind one of the many large cupboards that contained the library's treasures. Together the two monks attempted to move the cupboards, but, alas, they were too heavy. So then they began the systematic task of removing all the books from the shelves to lighten the cupboard. Once done, they were able, with some effort, to move the cupboards. One by one they lifted the cupboards away from the wall, only to find no secret passage behind them. It proved to be a long night, and by the time Thomas and Nicholas were finished putting all the books back in their proper places, it was almost time to attend *prime*.

The lack of sleep caused Thomas and Nicholas undue embarrassment as they yawned incessantly during early morning prayers. Both monks entertained thoughts of slipping off to bed after *prime*, but lost all desire for sleep when alarming news swept through the monastery.

Five

Thomas and Nicholas trailed the flow of monks that followed the call of alarm. They all congregated outdoors near the animal pens. In the goat pen, the beasts stood pressed to one side against the wooden fence that contained them. They huddled together, in that unerring instinct animals possess when they sense death close by. On the opposite side of the pen, away from the goats, lay Brother Gedeon, the parchment maker. He lay on his back with his arms and legs spread wide. A large mark in the middle of his forehead, as if from some incredible blow, was the only telling sign that could be seen.

Most of the black monks stood about, waiting for the abbot to arrive. Some were stricken with fear and unable to act, while others murmured in hushed tones to one another. Realizing this might be his only chance to examine the body, Brother Thomas opened the gate to the pen, and stepped inside.

"What are you doing?" one of the black monks demanded.

Nicholas looked anxiously about. He said, "Brother Thomas, do you think this is a good idea? Do you not think we should wait for the abbot?"

Thomas ignored all remarks directed to him or about him.

He bent down to examine Brother Gedeon's body. He felt several areas of the dead monk's flesh, and paid particular attention to the mark on his forehead. Looking around, he picked up a piece of wood that lay close by. The wood resembled the pieces that made up the fence around the goat pen. A section of the pen appeared to be broken. Brother Thomas examined the wood closely, then set it aside. He went to inspect the damaged portion of the fence, paying particular attention to the ground inside and outside the fence. With his hands clasped behind his back, he bent over to stare at the ground. Thomas walked back to the middle of the pen and picked up a crucifix on a broken leather strap that lay in the outstretched left hand of the dead monk. The crucifix and strap were identical to the ones worn by all the monks in the monastery.

Everyone outside the pen turned at the approach of the abbot, who was followed closely by the prior, Brother Vittorio. They made an almost comical pair, the tall, rotund abbot, and the short prior, who seemed to take two steps to the abbot's one. All the brothers knew that Brother Vittorio watched everyone, and reported everything that went on in the monastery to the abbot. The prior saw it as his sacred duty to keep everyone under a vigilant eye, for he honestly believed that without his closely observing and disclosing every move, the monks of the monastery would digress into sin and sloth. Secretly, most of the brothers regarded the prior with suspicion and dislike.

The abbot, on the other hand, regarded Brother Vittorio's role as a necessity that had to be tolerated. The abbot did not always agree with the prior, or with his method of skulking around the monastery to overhear every word and oversee every deed, but it did help keep many of the monks honest in their devotions. The day Brother Michael died, a new abbot would be chosen as the spiritual leader of the monastery. Abbot Michael knew Brother Vittorio had hopes of being chosen abbot on that day, but Michael also knew that it was not to be. For whoever was chosen abbot of the monastery would need to be worthy enough to inspire the unquestionable obedience and loyalty of every monk in his care. He would also need their respect, and few of the monks respected Brother Vittorio enough to make him abbot. Michael suspected Brother Vittorio would be prior all his life, and lucky to be that.

The abbot stood by the gate of the goat pen and looked from the prone figure on the ground to Brother Thomas who stood over it.

"What has happened here?" the abbot asked.

The abbot had a commanding presence, and many of the monks shrank back from the mere manner of the man. Only Brother Thomas found the nerve to answer. He spoke boldly, but with reverence.

"Brother Gedeon is dead," Thomas announced.

The abbot crossed himself and paused to consider both this disturbing news, and Brother Thomas's manner. He was in no mood for another of the German monk's incredible suppositions about murder in the monastery. The abbot decided he would not tolerate any wild conjectures from the monk. If Brother Thomas chose to press the issue, Michael would discipline Thomas severely in front of everyone.

"Does anyone know what happened to Brother Gedeon?" the abbot asked, keeping a watchful eye on Thomas.

As before, no one responded. Brother Thomas looked about the group expectantly, but said nothing.

Abbot Michael decided to entice Brother Thomas further. "Brother Thomas," he said, in a loud voice so everyone might hear, "do you know how Brother Gedeon died?"

"Yes, I do," Thomas said.

A series of gasps and murmurs ran through the assembly.

The abbot cast a rueful eye around, and waited for silence, before he asked, "And how is it that you alone know how he died?"

Thomas gestured to the body and said, "*Vel caeco appareat*—it would be apparent even to a blind man."

The abbot gestured for Thomas to continue.

"Brother Gedeon died from a blow to the head early this morning." Thomas pointed to the mark on the forehead of the dead monk.

"And do you know or suspect how that occurred?" the abbot asked.

"Yes, I do," Thomas said.

"Please illuminate, Brother."

Thomas paused a moment, weighing options in his mind before he spoke.

"I suspect Brother Gedeon came out to the pens early this morning, as was his custom," Thomas began. "He entered this pen to inspect the goats as he was known to do. I believe he then bent down to pick up his crucifix, which had fallen from his neck." Thomas held up the crucifix on the broken leather strap he had picked up off the ground. "See how the leather is worn and broken? It was a most unfortunate moment for it to break and slip off his neck, for when Brother Gedeon bent over to retrieve it, that ram charged Brother Gedeon and butted him in the head killing him instantly."

Heads turned to look at the horned ram that stood in the far corner of the pen. All the brothers were taken aback by Thomas's account, told in such a cold, detached manner.

"Well," the abbot said, after considering the matter, "we must have Brother Gedeon's body taken to the infirmary to be prepared for services."

Several monks entered the pen, gingerly picked up the body of their dead brother, and carried it into the monastery.

"Thank you for your assistance, Brother Thomas. You have been most helpful in clearing up this matter," the abbot said, then spoke to all the brothers present. "Come, let us away to the church to pray for the soul of our dear, departed brother." And he walked away, followed close on his heels by Brother Vittorio.

After the short service, Thomas motioned for Nicholas to follow him, and the two walked across the courtyard, and out of the monastery.

"That was quite remarkable how you recreated the manner in which Brother Gedeon met his demise," Nicholas said admiringly. "Each conclusion was supported by the facts."

"*Non semper ea sunt quae videntur*," Thomas responded. "Things are not always what they appear to be."

"What do you mean, Brother Thomas?" Nicholas asked.

"You may or may not have deduced by now that everything I told the abbot regarding Brother Gedeon's death was not entirely truthful."

"Do you mean to say you lied!" Nicholas exclaimed incredulously. "You lied to the abbot!"

"I will explain all," Thomas said evasively. "I was reluctant to tell the abbot the true events surrounding Brother Gedeon's death because of his opposition to my opinion on the cause of Brother Ryan's death. I knew if I were to tell him what truly happened to Brother Gedeon, he would not believe me, and I might be now on my way to another monastery."

"Brother Thomas," Nicholas said, speaking as if he feared each word, "what truly did happen to Brother Gedeon?"

"Can you not guess?"

"I would rather you tell me."

"Brother Nicholas, what I tell you now is between us, and we must keep it *in pectore*." Thomas tapped his chest with his fingertips. "It is not to be discussed with anyone. That also includes what we know about Brother Ryan. Agreed?"

"Agreed."

"Now, what you may have assumed is that Brother Gedeon was murdered."

Nicholas gasped. He was shocked and dismayed by what Brother Thomas had just revealed. Thomas's calm and even tone, as he said it, made the revelation even more disturbing.

"But your explanation about Brother Gedeon bending over to retrieve his crucifix, and the ram charging and striking him on the head sounded so viable."

"Yes," Thomas said in a self-satisfied manner. "I must admit to almost sinful pride at inventing that story, but I had to come up with a solution to fit the facts evident to an untrained eye. But if you or any of the brothers had observed the *corpus delicti* the way I did, and if you were to draw the correct inferences from those observations, then murder would be the only conclusion you could reach."

Nicholas shook his head, confused. "What did you see there in the goat pen?"

"A story," Thomas said. "Brother Gedeon did venture out early this morning to tend to his animals. While outside the goat pen, he was confronted by a monk of this monastery. The two struggled, and Brother Gedeon was struck on the head with a piece of wood from the fence and was killed."

Nicholas stared, mute and openmouthed at Brother Thomas. "Brother," he stammered, "how do you know this? Did you witness it?"

"No, of course not. I read the story from what was evident. I know it was Brother Gedeon's custom to go out every morning to see to his animals. A close examination of his body confirmed he died sometime this morning. From the footprints and broken fence, I know a struggle took place outside the pen."

"But Brother Gedeon was found inside the pen."

"The piece of fence I found by the body had a trace of blood on it. It was used to strike Brother Gedeon, and the blow sent him over the fence. The killer carried the wood with him when he walked over to examine the body, and there he dropped it. I know that a struggle preceded the blow because of the broken crucifix in Gedeon's hand."

"But it was Gedeon's crucifix."

"No, it was not. I only said it was to suit my false theory. No one else seemed to notice that Brother Gedeon still wore his own crucifix, and that was mainly because, while examining Brother Gedeon's body, I concealed his crucifix by tucking it underneath his habit. If anyone had noticed it, it would have invalidated my false theory."

"Then the broken crucifix belongs . . ."

"To Gedeon's killer. A brother of this monastery. He and Gedeon must have struggled, and the cross was broken in the struggle. Evidently, the killer did not realize he had lost his crucifix, and Brother Gedeon died still clutching it in his hand."

"So if we were to find out who is missing his crucifix . . ."

"We would have our killer."

"What is it, Brother Thomas?" Nicholas asked, when the German monk grew silent and thoughtful.

"Did you happen to notice who was present at the scene of the tragedy?" Thomas asked.

Nicholas thought a moment and said, "We all were; were we not?"

"Perhaps what is *notatu dignum* is who was not present at the scene."

"Who?"

"Brother Lazarus."

"But he does not have a crucifix similar to ours," Nicholas stated. "*Ergo,* he did not drop the one you found, *ergo,* he did not kill Brother Gedeon."

"Unless Lazarus left the crucifix purposely to divert our attention."

"That could be true," Nicholas conceded and asked, "But why was Brother Gedeon killed?"

"That may be more difficult to learn than the identity of the killer, yet I believe that when we have the latter we shall learn the former. At any rate, this last murder may very well be connected with the murder of Brother Ryan."

"In what way?"

"I do not know," Thomas admitted. "What I do know is that I am beginning to feel that dark malevolence our Benedictine brother, Anthony, wrote of more than four hundred years ago. I fear some evil mischief is afoot in the monastery."

Brother Nicholas had been walking with his hands folded. He brought them up to his lips in silent prayer. After a moment he said; "Still, Brother Thomas, you did lie. You lied to the abbot and displayed disobedience by secretly pursuing both Brother Ryan's death, and now the death of Brother Gedeon."

"Yes, that is true," Thomas reluctantly agreed. "And if you do not go to the abbot and tell him the truth, you will share in the culpability of my sin."

Nicholas stopped in his tracks as the realization of his predicament was thrust upon him. "Oh, dear," he uttered in dismay.

"Worry not, my young friend," Thomas said, putting a reassuring hand on Nicholas's shoulder. "We are not yet damned for all eternity. We will pray about it and ask for God's guidance and forgiveness."

For the next few days Thomas and Nicholas asked seemingly innocent questions regarding Brother Gedeon, hoping to acquire information that could lead to his killer. They also tried to discover which monk in the monastery was missing his crucifix, but that only proved to be embarrassing, although they did find one monk who was in possession of a crucifix that looked newer than most. It was Brother Marco, an elderly monk who was weak and moved very slowly around the monastery.

"Your crucifix looks new," Thomas remarked to the old monk. "Have you recently replaced it?"

Brother Marco looked down at the crucifix that hung from around his neck. He gently touched it with withered and trembling fingers. Brother Marco shrugged. "I do not remember replacing it," he said.

"Yet it looks quite new," Thomas reiterated. "How do you think that happened?"

"Perhaps it was a miracle," the old monk said, smiling a toothless grin.

"Surely you do not believe Brother Marco could be the killer," Nicholas said to Thomas later, when they were alone.

"No, of course not," Thomas said. "Brother Marco obviously does not possess the physical capability to have committed either of the murders. The true murderer, in all probability, noticed his missing crucifix, replaced it with a new one from the supply room and realizing it looked too new, traded it with the one belonging to Brother Marco while the old monk was asleep."

"Very clever," Nicholas observed.

"Yes," Thomas agreed. "This man is definitely intelligent and worthy of our best efforts." For the first time, Thomas started to wonder at the nature of the killer, and what would lead a monk of their order to not one, but two murders. This led Thomas to consider the works of Augustine. According to Augustine, every person was born with original sin—a term first coined by Tertullian—and thus prone to lead a sinful life. Indeed, man could not help but sin, for no one was without sin. This, of course, did not imply that man should accept the fact, and continue to sin purposely, rather that he should accept this sinful nature, and attempt to lead a sinless life. For if, in truth, one was not mindful of sinfulness and did not knowingly keep it restrained, it would undoubtedly grow and increase little by little, day by day. Since man was created by God and God was benevolent, and through His own Godly nature was capable only of creating good, it was man's free will that allowed him to turn away from God and do evil. Since man's nature was to sin, then it was not so unusual that he would turn to evil. Yet, as Augustine observed, if evil was merely the absence of God, then how, Thomas wondered, could such evil exist in this monastery where God was the main focus? How could a brother of theirs who ate with them, slept with them, and prayed with them, commit such gruesome and unholy acts? Was it possible, then, that some men were *mala in se*—inherently bad, and were incapable of redemption and salvation? It was baffling to Thomas, and he suspected he would have to give it further thought to understand it, for God's true nature could not be fully realized by man. Yet man's nature was accessible and needed to be understood.

Nicholas continued his work carefully cataloguing the library's eighty-three books. It was not the largest collection in the order, but for a monastery so remote and secluded as theirs, it was impressive. The monks considered the books the only treasure in their possession. Many of the books were copied in the monastery over the centuries by the brothers who saw it as their sacred duty to duplicate the word of God so it would live on and spread about the world. In the library there were few entire Bibles in one volume. Due to the size and time needed to copy out an entire Bible, many of the books in the library were individual books such as the Pentateuch, or the Prophets or the New Testament, and even smaller volumes such as the one Brother Thomas was working on. There, also in the library, were collected works of the Apostolic Fathers whose writings dated back to the first and second century. Though their library held few great works, each book was prized.

While in the library, Nicholas did note that the mysterious Brother Lazarus was making extensive use of the monastery's books. When he brought this to the attention of Brother Domitian, the chancellor replied that the abbot himself had given the Eastern Orthodox monk full use of the library.

Nicholas had not forgotten that before the death of Brother Gedeon, he and Brother Thomas had been looking for a secret passage in the library. Though Nicholas was not sanguine about deceiving anyone, he decided to question Brother Domitian slyly regarding a hidden room.

"I would certainly hate to see anything terrible happen to all these books one day, Brother Domitian," Nicholas said.

"What do you mean, Brother?" the chancellor asked, alarmed.

"All I mean is that the monastery has a very respectable collection, and it would be a pity if a disaster were to befall any of the books."

"Just what disaster are you anticipating?" Brother Domitian was clearly disturbed by these remarks.

"I was only recalling what I heard regarding the barbarian invasion hundreds of years ago when monks hid their books to keep them from falling into the hands of the invaders."

"Yes, that is so."

"Where did they hide them?" Nicholas asked, in what he hoped was an innocent tone.

Brother Domitian continued to scan a book while he spoke. "It was not unusual for monasteries to have secret rooms where treasures could be secreted in such cases."

"Does this monastery have a secret room?"

"No, I do not believe so."

"Oh," Nicholas said, disappointed.

"From what I have heard, the monastery was never overrun by barbarian hordes," Brother Domitian said. "But the library must have had many more books than we do now, for I heard tell the library was bigger years ago."

"Bigger?" Nicholas repeated.

"Yes," Brother Domitian said. "There is a story that at one time the library and the scriptorium were once one large room. That wall, there at the end of the room, was raised some time ago to separate them."

Nicholas regarded the wall closely. He had never thought about it before, but the scriptorium was on the other side of the wall. Hadn't Thomas told him he suspected the two rooms were once one? Nicholas exited the library and went down the hall to the scriptorium. Sitting at their tables were Brothers Bartholomew,

Gregori, and Thomas. None of them noticed Nicholas's presence. Nicholas stood near the door of the scriptorium and scrutinized the room, trying to determine the most likely location where the secret room or passage would be located. His eyes came to rest upon the lone cupboard at the rear of the room. If there was a hidden room in the scriptorium, it would have to be behind that cupboard.

Nicholas could not wait to tell Brother Thomas his discovery. Thomas assuredly would be proud that he, Nicholas, had discovered the door to a secret room or passage that might very well lead to a lost book of the Bible. Nicholas could barely contain his joy, as his heart pounded almost violently against his chest with excitement. Though Brother Thomas was twice his age and extremely knowledgeable, it was important to Nicholas that Thomas saw him as an equal. Though they lived as equals in this monastic *collegium*, Nicholas considered Thomas *primus inter pares*—first among equals. The trouble was that Thomas, himself, knew this to be only too true. In his Rule, Benedict of Nursia had called obedience the first degree of humility. In Thomas, Nicholas saw little humility. The German monk repeatedly disobeyed the abbot. He seemed overly proud of his heritage and education, and he never shied away from discussing his extensive travels or remarkable adventures. He was a very learned man, wise in the ways of the world and of his fellow man. Nicholas saw Thomas as a born leader, and the first to uncover things that seemed hidden to most others. But all this would change now with the discovery of the secret passage in the scriptorium, and perhaps Thomas would see Nicholas in a new light, with renewed respect.

It was time for *none*. When Nicholas sang during the service his excitement came out in his singing, his voice filling the church. There was a radiant quality that struck a chord deep in the souls of the monks. Each felt it and were moved by it. "Your voice is an instrument of the heart," Nicholas was often told by the precentor, Brother Bagnus, who oversaw the music and the organization of ceremonies. "Singing is an act of worship," he stressed to Nicholas. "It has the power to inspire others, transform us, and make us whole by connecting both the singer and listener to God in the perfect harmony of heart and mind and soul. Devotion comes from a total commitment and a total surrendering of our inner self, and through practice our voices reach out to heaven, and our spirits are elevated to new heights."

That was exactly the way Nicholas felt today. His singing reached a new apex, a oneness that seemed to come from within and without him. After the divine order, his fellow monks nodded to him as they exited the church in recognition of his soul-stirring rendition, but there was only one monk Nicholas was interested in seeing.

"Brother Thomas," Nicholas called to him, once outside the church. The brothers had left to attend their various tasks.

Thomas turned at the mention of his name and waited for his friend to approach him before they both walked on.

"You were in very excellent voice today, Brother," Thomas said sincerely. "I congratulate you."

"Thank you, Brother Thomas," Nicholas replied, grinning as if he were about to burst. "I have something very important to tell you."

By now they were alone, but still kept their voices to a whisper.

"Is it about the death of Brother Gedeon?" Thomas asked.

"No. It is—"

"Is it about the death of Brother Ryan?"

"No. It is—"

"What is it?"

"I believe I have found the entrance to the secret passage we have been searching for!" Nicholas said, barely able to suppress his excitement.

Thomas of Worms was taken aback. "You have?" he said half amused, and Nicholas detected a trace of doubt in the other's voice. "Where is it?"

"In the library, as the old monk said," Nicholas spoke quickly. "Well, not in the library exactly. The original library encompassed the scriptorium, as you once suspected. I believe we will find the secret passage behind the cupboard in the scriptorium."

"Are you saying you have not actually seen it?"

"Well, no. Yet I am certain it is there behind the cupboard."

"And how did you discover the scriptorium was once part of the library?" Thomas asked in a detached manner. Nicholas told him of how he had questioned Brother Domitian, but Thomas continued to question Nicholas's very reasoning and veracity.

This was not the response Nicholas had expected or hoped for. He had been certain Thomas would be pleased with the new information, and would in turn congratulate him, yet Thomas appeared bothered and distressed over the entire matter. Nicholas could not understand it.

"I thought you would be happy about this," Nicholas said, subdued.

"I am," said Thomas almost snapping. "But my happiness is not the issue."

"Then, what is the issue?" Nicholas asked, distressed.

"I should have thought of it myself," Thomas muttered, as he reflected out loud. "I always suspected the two rooms were once one. I cannot see how I came to overlook it."

"Brother Thomas, is there a problem?"

"No, nothing," Thomas answered curtly.

"Are we going into the secret passage?"

"Of course—since you went to all the trouble to find it."

Thomas did not, of course, explain to Nicholas that he felt resentful towards the younger monk for discovering something that should have been obvious to Thomas of Worms—he could not. Thomas realized he was being petty and that pettiness was unworthy of him. Nicholas was right. Thomas should have been pleased at the discovery, but since he had not been the one to discover it, instead he felt angry and insecure.

That night Thomas and Nicholas arose when they suspected all their brothers to be asleep. The monastery possessed an eerie, unsettling quality in the middle of the night. Though it was quiet during the day, the sunlight cast a bright natural ambiance, while the darkness of night lent the monastery an abhorrently silent and disturbing character. To Nicholas the building resembled a tomb with its cold dark walls and dim corridors. His young imagination conjured up ghosts and demons that lingered in the shadows just beyond his vision, while strange haunting sounds whispered and moaned sending shivers through his body. The silence of the night amplified the slightest sound; each furtive footstep echoed noisily, and every breath spoke out loudly. Nicholas was certain someone would wake and discover their actions. Several times he suspected they were being followed and observed. He did not know how he knew, for they had never actually seen anyone on their nightly excursions—he only knew that he knew it, as if by intuition. Nicholas wondered who it could be—Brother Vittorio, perhaps? Or was it someone else, or something more sinister? There were times when Brother Nicholas sensed an evil presence, something to be feared. Oh, how he prayed it was Brother Vittorio who was prowling about. Nicholas felt safer having Brother Thomas at his side.

The two monks moved stealthily down the hallway. Something caused Brother Thomas to stop and remain still. He placed a restraining hand upon his companion. The pair remained thus for what seemed to Nicholas an eternity. He did not know what had caused Thomas to halt, but he trusted in his friend's instincts. Thomas placed their candle in a niche in the wall and stood before it, so its light could not be seen.

From the library door, a light appeared. Nicholas gasped at the thought of a ghostly apparition crossing their path. He remembered the spectral glow from the scriptorium he and

Thomas had witnessed that night from the courtyard. Nicholas felt an uncontrollable terror creeping over him, and he started to tremble. An involuntary whimper escaped his lips, and an urge came over him to run screaming down the corridor.

Thomas noticed his friend's distress and laid a reassuring hand upon the younger monk's arm, to caution him and to put his mind at ease. They watched from the dark corner of the hallway, yet they knew if the light came out of the library and headed towards them, they would surely be seen.

Thomas motioned to Nicholas to put up his black cowl to help hide their faces and blend into the shadows. As the light came to the door, Nicholas held his breath, but he could not keep his heart from pounding so violently he thought it might come through his habit.

A figure appeared at the door, holding a candle in one hand and clutching an armful of books with the other. Thomas knew instantly that it was Brother Lazarus. Ever since the night he and Nicholas had seen the strange light in the scriptorium, Thomas had suspected that it was Brother Lazarus. But why had the Eastern monk been skulking around in the scriptorium late at night? What was he doing now coming out of the library with an armful of books?

At the door, the Orthodox monk blew out the candle and proceeded down the dark corridor passing within two strides of Thomas and Nicholas. Standing perfectly still and holding their breath, they hoped their black habits would keep them from being detected. When they were certain Brother Lazarus was out of sight, Thomas brought out their light and moved on to the scriptorium.

As always during the Great Silence, Thomas and Nicholas did not speak but communicated through gestures. In the scriptorium they went to the largest cupboard in the room and started to empty its shelves to lighten it, ensuring that nothing would fall from it when they tried to move the cupboard. Thomas inspected the floor in front of the cupboard, and there on the right-hand side he saw an arc-shaped scrape on the stone floor leading to the corner of the cupboard. At Thomas's silent urging, the two attempted to move the cupboard away from the wall by pulling on the right-hand side.

It would not budge. Thomas stood back and thought a moment. He picked up the candle they had brought from the dormitory and made a close examination of the cupboard. He was certain if this was a door to a secret passage, there would have to be a catch or a locking device to hold it securely in place. On the right-hand corner of the top shelf, he saw the small knob of a handle sticking out from the back of the shelf. He pushed it in and out, and up and down, until finally it moved with a dull click. Thomas turned and smiled at Nicholas, who now held the candle. Nicholas's comely face smiled back, and the two began to pull on the cupboard which moved only slightly. For the most part the cupboard stayed in place.

As they pulled, Thomas could feel that something continued to hold the bottom of the cupboard. Once again taking the light, he inspected the lower shelf, and there on the right-hand side he saw an identical knob protruding from the back of the bottom shelf. With Thomas working the top handle and Nicholas the bottom, they manipulated both handles and pulled on the cupboard. With a deep groan the cupboard pulled open like an old door on rusty hinges.

To Nicholas, the sound was deafening. He imagined the entire monastery had heard it. Despite their exertions the monks smiled at each other at their success. They embraced out of sheer delight, but Thomas pulled back quickly. He held a finger to his mouth and cocked his head as if listening. Then Nicholas heard it, too. Someone was moving outside in the corridor.

Perhaps Brother Lazarus had returned. Thomas moved to the door of the room and peered out. The corridor was dark, but he was certain he detected the scrape of sandals upon the stone floor. They were moving away, down the corridor. If it was Brother Vittorio, the prior, he might now be reporting to the abbot. Thomas considered his options. They could flee the room immediately and return to the dormitory undetected. If the prior brought the abbot, they would discover the secret passage and whatever lay inside it. If he and Nicholas stayed, they might be caught and severely disciplined. Thomas weighed all that against his curiosity and his desire to know. His curiosity won out, and he and Nicholas entered through the cupboard door together.

Instead of a passage, the monks were surprised to discover that behind the cupboard lay a small room containing a low wooden table, on which sat a single book. Thomas and Nicholas exchanged expectant looks. Thomas motioned to Nicholas to pick up the book. The younger monk laid his hands gingerly upon the cover and ran his fingertips along the edges. Nicholas picked up the book and pressed it to his breast, holding it tightly. Raising the candle high, Thomas examined the room in which they stood. Surely this room was constructed for the express purpose of hiding the monastery's treasures in case they were ever overrun by barbarian hordes. Why were there not more books here? Thomas wondered. He took a moment to look for a door leading to another passage. Finding none, he motioned to Nicholas, and the two stepped out of the room. Hastily they pushed the cupboard back into place, restocked the shelves, and put the room back into the condition in which they had found it.

Leaving the scriptorium, they were left with the problem of what to do with the book. As much as they wished to examine and study the text then and there, both realized they ought to get back to the dormitory before their absence was discovered. Standing in the corridor, Thomas considered their situation and led Nicholas down the hall to the library next door. What better place to hide a book than in the library, Thomas thought. Yet there was the chance Brother Domitian would notice a strange text upon his shelf, so Thomas took the book and placed it high upon the top of the tallest cupboard behind a shrine where it would remain out of sight. Once this was done, the two monks returned to the dormitory, though neither slept much that night.

The next day Thomas and Nicholas were faced with the problem of when they could read the mysterious book. They did not wish to be caught with it, so they would have to study the book in private. Each day the monks of the monastery took time to study Scripture and sacred writings. Thomas and Nicholas agreed to use this time to examine their recent find.

The book was actually a leather bound codex, an ancient form of the modern day book like the one Thomas was creating in the scriptorium. It was written in Greek, in a strong, but unusual hand. Nicholas estimated the text dated back to perhaps the third century, yet on closer examination he determined the book spanned decades, perhaps centuries. It was an abbot's journal, and though the handwriting changed from abbot to abbot it was all written in Greek and in upper case. Thomas found himself fascinated by the introduction which described the ancient Gnostics and their beliefs and read on with anticipation.

Six

I WRITE THIS SO THERE MAY BE A RECORD OF
THIS MONASTERY WHICH WE HAVE BUILT IN THE
THIRD CENTURY SINCE THE CRUCIFIXION OF OUR
LORD AND SAVOUR JESUS CHRIST MAY HIS LOVE
AND BLESSINGS RAIN DOWN UPON US.

I AND OTHER OF MY BROTHERS HAVE TAKEN
POSSESSION OF THIS OLD AND DESERTED
MILITARY STRUCTURE AND HAVE BUILT IT INTO
AN IMPRESSIVE DWELLING TO LIVE AWAY FROM
THE EVIL MEN DO. WE CAME HERE TWENTY YEARS
AGO AND CONTINUE TO BUILD ON AND MAKE THIS
A SELF – SUFFICIENT COMMUNITY OF DEVOUT
FOLLOWERS OF CHRIST JESUS.

WE ARE THE GNOSTICS, DEVOTED TO INNER
PEACE AND SALVATION. WE HAVE TAKEN OUR
NAME FROM THE WORD 'GNOSIS', WHICH MEANS
KNOWLEDGE. WE HAVE GIVEN OUR LIVES TO THE
ACCUMULATION OF KNOWLEDGE WHICH IS MAN'S
ONLY LINK TO GOD. ONLY IN THE ACCUMULATION
OF KNOWLEDGE CAN WE BECOME ONE WITH THE

INFINITE, THE ETERNAL.

THOUGH AT PRESENT WE ARE STRANDED HERE IN THE LAND OF PHYSICAL DARKNESS, THE LAND OF TANGIBLE EVIL, WE ARE FOREVER SEEKING INSIGHT TO THE OTHER WORLD; THE LAND OF THE SPIRIT WHERE OUR MIGHTY AND MYSTERIOUS GOD ABIDES. ONLY BY OUR CONSTANT SEARCH FOR TRUE KNOWLEDGE MAY WE DISCOVER THE DEEP THINGS OF GOD AND REALIZE ABRAXAS. NAMED FOR THE MYTHICAL CREATURE THAT CREATED THE WORLD, ABRAXAS IS THE EPITOME OF TOTAL KNOWLEDGE, AND THE STATE NECESSARY TO CROSS TO THE WORLD OF SPIRITUAL LIGHT. OH LORD, WE BESEECH THEE, DELIVER US FROM THE MATERIAL WORLD OF DARKNESS AND IGNORANCE. GRANT US, WHO ARE BLIND IN THE DARKNESS, THE ALL SEEING KNOWLEDGE.

BY STUDYING SACRED TEXT WE GROW CLOSER TO JESUS, THE REVEALER OF GNOSIS, THE BRINGER AND GIVER OF LIGHT. MAY HE BRING TO US THE FLAME OF ILLUMINATION, THE SAME FLAME THAT BURNS DEEP WITHIN THE WORTHY, THE SPIRITUAL, THE KNOWING. BY THIS LIGHT MAY WE ACHIEVE ABRAXAS AND SEE THE ONE TRUE FATHER AND OUR TRUE SELVES. THOUGH GOD MADE US IN HIS IMAGE, IN THIS WORLD WE ARE BLIND TO THAT IMAGE. ONLY THROUGH KNOWLEDGE MAY WE DISCOVER OUR TRUE IMAGE, OUR GOD – LIKE IMAGE AND THROUGH ABRAXAS HAVE A PERFECT KNOWLEDGE OF GOD.

Brother Nicholas was disturbed by this account, unlike Brother Thomas who was deeply fascinated. Thomas had always appreciated knowledge and intellect, and had never ceased trying to learn all he could. That was one of the reasons he travelled extensively, for the more he learned of his fellow man, he believed, the more he discovered himself. Thomas felt an almost instant respect for the Gnostics and their reverence for knowledge. As Thomas and Nicholas read on, they learned more about the Gnostics from generations of abbots who had made entries into the codex.

TODAY WE CELEBRATED GENESIS, AND RECOUNTED THROUGH STORIES AND RE-ENACTMENTS THE CREATION OF THE WORLD.

IN THE BEGINNING THE SUPREME FATHER CREATED THE DIVINE QUALITIES. THERE WERE THIRTY OF THESE IN NUMBER AND THEY WERE CREATED IN PAIRS OF MALE AND FEMALE. THERE WAS GOODNESS, TRUTH, CHARITY, PATIENCE, HOPE, WISDOM, UNDERSTANDING AND OTHERS. THE LAST FEMALE TO APPEAR WAS SOPHIA. IN HER BURNED THE PASSION TO KNOW THE UNKNOWABLE FATHER. THOUGH THAT SAME PASSION BURNED IN THEM ALL, IN SOPHIA IT BURNED MORE INTENTLY. SOPHIA'S DESIRE FOR THE SUPREME FATHER WAS SO GREAT, SHE REJECTED HER MALE PARTNER AND BY HERSELF CONCEIVED A MALFORMED AND OBSTREPEROUS CHILD. SHE NAMED HIM IALDABAOTH – CHILD OF CHAOS.

SOPHIA'S PASSIONS CONTINUED TO GROW, AND THEY MANIFESTED THEMSELVES INTO ELEMENTS OF THE MATERIAL WORLD. IALDABAOTH GREW AND BECAME WILD AND UNMANAGEABLE. HE TOOK THE ELEMENTS HIS MOTHER CREATED AND SHAPED THEM AS HE LIKED INTO THE DARK WORLD OF MAN. SOPHIA DID NOT TEACH HER SON IN THE WAYS OF THE SUPREME FATHER. IALDABAOTH DID

NOT BELIEVE THERE WAS A GREATER POWER THAN HIMSELF AND HE URGED PEOPLE TO WORSHIP HIM AS THE ONLY GOD. THOUGH MANY PEOPLE DID WORSHIP HIM AND TURNED THEIR LIVES TO THE UNRULY, THE DEFIANT, THE UNDISCIPLINED, YET ALL MEN ARE BLESSED BY SOPHIA'S GRACE AND HAVE DEEP WITHIN THEMSELVES A SPARK OF THE DIVINE WHICH WE NEED ONLY SEARCH FOR TO FIND.

"It sounds heretical," Nicholas confessed to Thomas.

"It is simply a myth, Brother Nicholas," Thomas said condescendingly. "A simple story to explain aspects of our lives. It is not unlike the Bible."

"The Holy Bible!" Nicholas exclaimed. "Brother Thomas, what are you saying? The Bible is not simply a collection of mythical tales."

"Brother Nicholas, do you actually believe God created the world in the manner the Bible relates, and that he did it all in six days, and that God, the supreme being of the universe, actually needed rest?"

"Sacred Scripture tells us so," Nicholas responded timidly, not able to look Thomas in the eye.

"And so it does," Thomas conceded. "But is it not logical to consider that the Bible's creation myth is there to make it easier for common people to understand God's greatness?"

Nicholas shook his head confusedly. He did not feel secure enough in his faith to stand up to arguments posed by Thomas of Worms.

Thomas, on the other hand, enjoyed taking part in a good argument. He felt it kept his mind and wits sharp, and believed it actually strengthened his faith. He was intrigued by the Gnostic codex, though. He found such study fascinating, and he was eager to read more.

IT IS VERY RARE WE ADD TO OUR NUMBERS, BUT TODAY WE WELCOMED TWO MEMBERS INTO OUR GROUP AND THEY WERE INDOCTRINATED WITH THE FEW AND SIMPLE RULES OF THE MONASTERY. SOME MEMBERS SUGGESTED WE INDOCTRINATE THE NEW MEMBERS WITH A RITUAL OF BAPTISM. I DISCOURAGE SUCH RITUALS AS HAVING LITTLE OR NO TRUE VALUE. FOR IT IS NOT THE BAPTISM OR ANY OTHER RITE THAT LIBERATES OUR MIND, BUT IT IS OUR GNOSIS, THE KNOWLEDGE OF WHO WE WERE, WHERE WE ARE FROM, WHO WE HAVE BECOME, WHERE WE ARE AND INTO WHAT WE HAVE BEEN CAST. WE MUST KNOW WHITHER WE HASTEN AND WHY, WHENCE WE ARE REDEEMED AND HOW, WHAT IS BIRTH AND WHAT IS REBIRTH.

The more Thomas read, the more he became entrenched in Gnostic beliefs. Here, for the first time, was a doctrine that inspired him, that suited his thinking, and Thomas allowed it to possess him. He had always known the significance of intellect. After all, hadn't God given man intelligence and the desire to know all things? What greater gift had God given man but the gift of his far-reaching mind? Early in the third century Clement of Alexandria had written that the thought and will of God exhorts, educates, and perfects the true Christian, while Clement's treatise, *Miscellanies,* was written to help guide developed Christians to perfect knowledge. Perhaps the Catholic Church had somehow lost some of this teaching down through the centuries, Thomas mused, and slowly, over time, their doctrine had been corrupted by outside forces.

More and more Brother Thomas began to suspect the Gnostics had been close to an answer with their method of finding God through knowledge. After all, he thought, what else was there? In the Gnostic writings Thomas had read the word Abraxas, which was defined as total and perfect knowledge. He suspected Abraxas referred to that perfect knowledge that only an enlightened spiritual conscience could obtain—something with which he was not wholly unfamiliar. There had been, after all, times in his life when he had reached a point of advanced reasoning that often escaped his colleagues. He sometimes wondered how his monastic brothers were not capable of developing thought patterns equal to his own. How was it his mind performed at a greater speed and on a different plane of reasoning than theirs? Though he did not know, he often thanked God for it.

He desperately needed to talk to someone regarding these newfound ideas, yet he was reluctant to make known the existence of the Gnostic book. Of course, Brother Nicholas already knew of the book. Although Brother Nicholas was not his intellectual equal, Thomas did trust the young monk with his deepest thoughts. There was a strong bond between them that was greater than knowledge.

"I fear you are taking that Gnostic nonsense too seriously," Nicholas told Thomas.

"You only say that because you are afraid to consider the possibilities."

"Perhaps I am," Nicholas admitted, his lip quivering slightly. "Yet I believe there are things in this world we should fear, Brother Thomas."

"Why?"

"Because there are powers in this world that would harm us."

"Nam et ipsa scientia potestas est," Thomas expounded. "For knowledge, too, is itself power."

"I fear for you, Brother Thomas."

"Do not fear for me, my young friend."

"I fear for your soul. I fear you are straying from us, and from God."

"I may be straying from this brotherhood," Thomas admitted,

"but I am getting closer to God, and is that not what we are all here to do?"

"I have been doing some reading of my own, since you began to study the Gnostics in earnest," Nicholas stated. "In the second and third centuries the church fathers spoke out against the Gnostics."

"Any new idea will attract criticism from all quarters," Thomas said lightly, "especially if it is a revolutionary idea. As much as I respect the early church fathers, they approached any new concept out of fear for their own beliefs, which were, in all honesty, also new and radical. In their day Christianity had not yet been fully and properly defined."

"What about sacred Scripture, Brother Thomas?"

"What about it?"

"The Book of Timothy: *Keep that which is committed to thy trust, avoiding profane and vain babbling, and oppositions of knowledge so called: which some professing have erred concerning the faith.*"

"'Knowledge so called,'" Thomas repeated. "And you take that to mean Gnosticism?"

"What do you take it to mean?" Nicholas countered.

Thomas paused to study his friend's face. He read judgement there, and Thomas resented it.

"Brother Nicholas, you are little more than a novice. Do not presume to instruct me," the German monk said, then thought better of it. He paused to regain his composure. "Expand your mind, my young friend," Thomas said, trying to hold his anger in check. "Perhaps you should consider leaving this sheltered life and seeing the world. Get to know God by knowing your fellow man. Serve Him by serving others. That is where true salvation lies."

Never before had Thomas spoken to Nicholas thus, and he felt extremely hurt and distressed by it. As a sensitive youth, Nicholas took this as a serious rebuke and found himself questioning his faith and his life here in the monastery. But he knew Thomas well enough to know that when the German monk got his mind onto an idea, he would not give up on it until all aspects had been considered.

"Do you plan to continue your secret study of the Gnostics?" Nicholas asked, choking back the tears that persisted.

"Yes, I do," Thomas replied defiantly.

"Then I shall pray for you, Brother Thomas."

SALVATION COMES WHEN JESUS IS SENT BY THE GOD OF LIGHT TO LEAD SOPHIA TO ENLIGHTENMENT AND SEPARATE HER FROM HER PASSIONS. JESUS IS NOT THE SON OF GOD IN HUMAN FORM BUT THE GREAT REVEALER OF GNOSIS. HE HAS CARRIED THE FLAME OF ILLUMINATION FROM THE DIVINE REALM TO THIS WORLD TO LIGHT THE FLAME THAT EXISTS IN THE TRULY SPIRITUAL, THE KNOWLEDGEABLE. FOR NOT EVERYONE HAS THE GNOSIS WITHIN HIM. BUT THE ONES WHO DO HAVE THE KNOWLEDGE WILL KNOW THEY DO. THOSE WHO DO POSSESS THE GNOSIS WILL SEEK THE TRUE REVELATIONS OF JESUS AND THESE SEEKERS WILL AWAKEN FROM THE STUPOR BROUGHT ON BY IALDABAOTH THE CHILD OF CHAOS AND THEY WILL FIND THEIR TRUE SELVES AND UNDERSTAND AT LAST THE TRUE GOD.

THE TRUE REVELATIONS OF JESUS CAN BE FOUND IN THE SACRED WRITINGS BUT ONE MUST SEARCH CAREFULLY FOR THE SECRETS ARE HIDDEN AND CANNOT BE FOUND IN THE LINES BUT BETWEEN THE LINES.

Thomas found this part of the codex extremely fascinating. He was one who possessed the gnosis, of this he was certain, and if Abraxas were to be obtained, the answers could be found in

Scripture. A hidden meaning lay somewhere in the Gospels. They were never meant to be taken at face value—Thomas often had suspected as much.

Thomas of Worms began to study the Gospels in a new light, looking for secret messages that could only be interpreted by those possessing gnosis. He started to develop fantastic theories and suppositions, but was forced to discard each as they grew more bizarre and meaningless. After weeks of what seemed to be futile study, he returned to the Gnostic codex for further illumination.

HERE WE HAVE LED A LIFE AWAY FROM THE MATERIAL TO COME TO KNOW THE SPIRITUAL. BUT AS ABBOT I HAVE BEGUN TO NOTICE SOME OF THE BROTHERS ARE TRANSGRESSING. SINCE, AS OUR BELIEFS TESTIFY, THE MATERIAL DOES NOT HAVE RELEVANCE, SOME OF THE BROTHERS HERE IN THE MONASTERY ARE INDULGING IN ACTS THAT ARE NOT OF THE HIGHEST ORDER. WHEN I OR ANY OF THE BROTHERS CONFRONT THEM ON THIS THEY PROCLAIM THEIR ACTIONS HAVE NO CONSEQUENCE SINCE THESE LIVES IN THE MATERIAL WORLD ARE INCONSEQUENTIAL COMPARED TO THAT OF THE SPIRITUAL REALM. AS WE DO NOT BELIEVE THERE IS ANY POTENTIAL GOODNESS IN MAN, THESE BROTHERS DO NOT MAKE ANY ATTEMPT TO PRACTICE ASCETICISM. AS ABBOT I BELIEVE WE ARE DESPERATELY IN NEED OF SPIRITUAL GUIDANCE.

WORD OF A HOLY MAN LIVING IN A CAVE NEAR ROME HAS REACHED US. HIS NAME IS BENEDICT AND I HAVE SENT THREE UPSTANDING AND RELIABLE MEN TO APPROACH BENEDICT AND REQUEST HE COME TO OUR MONASTERY AS WE

ARE IN NEED OF SPIRITUAL GUIDANCE.

IT IS A HAPPY DAY AT THE MONASTERY AS BENEDICT OF NURSIA ARRIVED AND HAS AGREED TO BE OUR SPIRITUAL LEADER. FOR HIS FIRST STEP IN TAKING ON THIS ROLE BENEDICT HAS WRITTEN OUT NUMEROUS RULES WE IN THE MONASTERY MUST FOLLOW. I CAN ONLY HOPE THAT THESE RULES AND BENEDICT'S PRESENCE WILL HELP US ALL REACH A MORE SPIRITUAL PLANE IN THIS WORLD.

NOT EVERYONE IS PLEASED WITH THE MANY STRICT RULES BROTHER BENEDICT HAS PUT INTO EFFECT. THOUGH IT MAY BE JUST WHAT MANY OF THE MONKS HERE NEED, SOME ARE RESENTFUL OF BROTHER BENEDICT AND HAVE SAID UNKIND THINGS ABOUT HIM. I CANNOT FAULT THE MONKS WHOLLY AS BROTHER BENEDICT TENDS TO FORCE HIS WILL AND HIS OWN PERSONAL BELIEFS UPON US. HE HAS EVEN GONE AS FAR AS TO DISCLAIM ONE OF OUR MOST PRECIOUS AND SACRED TEXTS AND ORDERED US TO DESTROY IT, DENOUNCING THE TEXT AS BLASPHEMOUS. MANY OF THE BROTHERS WERE ANGERED AT BROTHER BENEDICT'S WORDS. TO PLACATE EVERYONE I HAVE ORDERED YOUNG BROTHER ALAMAR TO HIDE THE TEXT IN THE CRYPT BENEATH THE MONASTERY AND BROTHER BENEDICT WAS SHOWN A PILE OF ASHES TO PROVE WE BURNED THE BOOK.

A VERY DISTURBING EVENT HAS TAKEN PLACE TODAY. UNBEKNOWNST TO ME SEVERAL OF THE MONKS PLOTTED TO MURDER BROTHER BENEDICT.

IN WHAT I CAN ONLY DEEM A FLEETING ACT OF INSANITY SOME OF THE BROTHERS CONSPIRED TO POISON BROTHER BENEDICT'S WINE. SOMEHOW HE MUST HAVE SUSPECTED SOMETHING WAS AMISS FOR PRIOR TO DRINKING THE DEADLY WINE BROTHER BENEDICT BLESSED THE CONTENTS OF HIS GOBLET. AS HE MADE THE SIGN OF THE CROSS ABOVE THE GOBLET, BROTHER BENEDICT KNOCKED THE DEADLY DRINK OVER SPRAYING IT UPON THE CONSPIRATORS AND MARKING THEM. NOT SURPRISINGLY BROTHER BENEDICT FLED THE MONASTERY AND I AM CERTAIN WE WILL NOT SEE HIM AGAIN.

Thomas of Worms stared at the words of the Gnostic codex with an open mouth. He could barely believe what he was reading. Every Benedictine monk had heard the story of how Benedict of Nursia, before he began the monastery at Montecassino, had been invited to a monastery in the north, and how certain resentful monks had tried to poison him. Thomas could never have imagined this was the very monastery where his patron had escaped death. He found it difficult to believe that Gnostic monks had been the ones who tried to kill him. Thomas was reluctant to tell Brother Nicholas, but the truth could not be avoided.

Thomas found Nicholas alone in the library.

"Brother Nicholas! Brother Nicholas! Thank heaven I found you," Thomas exclaimed in a hushed voice. "There is something I discovered in the Gnostic codex that you simply must hear."

Nicholas did not approve of the Gnostic codex—did indeed fear it and how it was seducing his friend. Though he acknowledged Thomas's presence, Nicholas endeavoured to appear aloof and showed little interest.

"This is the very monastery Benedict of Nursia came to early in his life and where he was almost poisoned!" Thomas told a detached Nicholas. "The old Gnostic monk, Alamar, mentioned in the sixth century Benedictine text, is mentioned in the Gnostic codex as well. He knew Brother Benedict and what happened. He was reluctant even to admit he knew anything of Benedict, and now I know why."

Brother Nicholas turned wordlessly away to place the book he was inspecting onto another cupboard. Thomas followed him persistently.

"Brother Nicholas, do you not understand what this means?" Thomas asked him. "This is of incredible historical importance." When Nicholas still did not respond, Thomas asked more forcefully, "Do you understand what I am saying?"

"Yes, I understand," Nicholas spoke for the first time. "I understand that these Gnostics—whom you hold in such high regard—tried to murder our patron."

Thomas paused and released a long, exasperated breath. Though it was difficult, Thomas came to the self-realization that he had indeed been caught up in the glamour of Gnostic beliefs. So much so, that for the past week he had not spoken to Brother Nicholas or to anyone else. So occupied had he been that Thomas had almost forgotten the two murders in the monastery, and he had neglected his work in the scriptorium. But harder than admitting to himself he was wrong in advocating the Gnostics, Thomas now had to admit to another human being that he was in error. For Thomas of Worms it was a hard lesson in humility.

"Brother Nicholas, I know that I have neglected you as of late, and I apologize. Where it does seem that the Gnostics may not be everything I hoped, I still believe not all their ideas are without merit. What I am trying to say is that . . . I seem to be in . . . What I mean to say . . . it . . . there may be some aspects . . ."

"Brother Thomas," Nicholas said with wonder, "are you trying to say you were mistaken?"

Thomas felt his stomach churn at the prospect. "Yes," he said, almost choking on his words. "I'm afraid I was."

"Fear not, Brother," Nicholas spoke tenderly to him. "I shall tell no one."

Seven

Brother Nicholas did not approve of the Gnostic codex and what it contained, and especially did not like the negative influence it had had over his friend, but he did agree to read the text as a work of historical importance at Brother Thomas's request. While reading of the Gnostic's beliefs and practices, Nicholas skimmed the words lightly so as not to be seduced by the unholy glamour they possessed.

When he finished reading the codex, Nicholas felt a current of suppressed excitement at a discovery Brother Thomas had obviously overlooked. Nicholas suspected Thomas was so caught up in Gnosticism that he had failed to recognize two significant facts that were obvious to the younger monk. Eager to relate his discovery, Brother Nicholas went off in search of Thomas.

Nicholas found Brother Thomas at his desk in the scriptorium, once again working on copying the book of Revelation. Fortunately, aside from the two of them, the scriptorium was empty and they were free to talk, though they did so in hushed tones.

"Ah, Brother Nicholas," Thomas spoke in a calm and friendly manner, "you've come to visit a lonely prisoner, have you? You've come with word of my exile? Tell me, what is transpiring beyond this room? Is our dear Sylvester still pontiff? Is Christianity still the true faith of the world? Alas, I have lost all track of time, but I fear it is almost time for lunch, for even from here I can smell one of Brother Bernard's concoctions wafting up through the halls to assault my olfactory senses."

"Lunch will have to wait, Brother Thomas," Nicholas said.

"You have something important to tell me; that much is evident. There hasn't been another murder, has there?"

"No, thank God, nothing as gruesome as that, yet something just as nefarious."

"Then speak, dear Brother, so we may combat it."

"I have just finished reading the Gnostic codex," Nicholas explained. "And I have stumbled upon something you may have overlooked."

Thomas looked down his long, straight nose, and his face revealed both surprise and indignation. Despite the slight affront, he allowed the young monk to continue.

"Though they may have begun with good intentions of reaching a high spiritual plane, over the years the Gnostics of this monastery transgressed horribly."

"The abbot himself admitted that," Thomas said.

"Yes, but what a transgression it must have been to lead to an attempted poisoning of one of the holiest, most righteous and Godly men of that time, Brother Benedict of Nursia!"

"Brother Nicholas, what are you trying to say?"

Nicholas paused, as if only now realizing what he was trying to tell his friend. So eager was he to speak with Thomas, he had not taken the time to think it through, and now he began to doubt himself. Regardless, Nicholas continued, forming thoughts and ideas as he spoke.

"What I am trying to say is," Nicholas said, slowly and methodically, "that perhaps because of their beliefs, or because of their sinful nature, or for whatever reason, evil entered the hearts of those monks who tried to murder our patron."

Thomas could only stare at Nicholas.

"Don't you see, Brother," Nicholas continued, hoping to rationalize his thoughts, "those monks turned away from the earthly life in hopes of finding God, and yet they grew wicked and sinful. Their lives were pointing one way, and ended up in the totally opposite direction."

Thomas continued to stare at his friend and admitted, "I still do not think I follow your line of thought."

The young monk's body shook slightly as he groped for words to express his incomplete ruminations. His blue-green eyes darted back and forth as he searched for the right words. "Something outside themselves drove them to it," he said, still groping. "Something outside this monastery breached these walls to enter and corrupt the hearts of those misguided Gnostics."

"And you believe that this evil abides here still?" Thomas queried.

Nicholas looked back puzzled, a little afraid at his friend's words.

"Because of the recent murders?" Thomas added.

"Yes!" Nicholas exclaimed. Though his rational mind had not truly thought that far ahead, he now knew that was the conclusion he was ultimately trying to reach.

"That is a very interesting idea, and one that I myself was contemplating a short time ago," Thomas said, biting down gently on the end of his quill pen. "What do you propose we do now?"

"We must tell the abbot," Nicholas said. "He must be made aware."

"My dear Brother," Thomas said, sadly shaking his head, "the abbot does not want to hear anything about murder in his monastery. He went so far as to tell me that if I mentioned it again, I would be cast out."

"Then I will tell him!" Nicholas said with pluck.

"Then you will be cast out."

"What are we to do?" Nicholas asked in desperation.

"We could solve the murders," Thomas proposed. "Though we would have to conduct our investigation in secret, plus we have very little evidence to consider."

"Brother Thomas," the young monk said, as his lower lip quivered, "I am afraid."

"Perhaps we should be," Thomas said, then thought better of it. "For now we will trust in God and remember: *All works for good for those who love the Lord.*" And Thomas gripped Nicholas's shoulders to encourage him.

Just then the bell tolled for lunch.

Despite Thomas's derogatory comments regarding the food, Nicholas did not think Brother Bernard's meals were completely unpalatable. The midday meal was the main meal of the day, and today they were having soup and bread with cheese. Since it was a fast day, there was no meat or fish served with the meal.

The monks ate in silence as they listened to a reading from sacred Scripture. Today's reading was from the Old Testament, and told the story of how Joseph's jealous brothers sold him into slavery. Afterwards, in order to explain their brother's disappearance, they showed their father Joseph's bloodstained coat and claimed he had been eaten by a wild animal.

As Nicholas listened to the story, he recollected that there was something else he wished to tell Thomas, but with all the talk about the Gnostic attempt to kill Benedict of Nursia, he had forgotten. Nicholas was anxious to speak with Thomas on this new subject and eagerly attempted to gain Thomas's attention. Through a prearranged signal, Nicholas relayed to his friend that he wished to speak with him.

After dinner the monks of the monastery could rest until *none,* and Nicholas and Thomas chose this time to meet in secret to talk.

"There was something else I found in the Gnostic text that was of interest," Nicholas told Thomas.

"What was that?" asked the other.

"Towards the end of the entries the abbot mentioned a precious text that Brother Benedict did not approve of and ordered destroyed."

"Yes?" Thomas said, barely recalling the passage.

"The Gnostic abbot said he could not bring himself to destroy the text, and instead ordered the work hidden."

Thomas fully recalled the passage now. "So the wily old abbot showed Benedict a pile of ashes as proof of the book's destruction."

"Much in the same way Joseph's brothers showed their father Joseph's blood-soaked coat so he would think Joseph was devoured by a wild beast," Nicholas said eagerly, then added, "But like Joseph, the book was not destroyed!"

"The abbot ordered it hidden in the crypt by Brother Alamar," Thomas said enthusiastically.

"But does the monastery even have a crypt?" Nicholas asked.

"There must be a crypt," Thomas said. "The Gnostic text explicitly refers to one."

Nicholas was slightly repulsed by the subject, yet asked; "And if we were to look for this missing sacred text, we would need to find this crypt?"

"Oh, we are indeed going to look for the hidden text, my dear Brother Nicholas," Thomas reassured his friend. "As to the location of the crypt, I believe we will find it beneath our feet."

In their quest to find a passage to the crypt, Thomas and Nicholas discreetly questioned every monk in the monastery. When that proved futile, they decided to search for an opening or door of some kind themselves. Yet, alas, that also proved fruitless. Thomas suspected the most likely entrance to the crypt would be in the hidden room in the scriptorium, but remembering his initial inspection of the room he concluded it was not to be found there.

"There must be a way into the old crypt," Thomas said. "There must be."

"Perhaps there is no crypt," Nicholas said.

"There is," Thomas countered with frustrated impatience. "Before the Church began to provide burial sites, crypts beneath churches and monasteries were common. The Gnostic abbot mentioned a crypt. There is a crypt beneath this monastery. I am as certain of that as I am that the sun revolves around the earth."

"But how are we to find it?"

Thomas interlocked his fingers as if in prayer and pressed his knuckles to his chin contemplatively. "None of our brothers seem to know anything about a crypt," he said, almost to himself. "Not even any of the older ones seem to know about it."

"If only we could speak with an old Gnostic monk," Nicholas said, with a humour born of impotence. "I am certain he could tell us how to find it."

"What did you say?" Thomas asked, turning on him seriously.

"I am sorry, Brother Thomas," Nicholas apologized, realizing his attempt at humour was misplaced. "I spoke without thinking. I did not mean to—"

"No, no!" Thomas interjected. *Rem acu tetigisti*—you touched the thing with a needle. 'Speak with an old Gnostic,' you said."

"Yes."

"Do you not see, Brother Nicholas?" Thomas said smiling. "We can speak with an old Gnostic."

"Yet the Gnostic codex holds no clue to the crypt," Nicholas argued. "I have read it over closely, and there is only one reference to the crypt, and that being only that the sacred text was placed there."

"I am not speaking of the Gnostic codex," Thomas explained. "I am speaking of the Benedictine book you discovered in the library."

Hastily the two monks retrieved the book they secreted in the library and scanned the pages. They came across the passage that described the end of Brother Alamar's life when he lay upon his deathbed, and the Benedictine brothers believed he was delirious.

"'A key that is not a key, to a door that is not a door,'" Brother Thomas read aloud.

"What does it mean?" Nicholas asked.

"I am not certain," Thomas of Worms said, "yet I am certain once we discover the meaning, it will lead us to the crypt."

For the next two days Brother Thomas devoted much time to the hidden meaning of the Gnostic monk's cryptic words. Several times he admitted to himself that he was completely baffled, but every time he went back to the problem and approached it from a new perspective. It was not in his nature to give up on a problem, and like a mongrel with a bone, he would not let it go.

Brother Thomas's musings were interrupted by yet another tragedy to befall the monastery.

Brother Bartholomew, the *armarius,* was found in the north cloister. It appeared he had met his end while taking a solitary walk with his head bowed in silent prayer.

"Better that he had been looking up to heaven," Brother Thomas whispered to Nicholas after they arrived at the scene, for there lay Brother Bartholomew in the cloister with the back of his head crushed in. Lying next to the body was the instrument of his death—a stone that had worked loose from the wall at a very inopportune time.

By this time many of the monks had arrived to witness the awful tragedy and pray for the soul of their recently departed brother. Thomas, however, used the time to study the scene. He examined the wound on the back of the dead monk's head. It was a terrible wound, and Thomas assumed the old monk had died instantly. Thomas inspected the stone that had done the deed. It was heavy, and falling from a considerable height it could indeed have caused such a wound. Looking up above the scene, Thomas observed the spot from where the stone had fallen. It was a ledge on the wall of the cloister that stood taller than a man and directly above an old wooden riddle carving. Not many of the brothers knew that these wood carvings pre-dated the Benedictine's occupation of the monastery. There was one carving on each of the four walls of the cloister, and when a monk was welcomed or indoctrinated into the monastery, his acumen was determined by contemplation of the riddle and how quickly he could analyse it. Thomas himself had worked out three of the four in his first week, but he was still stumped by the fourth. That was the same one that overlooked Brother Bartholomew's death.

"Who discovered the body?" Thomas asked the black monks who stood about.

After a brief pause, one of them said, "I believe it was the Orthodox monk, Brother Lazarus."

Thomas looked about the group but did not see Brother Lazarus among them. His gaze continued to scan the area, until it came to rest upon a wooden ladder that lay nearby in the grassy courtyard. Enlisting the aid of Brother Nicholas, he moved hastily between the columns and retrieved the ladder, bringing it to the scene of the recent tragedy. Thomas had Nicholas hold the ladder while he climbed up the steps to examine where the stone had come loose.

"Brother Thomas!" a voice spoke sternly.

So engrossed was Thomas on his inspection of the stonework, he barely heard his name.

"Brother Thomas!" the voice repeated louder and more forcefully.

Thomas looked down to see the abbot staring up angrily at him. As always, next to the abbot stood the prior, who endeavoured to look equally as angry.

"Brother Thomas, you will come down from there immediately!"

Reluctantly Thomas climbed down the ladder and faced the

abbot.

"Brother Thomas, what is the meaning of this?" the abbot demanded.

"I was merely inspecting the stonework —"

"I know what you were doing!" the abbot shot back. "How can you carry on thus with Brother Bartholomew lying here in this condition?"

"It was Brother Bartholomew's condition that led me to inspect the stonework."

"That is enough, Brother Thomas," the abbot said. "We will show our departed brother the proper respect. His body will be taken to the infirmary and prepared for burial." He directed some of the monks on hand. Then he bowed his head and drew in a laboured breath, for now he knew what was called for. With another deep breath, the abbot spoke in a voice loud enough for all present to hear.

"It appears, Brother Thomas, that you insist on conducting yourself in a very undisciplined and disruptive manner, which is contrary and unacceptable to the ways of this monastery. I have previously spoken to you regarding this, for which you have received an act of penitence, yet it appears that was not enough. Out of the goodness of our hearts we have welcomed you into this monastery, and how have you repaid this act of kindness? You have consistently disrupted the peace and tranquility of this sanctuary."

While receiving this public rebuke, Thomas looked about at his brothers, some who looked at him austerely, some with contempt. Others looked on with pity, yet were secretly relieved it was not they who were receiving the rebuke.

"I am sorry," Thomas began graciously, "but as to disrupting the peace and tranquility of the monastery, it was not I who murdered Brothers Bartholomew, Gedeon, and Ryan."

The abbot grew enraged at this statement and shouted harshly, "That will be enough, Brother Thomas! I will see you immediately *ianuis clausis!"*

In the privacy of the abbot's chamber Thomas stood with his hands clasped before him, and his head slightly bowed. Behind him the abbot paced about the room, trying to regain his composure. When he finally did speak, the abbot continued to pace in back of the German monk.

"So, Brother Thomas," the abbot said calmly and evenly, "you undoubtedly have some theory regarding Brother Bartholomew's death."

"Yes," Thomas said.

The abbot made a thoughtful sound in his throat. "Brother Bartholomew's death was accidental," the abbot insisted, "and I have seen little that would say otherwise."

Multum in parvo—much in little," Thomas declared as he studied the abbot's character. Something inside Thomas had compelled him to reveal his true belief in the affair, and now he would have to disclose all he knew in support of his theory to the highest authority in the monastery. The situation was not wholly devoid of appeal for him. Though he would never admit it—even to himself—Thomas needed to display his intellect and manner of reasoning.

"The wound on Brother Bartholomew's skull was too far back to coincide with a stone falling from the ledge. He was most likely hit from behind."

"Yet if you take into consideration that Brother Bartholomew was in prayer with his head bowed, then the wound would not be out of place," the abbot managed to say as if it were an effort to move his mouth.

Thomas conceded that point, but was not prepared to abandon his theory.

"It seems highly unlikely that the stone would come loose at the precise moment Brother Bartholomew was passing beneath it," Thomas stated. "The instrument of his death is also in question in that I inspected the stonework and found the masonry to be secure. *Ergo,* the stone that killed Brother Bartholomew could not have come loose by itself, but rather was pried away from the ledge."

"Are you proposing that his would-be killer sat upon the ledge undetected, waiting for Brother Bartholomew to pass by, and as he did, the killer dislodged the stone to drop it on him?"

"No," Thomas said. "Most likely the killer worked the stone loose beforehand, probably using the same ladder I used."

"And he came up behind Brother Bartholomew on the exact spot where the stone would have fallen, and killed him with it— for what purpose?"

"To make it appear to be an accident," Thomas proposed.

"But why kill Brother Bartholomew, and why make it look like an accident?"

"I have not worked my theory out to its completion. But if I were to pursue this I would first question Brother Lazarus and ask how he came upon the body of Brother Bartholomew."

"Brother Thomas, you will not question Brother Lazarus, or disturb him in any way," the abbot said sternly.

"May I ask why?"

"You may not."

"My good Lord Abbot, whatever secret you may be protecting, it is not wise to hide the truth," Thomas began respectfully. "These murders all started shortly after Brother Lazarus arrived here. We cannot presume to judge him because he is Orthodox, nor can we ignore that the strain between the Roman Catholic Church and the Greek Orthodox Church has grown considerably in the last century. Brother Lazarus has been seen lurking about the monastery late at night and was observed at least once taking books from the library. If you are trying to protect Brother Lazarus, consider that you may be protecting a murderer."

"Brother Lazarus is not a murderer," the abbot said with conviction.

Thomas waited in silence.

Brother Michael regarded Thomas of Worms and saw he was expecting some kind of explanation. The abbot was reluctant to give it, not believing it necessary that he should do so. All the monks under his leadership were expected to trust and abide in his decisions, and he believed all of them did—all of them except for Brother Thomas.

The abbot drew in two long, laboured breaths. Then he began, "Brother Lazarus came here at my request. He and I have known each other for a number of years, and I consider him to be a trusted friend. He is the abbot of a monastery in Constantinople. For many years we have corresponded, and one of our common concerns has always been the schism between the East and West churches. You, yourself, mentioned it, and both Brother Lazarus and I feared that the differences between our two respected churches might cause an ultimate and final separation—a separation between the two churches that would only weaken us as Christians. Neither Brother Lazarus nor I could live with that consequence without taking steps to prevent it. So we decided that before the new millennium we would try to collaborate upon a solution.

"I invited Brother Lazarus to Saint Benedict's and we both thought it best that, while here, Brother Lazarus would keep his presence as quiet and unobtrusive as possible. Brother Lazarus, of course, hoped to find some solution to the problem in the writings of the Fathers and Doctors of the Church—hence the reason for his removing books from the library late at night. His presence in the library during the day drew too much attention to him. But I do not believe you have further reason to concern yourself regarding Brother Lazarus."

"Why is that?"

"Because, Brother Thomas, as of this afternoon, Brother Lazarus has left us to return to his own monastery in Constantinople."

"What!" Thomas exclaimed. "Despite what your personal

feelings are for Brother Lazarus, he is still very much a suspect in these murders."

"Then we shall learn for certain, shan't we," the abbot said calmly. "For if there is no longer any trouble you may assume that Brother Lazarus is the perpetrator, and we are well rid of him. But if anything else shall occur after his departure, then you shall know he is innocent and the culprit is still within our walls. One way or another, I do not believe we will be experiencing any more incidents."

Thomas was taken aback at the abbot's cavalier attitude. "Why is that?" he asked heatedly.

"Because, Brother Thomas, as I have told you, I do not believe these deaths were anything more than what they appear. And I will not spend any more time thinking about them—nor will you," the abbot said, with finality. "Brother Thomas, you will cease speculating on Brother Bartholomew's death and the previous deaths this monastery has witnessed. All of them were clearly accidents, and you are not to make something more out of them. I trust I have made myself understood?"

"Yes, Abbot."

"Brother Thomas, I went up to the scriptorium and spoke with Brother Bartholomew prior to his death regarding your work in copying out Revelation, as you were ordered to do. Your work, thus far, is not progressing as it should. *Nulla dies sine linea*— not a day without a line. You have also been seen much in the company of Brother Nicholas. It appears the two of you have been seen speaking more than usual."

He said the word "speaking" as if it were distasteful.

"We are justified by our works, and not our words," the abbot said.

"St. Clement I again?" Thomas said, with a note of sarcasm.

The abbot gave Brother Thomas a stern look, and said, "Learn to submit yourself, Brother Thomas, laying aside *the arrogant and proud stubbornness of your tongue.*"

That, too, was St. Clement, and Thomas wondered to himself why the abbot was prone to quote the first-century pontiff.

"Brother Thomas, this is not the first time I have had to speak to you about your transgressions. The Rule is quite clear in these matters. First there is a private admonition, which you have already had. Next there is a public reproof, then a separation from the brotherhood. I am now restricting you to a diet of bread and water for two weeks. If these infractions persist, then comes the scourging and finally expulsion from the monastery. These, of course, are at the discretion of the abbot. Brother Thomas, I wish you to look upon this as your final warning."

The abbot's voice took on additional firmness. "If you choose once more to go against my will and the will of this monastery, if you once more willingly and purposely transgress against the Rule—which you have sworn to obey—then I will have no choice but to banish you from this monastery. In addition, I will send out letters to other monasteries and recommend that you be *persona non grata*.

"I trust, Brother Thomas, that you will seriously consider everything I have said to you, and that you will make an effort to curb your pride, which is the devil's own vehicle, and strive for modesty. Forget your fantastic theories, but rather concentrate on God's love and on emulating the life of our Saviour. We must wear the ways of the world as a loose garment, and not allow it to corrupt us or hinder our spiritual journey. Return to your sacred work in the scriptorium, Brother Thomas, and allow nothing to hinder that. Pray for guidance and humility. That is where our salvation lies."

Thomas paused, overcome by a wave of doubt. Could he be wrong? he contemplated. Time and again the abbot found it necessary to rebuke him. Was Thomas straying from his mission in life? Was it not more important to strive for personal salvation, rather than these earthly mysteries that he sought out? Or was it the mysteries that sought him out? What were these temporal conundrums compared to God's glory? Thomas did lack humility, he freely admitted that. And yet . . . how was it his mind functioned on such a level? How was it possible that Thomas saw with the eye of illumination, while others stood in the dark? Perhaps God had made Thomas for just such a purpose.

These were indeed dark times. It had been centuries, it seemed, since anyone in the Church had brought some illumination to the Faith. The Church was stagnant, Thomas felt. It had not advanced, and he wondered why. Perhaps now was the time for some new growth. It was time to move forward, and Thomas believed intellect coupled with faith could only enhance Christianity. More and more he was certain he was on to a new direction for the Church—a new faith for the new millennium. Still, he would have to pray about it.

"I will, Brother Abbot," Thomas said humbly with his head still bowed. "And thank you."

Thomas left the abbot and went directly to the church to pray. He remained there a long time not only in prayer, but in silence, waiting to hear God's voice. From there he went to his work station in the scriptorium. With the death of Brother Bartholomew, the duties of the scriptorium fell to Brother Gregori, who was not overly friendly, but did lack Brother Bartholomew's gruffness.

Brother Gregori was an excellent choice to take over as *armarius,* Thomas thought. Though younger than Brother Bartholomew, Brother Gregori was vastly experienced as a scribe. Two days later, in one of their rare talks Brother Gregori told Thomas that he had travelled some before coming to this monastery five years ago.

"I spent three years in England and Ireland studying script," Brother Gregori said, not boastfully, but matter-of-factly. "I saw the Irish manuscript Cathach, or 'Battler,' so called because it is said to bring victory when carried thrice around a battlefield. In Northumbria, I studied the eighth-century Gospel According to St. Luke where a space was allowed between words. In the East I studied Targums written in Aramaic on scrolls. I have also read the Codex Argenteus written in silver ink on purple parchment, and the Moutiers-Grandval Bible created in the monastery of St. Martin in Tours where the monks there perfected the Carolingian minuscule. All these works have greatly inspired me in my own work."

"I have seen a sample of your work, Brother Gregori." Thomas said sincerely, "It is truly wonderful. You are to be commended."

"Thank you, Brother, and may I say your work is beginning to show promise."

"I think you are being too kind. I do not believe I was meant to be a scribe."

"I believe that the great Thomas of Worms is capable of anything he sets his mind to. If you need any assistance while in the scriptorium, please let me know."

"Thank you, Brother Gregori, I shall."

Brother Thomas worked for three entire days upon his manuscript, and he allowed only sleep, meals, and Divine Order to interrupt his work in the scriptorium. He did not even speak with Brother Nicholas for those days, mainly because he knew the prior, Brother Vittorio, was keeping a strict eye upon his movements, and would undoubtedly report everything to the abbot. Thomas could be a patient man when it was required of him, so he waited, and as he waited his mind worked upon the mysterious deaths that plagued the monastery.

He wondered what Brother Ryan, Brother Gedeon, and Brother Bartholomew all had in common that had brought them to their deaths? Had all the murders been staged to look like accidents? And, if so, why? He was certain all the murders had been committed by the same man, for Thomas could read the same signature on each. The last murder vexed him the most. The method of Brother Bartholomew's murder was most peculiar in that the murderer had gone to unusual lengths to pry the stone loose from the ledge in the cloister. Was there some significance to the spot where he was found? Thomas wondered. Try as he might, he could find no solution.

He found this difficult to admit to Brother Nicholas when the time came that they could risk being seen together again.

"Are you certain Brother Bartholomew was murdered?" Nicholas asked, sincerely troubled by the entire affair.

"You might as well ask if I am certain the earth is flat," Thomas replied, not hiding his resentment at this insulting question.

"What could it all mean?" Nicholas asked, in a tone of desperation.

"The ways of man are not as mysterious as the ways of God," Thomas proclaimed. "Man kills for greed, revenge, or self-preservation. We already know the manner. If we discover the motive, we might be a step closer to the man."

"How can you be so analytical, Brother Thomas?" Nicholas asked, confused. "We are talking about murders here in the monastery, perpetrated by a Benedictine monk and a brother of ours!"

"My dear Brother Nicholas, since the betrayal of our Lord by Judas Iscariot, nothing men can do surprises me."

Nicholas shuddered. Thomas's remark forced him to recall the incident in the woods with Brother Sebastian. He had never told Brother Thomas the story, and he tried not to think of it. It was a painful and disturbing memory for him. Sometimes when Nicholas lay in his cot at night he would see the face of Brother Sebastian staring down at him, and Nicholas knew the man had not acted under his own volition, but rather the will of something else—something sinister.

"We are not speaking of men here, Brother Thomas," Nicholas said, as his tone turned quite serious and low. "These murders can only be attributed to unspeakable evil."

"What are you saying, Brother? That the devil is responsible for these murders?"

"Is that not obvious?" Nicholas said incredulously.

Thomas let out a sigh. "My young friend, I know how tempted

you are to believe that to be so, but you must trust me. When we find the perpetrator of these atrocious acts, it will not be a demon or devil, but a flesh and blood man. What his motive is I cannot say. What his mental and spiritual condition is I cannot guess, but as surely as we stand at the centre of the universe, it is a man we seek. But to put your mind at ease, and so to give your soul strength, we shall pray about it."

And so they prayed.

The next day Brother Thomas used his free time to walk the cloister while he prayed. Between prayers he contemplated the murder scene where Brother Bartholomew met his end. He stopped to observe the spot in hopes that divine inspiration would descend upon him. He was deep in thought, when a voice spoke to him and called him by name. Thomas turned to see Brother Nicholas standing beside him. Thomas gazed around to see if Brother Vittorio was in view. No one seemed to be in their vicinity.

"Have you been able to come to any conclusions?" Nicholas queried.

"No, nothing I am afraid," Thomas admitted, as he stared up at the spot where the stone had been pried loose from the ledge.

Nicholas followed his gaze. Beneath where the stone had been removed, Nicholas studied the wood-carved riddle that hung below it.

"I have a confession to make, Brother Thomas," Nicholas whispered.

"I do not believe now is the proper time or place for that."

Nicholas let out a disappointed sigh and grew silent. After a moment, Thomas thought better of it and asked, "What is your confession, Brother?"

"I have never been able to solve one of them."

"You have never been able to solve one of what?"

"I have never been able to solve one of the wood-carved riddles on the cloister walls."

"How long have you been here now?"

"Since I was thirteen. Five years," Nicholas said, a trifle embarrassed.

"And in five years you have not been able to solve one of the riddles?"

"No."

"Come with me," Thomas said, and they walked around the cloister to the south wall. There, they stood looking up at another wood carving.

"I believe these carvings date back before the Benedictines," Thomas informed the younger monk, "which means they were done by the Gnostics, towards whom you have such strong feelings. Now, whatever you may think of the Gnostics, they were intelligent and had a sense of humour about them. Look at this wood carving and tell me what you see."

Nicholas stared at the familiar carving and described it. "It is of a woman dressed in nothing but a net, half-riding a goat, but with one foot on the ground. In her arms she is holding a rabbit."

"Now what does that suggest to you?" Thomas asked.

Nicholas thought for some time, yet in the end he shook his head, and confessed he could think of nothing.

"Though it is not allowed, I will help you with this one," Thomas said conspiratorially. "But you must promise to tell no one."

"I promise," Nicholas said, with the same conviction as when he took his vows.

"This riddle is not so difficult," Thomas said. "It involves a woman neither naked nor dressed. Neither driving nor riding nor walking. Not in the road or out of it. And bringing a gift that is not a gift."

As Thomas revealed the riddle, Nicholas's face shone as if he had been told the secret of life itself.

"But the rabbit?" Nicholas questioned. "Why is it a gift that is not a gift?"

"Because once it is given it runs away."

Nicholas stifled a laugh that barely escaped his lips. "It is all so simple!" he exclaimed.

"Yes," Thomas said blandly. "The mysterious often is once it is explained."

"And yet it does require special thought."

Thomas nodded and said, "We must alter the manner in which we think. Solving problems requires a flexible mind that allows us to look at situations slightly askew. Now, come with me."

Thomas led Nicholas back to the north wall of the cloister to where Brother Bartholomew had been discovered.

"Now, Brother, what do you make of that?" Thomas said to Nicholas indicating the wood carving upon the wall.

It was a very simple carving of a donkey with a small jug upon its back.

Nicholas stared at the carving for a considerable length of time. Finally he conceded, he could make nothing of it.

"Do not feel too bad," Thomas said. "I have yet to decipher it myself."

That night Thomas retired to his cot in the dormitory. He had a difficult time falling to sleep as his mind still worked on the many mysteries in the monastery. Finally, exhausted, his body slept, yet his mind continued to churn.

Sometime in the middle of the night, he woke out of a sound sleep and exclaimed aloud, "My God!"

Thomas sat up in bed to make certain he was not dreaming. He rose from his bed by the dim light of the candle that lit the dormitory and in the dark made his way to the north wall of the cloister. It was a clear cool night, and there was just enough light for Brother Thomas to make out the wood carving of the donkey with a clay jug upon its back. As Thomas gazed at the carving he laughed out loud, then gave thanks to God for all the blessings

He bestowed upon him.

Thomas was careful that day to report to the scriptorium, and attend to his work. During his free time he walked the cloister in prayer, and one of his prayers was that Brother Nicholas would seek him out and find him there. His prayers were answered in the afternoon.

Brother Nicholas walked with Thomas for some time before either of them spoke, and the first one to speak was Thomas.

"I believe I have solved it," the elder monk whispered out of the side of his mouth.

"Brother Bartholomew's murder?" Nicholas asked.

"No. The riddle of the wood carving."

"Oh," Nicholas said.

"Do not take it lightly," Thomas said. "The riddle of the wood carving is the way to the crypt."

Nicholas turned his head sharply towards his companion and stared at him doubtfully.

"What was it the old Gnostic said?" Thomas spoke to Nicholas in a Socratic manner.

"'A key that is not a key to a door that is not a door.'"

"Exactly," Thomas said, as they stopped and stood before the wood-carving. "If nothing else those old Gnostics had a singular wit. It is a play on words, don't you see. A key that is not a key is a don-key. And a door is not a door when it is a-jar. A donkey and a jar. It is a jar on the donkey's back, not a jug or a pot, but a jar."

Nicholas stared at the wood carving and shook his head. "Brother Thomas, I don't see how you do it. What are we to do now?"

"We are not to see each other for the remainder of the day. We will come here after the Great Silence. Farewell until then."

Eight

Nicholas lay in his bed waiting for the signal from Brother Thomas to arise and begin yet another nocturnal adventure. In the past weeks he had looked forward to these secret excursions. They were mysterious and exciting, and Nicholas felt these adventures brought him and Brother Thomas closer.

Most of the brothers in the monastery were not close. They lived, worked, and worshipped together. Yet how well did they know each other? Nicholas wondered. How would any of them react if they knew his secret?

At times he wished to tell someone, anyone, but fear held him back. He felt closest to Brother Thomas, but what would Brother Thomas think of him? Would Thomas consider him a deviant, a spawn of the devil? Nicholas could not bear to have Thomas turn away from him. At times he felt tormented by his own feelings and desires. Nicholas knew he should not feel these emotions in a monastery, and he had for years tried to suppress these feelings, but sometimes the urges were too strong. How long could he fight off these urges? How long could he deny his true self? The fear of being found out was almost overpowering. *Be sure your sin will find you out,* he had once read in Numbers. As he lay in his cot, he prayed for strength.

Thomas had no trouble fending off sleep. He lay awake and his mind raced with possibilities, theories, conjectures, and hypotheses. He wondered what they would find in the crypt, and how it could affect Christianity. Perhaps Thomas would become as well-known as Ignatius, Eusebius of Caesarea, and Athanasius of Alexandria. It would surely garner him an invitation to Rome, an audience with his Holiness, and the respect of all the bishops.

Thomas's musings were interrupted by very loud snoring. It was Brother Anthony. Over the years Thomas had become well-acquainted with all the nighttime noises in the dormitory. In the dark he could differentiate the wheezing breathing of Brother Corbini from the whistling exertions of Brother Gudula. He knew Brother Sabinus talked in his sleep, but only in Latin, and also that if Brother Ethelbert did not tie his cord around the bed frame, he would rise in his sleep and walk about.

Thomas realized that he would leave this place one day, and he would miss the monastery of St. Benedict, but no more than any of the many monasteries where he had sojourned in his travels. In his spiritual quest for God, Thomas had lived in the natural desert caves of Egypt, and in the simple cells cut out of the rocky cliffs by monks in Cappadocia. Thomas found that same simplicity in the beehive huts built of flat stone by the monks in the Celtic Kingdoms. The churches of Ireland were as crude as their huts, constructed of timber and sod, while the churches and abbeys of Britain were a bit more stately and built of stone. During his travels Thomas had witnessed some of the finest structures in all of Christendom, such as the old fortified Monastery of St. Catherine at the foot of Mount Sinai. One of the two of the grandest structures that Thomas had ever visited was the magnificent Hagia Sophia—the Church of Holy Wisdom, built by Emperor Justinian I in Constantinople, and completed in the year 537, with its gold altar, multiple marble flooring, and tall dome. The second was Aix-le-Chapelle built by Charlemagne at the beginning of the ninth century, with its splendid octagonal palace chapel. All these he had visited and prayed in, both the humble and the grand, yet he could not say in which God was more likely to be found.

Thomas rose silently from his cot and walked past rows of sleeping monks to where Nicholas lay. Thomas tapped the young monk's head lightly. Nicholas arose without a sound and followed him out of the dormitory and down to the north wall of the cloister. As before, during the Great Silence, Thomas and Nicholas communicated with gestures.

Thomas knew that the wood carving was the key to the crypt entrance. Not finding the ladder he had used earlier, Thomas motioned to Brother Nicholas to climb up on his shoulders, so to reach the wood carving.

Nicholas considered this and quickly shook his head.

Thomas furrowed his brow in consternation and silently asked, "Why not?"

Nicholas continued to shake his head.

Thomas looked at him sternly. With reluctance, Nicholas agreed and carefully climbed upon his friend's shoulders. From this very awkward position Nicholas pushed and pulled, twisted and turned the wood-carving until he heard an audible click, and felt a catch released. Excitedly, Nicholas climbed down off Thomas's shoulders, and the two monks felt around the wall beneath the wood-carving for an entrance. The wall of the cloister was of uneven stone, and it was difficult to find a break or seam.

Persistence won out. After much pushing a noticeable crack appeared, and then a definite opening. It was not an exceptionally large door, and Thomas had to turn sideways and stoop as he entered, holding the lit lantern he had brought. Nicholas followed apprehensively. They found winding stairs leading down into a dark oblivion that Nicholas imagined was the path to hell. Thomas held the lantern low, so they could see their own feet as they descended the stone steps. Nicholas walked warily, hoping he would not misplace a step and go tumbling down into the unknown depths. The image of Brother Ryan's body lying at the foot of the tower steps came into his mind. He tried not to think of it.

They descended slowly, seeing very little. The light of the lantern seemed to fight against the darkness. To Nicholas, it was a darkness that could almost be felt. A damp coldness drifted up to meet them and found its way beneath their habits, lending the monks an unearthly chill. The air smelled stale and lifeless, and they could practically taste it on their tongues. It tasted of death. Their sandalled feet scraped against the stairs, making hollow echoes. They stepped furtively and slowly. At one point Nicholas stumbled and fell against Brother Thomas, who caught him solidly. After a brief pause they proceeded.

They reached the bottom of the stairs and walked along a narrow passage. Nicholas inadvertently clutched at Brother Thomas's habit. They soon came to a room that was so large Thomas had to carry the lantern over to see the walls. Nicholas shrank back in dread as he realized that cut into the walls were burial chambers, each one filled with a corpse clothed in a rotting habit. Nicholas gasped in revulsion. Brother Thomas barely noticed, as he moved on inspecting all the burial chambers in the room.

Thomas counted seventeen, and he began to search each for the sacred Gnostic book. He motioned for Brother Nicholas to do the same, but the younger monk shook his head in protest. Thomas gave Nicholas a stern look, yet so great was the younger monk's fear that he defied any urging, and could not bring himself even to watch as Thomas poked his hand among the bones. Nicholas turned his head and wrapped his arms around himself in an attempt to stop trembling. The book was not in that chamber, so they moved on to the next.

The second room was similar to the first. Eventually, Brother Nicholas summoned up enough courage to aid in the search.

Gingerly he placed his trembling hands among the decaying bones and rotting habits. On the fourth such search Nicholas put his hands into a burial chamber and felt something furry and alive. The thing screeched like evil incarnate. Nicholas experienced a sharp, stabbing pain that burned like what his terrified mind took to be hellfire. The demon's screeching blended into Nicholas's own. For an instant he stood petrified with fear, screaming at the top of his lungs, then he fled into the darkness, still screaming with unimaginable terror.

Thomas turned in time to see Nicholas flee the room in horror. The look on the young monk's face both shocked and surprised him. Nicholas's face had grown distorted, so much so that Thomas barely recognized his companion. Before he knew it, Nicholas had disappeared into the darkness, and Thomas followed in pursuit. Thomas attempted to follow the whimpers and gasps of his friend, but the echoing acoustics proved deceiving. The underground tunnels of the crypt broke off in different directions. Thomas could not guess how far the tunnels ran. He began to fear for Nicholas's safety, and worried that if his friend became lost, he would not be able to find him again. Slightly disoriented himself, Thomas decided to break the Great Silence, and call out to his companion. Pausing a moment before doing so, he prayed.

Panic-stricken, Nicholas ran on aimlessly and blindly, as the crypt was perfectly dark. He heard only his own laboured breathing, and in his ears echoed that horrible scream that had mingled with his own. Several times he ran into a wall, but fuelled by fear he ignored the pain and ran on. Where he was headed, he did not consider. Finally he slowed down, then stopped, his panic abating. Nicholas did not know how far or in what direction he had fled. Finding himself in a corner, he sat upon the ground. He brought his knees up to his chin and hugged them tightly. As he rocked back and forth, he wondered what he was doing in such a hellish place. Ever since he had been a child, he had feared the dark, and dark places. He never should have let Brother Thomas lead him down here to this place of death. Nicholas had let his feelings for Brother Thomas influence his judgement. He never would have come here of his own volition. Now he had come across some demon in the dark.

Nicholas did not know what to do. He might be lost down here forever with the dead and the demons. He might very likely become one of them. Pausing a moment, he prayed. Beyond his prayers, Nicholas thought he heard God calling out to him.

Thomas searched frantically for his fellow monk. With all the twists and turns in the crypt Thomas began to fear he might never find him. He continued to call out, yet no answer was forthcoming. Suddenly, something caught the light of the lantern. Thomas moved the light towards it. At first, it appeared to be a disembodied head floating in mid-air. On closer inspection Thomas saw that it was only the effect of the black habit, for there sat Brother Nicholas on the floor of the crypt with his eyes closed, and his lips moving in prayer between whimpers.

"Brother Nicholas!" Thomas exclaimed, and rushed over to him. Thomas set the lamp down and knelt beside him, putting his arms around his friend. He could feel that Nicholas was shaking with fear and dread, and Thomas tried to comfort him. "Now, now," Thomas said soothingly, "everything is all right. There is no need to fret. *Shh, shh, shh.* There, there. Do not cry, Brother Nicholas. I am here."

Nicholas's sobs slowed as Thomas patted him and stroked his tonsured head. Thomas's presence had a decidedly calming effect, but Nicholas clutched onto him for security. Several minutes passed before Nicholas could bring himself to release his hold on Thomas, and still several more minutes after that before he could speak.

"I am sorry I ran away," he said, as his voice still trembled. "I am not certain what happened back there. Some demon—"

"It was a rat."

"It was what?"

"It was a rat," Thomas repeated. "You obviously disturbed it, an act to which it took exception."

"But I felt it burn me with hellfire," Nicholas protested. "I heard its awful scream."

"It screeched—you screamed—and then it bit you," Thomas informed the other as he rolled up the sleeve of the young monk to show him the bite marks on his right wrist.

"I do not like rats, Brother Thomas," Nicholas stated with conviction.

"No. I am certain you do not."

"I am sorry that I ran off like a coward," he said timidly. "Thank you for coming to find me."

"You are welcome."

"Have . . . have you . . . ever been afraid, Brother Thomas?"

"We have all been afraid at some time or other, Brother. It is a human condition. But when we fear, we are not showing faith and trust in our Lord, and that must displease him terribly. So in our lives we must attempt to rid ourselves of fear."

"But you, Brother Thomas, have you ever personally been afraid?"

Thomas paused, then said, "Yes. I have experienced fear."

"When?"

Thomas sat down on the floor next to Nicholas. He said nothing for a long moment. Then he spoke slowly and quietly.

"Do you recall when you joined the order, you were required to reveal your conversion of life—what great revelation in your life led you to want to serve God in this way? It is a requirement of everyone who wishes to join the Benedictine order. When it came my time to reveal my revelation, I was very, very afraid. I believed that if I told my story, I might be refused entry into the order."

"Because of something terrible you had done in your past?" Nicholas asked timidly.

"No. It was not anything like that," Thomas said, stifling a grin. "It was simply that I had no great revelation that led me to join the order. There I was, having heard incredible stories from Benedictines proclaiming wondrous revelations, and I had no conversion of life to share."

"And your fear was that they would not allow you into the order without one?"

"No, it wasn't that."

"Then what was it?"

"Well, since I had no great conversion of my life to proclaim, I simply made one up."

"You did what?"

"I made up a revelation, and I feared for the longest time that my deception would be discovered. I was afraid that when that happened I would be disgraced, branded a liar, and ejected from the order. But more than that, I feared God would punish me for such a lie. I feared I had damned my soul for all time."

Nicholas shook his head in disbelief. He said, "How were you able to do that? I do not mean simply lying, but how were you able to think up something to tell them? What did you tell them?"

"To tell you the truth, I cannot recall exactly what I said. I am certain it was spiritually uplifting without being overly dramatic. As for how I came up with the story, the imagination is a glorious thing, and I must admit mine is quite extraordinary."

"I could not imagine making up such a story," Nicholas said.

"Then, you are an honest man, and I respect you for your honesty," Thomas said, looking the young monk in the eye.

Nicholas turned away from Thomas's gaze.

"What is it?" Thomas asked, picking up on his friend's distress.

Nicholas could not bring himself to look at his companion, and when he spoke it was with some embarrassment.

"I am not as honest as you might think," he said finally. "Something happened several weeks ago—something appalling. I

never told you. I never intended to tell you. I was too embarrassed."
Nicholas proceeded to tell Thomas what had happened to him in
the woods, of how Brother Sebastian had found him and accosted
him, and how Brother Gregori had come to his rescue.

"The incident in the woods brought back memories which I
had tried to forget," Nicholas said. "They are memories so painful
that up until now I have not shared them with anyone."

Nicholas fell silent. Thomas did not prompt him, but waited
silently, staring straight ahead. Finally, Nicholas spoke.

"I was always a disappointment to my parents. They often
made me feel that I was not the son they wanted. I was small and
physically weak, and not much help with chores around the farm.
My mother was a pious woman, and taught me to pray and love
God. Unfortunately, she could not save me from my father. My
father was not a tall man, but he was broad and strong. When I
was young—I do not recall how young—my father found me in
the barn while I was doing my daily chores. When he came in, I
knew he was drunk on wine, as he often was. I looked at him, and
he at me. I do not think I can ever forget that look; it haunts my
dreams.

"The innocence of a child is a blessing from God. I lost my
childhood innocence that day. My father took me many times
after that. Though I feared him, I never hated him for it. I began
to hate myself. I hated who I was, and my size, and my lack of
strength. If only I could fight him off, I thought, then I would be
safe, but I could not. I began to imagine myself as someone else,
someone larger and stronger. Somewhere in my young life I lost
myself. I lost who I was and what I was. As I grew older, I began
to have certain . . . desires that I knew were unnatural. When I
entered the order, I did not tell all of this, only part of it. I made
my revelation sound as if I were a lost soul in need of salvation
through God's graces, and that I intended to spend the remainder
of my life in dutiful service and gratitude to God. In some ways,
I do not believe I was totally dishonest."

Nicholas ceased his narrative. The two sat in deep silence for a long moment. Turning towards Nicholas, Thomas was caught by how the young monk's blue-green eyes reflected the dim light and glistened like twin pools of water. Thomas suspected Nicholas was on the verge of tears.

"You are the only person who has ever heard my story," Nicholas said, still unable to look Thomas in the face. "I have always been afraid to tell anyone the truth, for fear of what they would think of me. Your friendship has always meant very much to me, Brother Thomas. I feel I have now placed that friendship in jeopardy by revealing so much of myself."

Thomas paused to absorb all he had heard. He chose his words more carefully than usual, so they would be effective. "You have displayed great courage just now," he told Nicholas. "You have revealed a strength of character not found in many men today. What we have shared here today will remain *inter nos*—between us."

"And God," Nicholas interjected.

"Yes," Thomas agreed. "Between us and God. I can only say that by telling each other our flaws and imperfections we have become closer, and an inseparable bond exists between us, now and forever. In this monastery we call ourselves brothers, but what occurred here in this cold, dark place has made you and me true brothers, and our love for each other has grown to a level that was first known by our Saviour's apostles. Brother Nicholas, we have been participants in a small miracle."

As Nicholas turned to face Thomas, tears welled in the young monk's eyes, and he fought against a smile. The two embraced each other, and remained locked in love for a long moment.

"Brother Thomas," Nicholas said, breaking the silence of the crypt, "there is something else I need to tell you, something I must reveal about myself."

Thomas half-suspected what Nicholas was about to say, and he was not wholly comfortable with the subject. He thought it best to put off this particular revelation.

"I think we have had enough disclosure for the time being," he said good-naturedly, and, smiling, Thomas rose and put out his hand to help his friend to his feet. "But for now we must turn our attention to finding the sacred Gnostic book, and leave this place before our absence is discovered."

Brother Nicholas sniffed, wiped his eyes, and nodded in agreement.

Raising the lantern high, Thomas was able to observe the room they had been in all this time. It was not typical of the burial chambers they had seen prior to this one. Though this room was made to be a burial chamber, there were no bodies buried here. On close inspection only one niche was cut into a wall, and that being high and small.

Thomas walked over to the niche, and passed the lantern to Nicholas. Reaching up, Thomas put his hands into the small recess and carefully felt around. His hands came to rest on something solid with edges. He picked up the article and gingerly extracted it from its resting place. It was a book wrapped in a coarse, worn cloth. Thomas stared open-mouthed at the object, then looked at Nicholas and smiled. He did not unwrap his prize but clutched it eagerly to his breast.

"Let us give thanks," Nicholas said to Thomas, and both said a silent prayer.

"We will again observe the Great Silence and find our way out of here," Thomas instructed once they had prayed.

With some difficulty they were able to retrace their steps in the crypt. Fortunately there was a deep layer of dust upon the floor, and Thomas was able to backtrack using their footprints in the dust as a guide. The method did prove confusing at times, for there often seemed to be an extra set of footprints, but after a long while the brothers eventually found the correct passage that led them back to the secret door in the cloister.

Just as the two monks emerged from the passage, they heard

the bell toll for *prime*. Thomas and Nicholas hastened to join their brothers in Divine Office.

Thomas had no time to hide the book, but kept it tucked securely beneath his black habit. During worship, Thomas made all the correct responses, but his mind dwelt upon the book, and all the wonders it might hold. It was all he could do to suppress the excitement that gripped him.

When *prime* worship ended, Thomas rose quickly to leave the church. He was almost out the door when he heard someone call his name. Thomas did not hesitate but pretended not to hear and kept walking. The voice called out to Thomas again, this time louder and with definite authority. Thomas recognized the abbot's voice, and thought it best to stop. He kept his long, full sleeves in front of him to help conceal the book's presence beneath his robe.

"Brother Thomas," the abbot asked suspiciously, "where do you hasten?"

"Why, Abbot, to the scriptorium, of course." Thomas raised his arm in the direction of the room, but when he did so he felt the book slip and he brought his hand back quickly to steady it.

"Ah, yes," the abbot said, peering closely at Thomas. "How is your work progressing?"

"Very well, thank you, Lord Abbot."

"I was speaking to Brother Gregori about you, and he said you have the talents of a very good scribe."

"Brother Gregori is too kind."

"Yes, he is. He also said that you are a very quiet worker, and he seldom even knows you are there."

Thomas said nothing, wondering if there was a hidden meaning in the abbot's words.

Looking him up and down, the abbot said, "Are you certain you are getting enough sleep, Brother Thomas? You looked quite tired."

"Yes, thank you. I have been sleeping just fine."

"Very good, Brother Thomas, you may proceed to the scriptorium."

Thomas turned to leave, but the abbot called out to him again.

"Have you seen Brother Nicholas?" asked the abbot.

Thomas looked about and said, "I am certain he is here somewhere. Why do you ask?"

"No reason," the abbot said. "It is simply that Brother Nicholas, also, looks as if he is in need of sleep."

Thomas hesitated, trying not to betray anything by word or look.

"Good day, Brother Thomas," Abbot Michael said slowly.

As the abbot turned and walked away, Thomas felt certain the man knew something. But how he knew, and how much he knew, Thomas could not guess.

In the scriptorium Thomas went directly to his work station and carefully removed the book from beneath his habit and placed it, still wrapped in its cloth, under his desk. Brother Nicholas entered the scriptorium and approached Thomas. Wordlessly, they exchanged looks that translated into:

Nicholas: "Where is the book?"

Thomas: "Under the desk."

Nicholas: "Take it out and let us have a look at it."

Thomas: "Now is not a good time."

Nicholas: "When then?"

Thomas: "Later. Meet me among the berries after dinner."

After the midday meal Thomas strolled out and walked the cloister. He walked around it twice to determine if he were being followed or observed. Satisfied that he was not, he casually slipped out the rear gate and strolled towards the grove of pine trees. He found Brother Nicholas already there, eagerly awaiting him.

"I thought you would never arrive," Nicholas said.

"Youth is synonymous with impatience," Thomas told him.

"You must learn to bide your time. I did not wish to make a fool's rush, lest I was followed."

Nicholas accepted the slight and ungraciously replied, *"Magister dixit*—the master has spoken. Well, did you bring it?"

Thomas glared briefly at his young friend, then paused to look around him, and proceeded to draw the book from beneath his habit. They sat down side by side upon a fallen poplar tree, and Thomas placed the book upon his lap, while Nicholas looked on. In his own peculiar way Thomas took a moment to examine the coarse, heavy cloth that enshrouded the book. It was old and well worn.

"Well, open it," Nicholas spoke impatiently.

Thomas gave him another disapproving look before he slowly unwrapped the book.

It was a modest unveiling for an object that was very modest in appearance. A worn, faded leather wrapping covered the book, which was in truth a codex. At first sight, Thomas estimated the codex to be hundreds of years old. Carefully, he opened the leather cover to reveal the first page, which was not made of parchment, but very old papyrus. There was a stiffness to it and the ends were brittle. The entire look of it spoke of antiquity. Both Thomas and Nicholas read the title. The title, centred at the top of the first page, was written in Greek, as was the entire text. As they read the title, the two were amazed by it. Even more amazing was the epistle that followed.

Nine

JUDAS

IT IS WITH GREAT JOY AND ANTICIPATION THAT I PUT DOWN THESE WORDS SO THEY MAY SURVIVE MY PASSING, AS I AM IN MY SEVENTY-EIGHTH YEAR AND DO NOT KNOW HOW MUCH LONGER I MAY REMAIN UPON THE EARTH. MY NAME IS JUDAS, TAKEN AFTER MY LORD WHOM I SERVED MANY YEARS. HE IS LONG DEPARTED NOW, HAVING LIVED THE LATTER PART OF HIS LIFE IN EXILE UPON THIS ISLAND OF PHAROS OFF THE COAST OF ALEXANDRIA. HE HIMSELF DID NOT WISH TO RECORD THE EVENTS THAT GAVE BOTH JOY AND SORROW TO HIS LIFE, BUT HE HAS TOLD ME HIS TALE ENOUGH TIMES THAT IT COULD BE MY OWN. HERE, DURING THE REIGN OF TRAJAN, WORD IS SPREADING OF A HEBREW MESSIAH WHO WAS CRUCIFIED BY THE GOVERNOR OF JUDEA, DURING THE REIGN OF TIBERIUS. ALONG WITH THESE STORIES ARE ALSO TALES OF MY LATE LORD

OF THE MOST UNTRUE NATURE. I HAVE VOWED TO
SET DOWN THE TRUTH REGARDING THE HEBREW
KNOWN AS JESUS OF NAZARETH AND OF ONE OF
HIS DISCIPLES, MY LORD, JUDAS ISCARIOT.

IN THE TIME WHEN TIBERIUS RULED ROME,
AND PONTIUS PILATE RULED OVER JUDEA, AND
HEROD ANTIPAS WAS THE TETRARCH OF GALILEE,
AND JOSEPH CAIAPHAS WAS THE HIGH PRIEST OF
THE TEMPLE IN JERUSALEM, THERE LIVED HOLY
MEN IN THE JUDEAN DESERT ON THE EDGE OF A
DEAD SEA. THEY WERE A SOLITARY RACE WHO
HAD RENOUNCED THE PRIESTS OF THE GREAT
TEMPLE IN JERUSALEM, AND THEY FLED SOCIETY
TO LIVE AWAY FROM ALL THINGS EVIL AND
CORRUPT. WITH THEM ALL GOODS WERE HELD IN
COMMON, AND MEALS WERE TAKEN IN COMMON,
AS WERE PRAYERS, AND DAILY RITUAL BATHS.
THEIR TOWNS WERE SELF-SUFFICIENT, MAKING
AND GROWING EVERYTHING THEY NEEDED, AND
ALL SHARED IN THE WORK. THEIR OATH WAS TO
PRACTICE PIETY TOWARDS GOD, TO ACT JUSTLY
TO ALL MEN, TO HATE THE UNJUST, TO INJURE
NO ONE, NEVER TO LIE OR STEAL, TO KEEP NO
SECRETS FROM BRETHREN, NEVER TO REVEAL THE
SECRETS OF THE ORDER TO OUTSIDERS, AND MOST
IMPORTANTLY TO SHUN EVIL AND TURN ONLY
TOWARDS WHATEVER IS HOLY AND GOOD. FOR
THE WORLD, THEY BELIEVED, WAS DIVIDED INTO
TWO OPPOSING FORCES: THE SONS OF LIGHT AND
THE SONS OF DARKNESS.

OUT OF THIS GROUP OF HOLY MEN CAME A
DESERT PROPHET NAMED JOHN WHO BADE PEOPLE
TO RENOUNCE SIN AND CLEANSE THEMSELVES
IN THE JORDAN RIVER. ONE OF JOHN'S MOST

DEVOTED FOLLOWERS WAS A MAN FROM NAZARETH NAMED JESUS. FROM JOHN, JESUS LEARNED MANY THINGS, PRAYERS AND PARABLES, AND HEALING TECHNIQUES. JOHN SENT JESUS OF NAZARETH OUT TO TEACH TO THE PEOPLE OF THE TOWNS AND VILLAGES, AND IN THIS WAY JESUS HIMSELF ATTRACTED FOLLOWERS, MY LORD JUDAS ISCARIOT BEING ONE OF THEM.

ALONG WITH HIS FELLOW DISCIPLES, MY LORD LEARNED MANY THINGS FROM JESUS OF NAZARETH WHO WENT FROM TOWN TO TOWN TEACHING PEOPLE AND ADMINISTERING TO THE SICK, AS HE WAS AN EXPERT WITH THE HEALING POWERS OF HERBS AND GEMSTONES. HEALING THE SICK BECAME A LUCRATIVE PRACTICE, AS MOST PEOPLE WERE GRATEFUL ENOUGH TO RECOMPENSE. JESUS TRUSTED ENOUGH IN JUDAS ISCARIOT TO MAKE HIM THE TREASURER OF THEIR MONEY. FOR THIS REASON AND OTHERS, SOME OF THE DISCIPLES WERE JEALOUS OF HIM, BUT JUDAS WAS NOT RESENTFUL.

IN HIS TEACHINGS THERE CAME A TIME WHEN JESUS SPOKE AGAINST ROME AND THE HIGH PRIESTS OF THE TEMPLE, WHICH GARNERED HIM ENEMIES. MANY TIMES MY LORD JUDAS AND HIS BROTHERS ASKED THEIR MASTER TO FLEE, AS THEY FEARED FOR HIS SAFETY. FINALLY JESUS AGREED TO LEAVE NAZARETH BUT BEFORE HE COULD ESCAPE JESUS WAS ARRESTED.

FALSELY THE MAN WAS ACCUSED, PUT ON TRIAL AND CONDEMNED TO DIE. DISTRAUGHT OVER THE IMPENDING FATE OF HIS MASTER, JUDAS ISCARIOT APPROACHED HIS FELLOW DISCIPLES AND PROPOSED THAT THEY PAY THE HIGH PRIESTS TO

WITHDRAW THEIR CHARGES. THE OTHER DISCIPLES REFUSED, STATING THAT IT WOULD DO NO GOOD AND WOULD PROVE A WASTE OF MONEY. JUDAS WAS DETERMINED TO SAVE JESUS, SO HE TOOK THE MONEY WITHOUT THE CONSENT OF THE OTHERS.

HE GAVE THE MONEY TO THE PRIESTS OF THE TEMPLE IN HOPES OF FREEING HIS MASTER. THOUGH A BARGAIN WAS STRUCK AND THE PRIESTS TOOK THE MONEY THEY DID NOTHING TO HELP SAVE JESUS. TRY AS HE MIGHT, MY LORD JUDAS COULD NOT SAVE HIS MASTER FROM HIS IMPENDING FATE. THE NAZARENE WAS CRUCIFIED AT THE COMMAND OF PONTIUS PILATE, THE GOVERNOR OF JUDEA.

ONCE HE WAS DEAD THE BODY WAS TAKEN DOWN OFF THE CROSS AND PLACED IN A TOMB. THE FOLLOWERS OF JESUS WERE FEARFUL THAT THE BODY WOULD BE STOLEN BY THE ROMANS OR THE JEWISH ELDERS. JUDAS AND HIS BROTHERS DECIDED TO TAKE THE BODY FROM ITS TOMB AND BURY IT SECRETLY WHERE JESUS'S ENEMIES WOULD NEVER FIND IT. SOON AFTER THE BODY WAS DISCOVERED MISSING, RUMOURS BEGAN TO CIRCULATE THAT JESUS HAD RISEN FROM THE DEAD. PEOPLE AROUND JERUSALEM EVEN CLAIMED TO HAVE SEEN HIM AFTER DEATH. IT WAS DECIDED BY JESUS'S DISCIPLES THAT THEY WOULD PERPETUATE THE MYTH WHICH THEY DID BY CREATING STORIES THAT HE WAS THE JEWISH MESSIAH AND HAD PERFORMED MIRACLES WHILST HE LIVED.

MY LORD JUDAS, WHO LOVED JESUS MORE THAN THE REST, WAS AGAINST SUCH A DECEPTION AS HE DID NOT WISH TO MAR HIS DEAD MASTER'S

MEMORY WITH LIES. BUT BY HIS FELLOW DISCIPLES WAS MY LORD'S LIFE PLACED UNDER THE THREAT OF DEATH IF HE WERE EVER TO REVEAL THE TRUTH.

BELIEVING HIS LIFE TO BE ENDANGERED, MY LORD JUDAS FLED HIS COUNTRY AND AFTER SEVERAL YEARS OF TRAVELLING CAME TO REST HERE ON THIS PEACEFUL ISLAND. SOON AFTER HIS ARRIVAL I CAME TO BE HIS DEVOTED SERVANT. NEVER HAD A SERVANT A MORE NOBLE AND WORTHY MASTER.

AFTER A TIME, STORIES OF JESUS OF NAZARETH FOUND THEIR WAY TO THIS ISLAND. AMONG THESE STORIES WERE THE FOULEST LIES REGARDING MY MASTER JUDAS ISCARIOT. THEY WERE STORIES OF THEFT, BETRAYAL AND DEATH. I CAN SAY BEYOND ALL DOUBT THAT NEVER WAS THERE A MORE HONEST MAN, NEVER WAS THERE A MORE LOYAL MAN THAN JUDAS ISCARIOT. THE RUMOURS OF HIS DEATH IN JERUSALEM ARE GREATLY EXAGGERATED WHEREAS I CAN ATTEST THE MAN WAS VERY MUCH ALIVE AND WELL AND LIVED FOR MANY YEARS IN MY COMPANY.

THOUGH HE WAS DISTRESSED OVER THESE DEFAMATIONS, MY LORD WAS PHYSICALLY STRICKEN WHEN HE HEARD THE INCREDIBLE UNTRUTHS REGARDING HIS FORMER MASTER, AND HOW THE MAN'S MEMORY WAS BEING PERVERTED TO SERVE SOME BLASPHEMOUS POLITICAL AGENDA. I NEED NOT GO INTO DETAIL REGARDING THESE LIES AND EXAGGERATIONS OF JESUS OF NAZARETH BEING THE SON OF GOD, AS THEY WILL IN ALL PROBABILITY COME TO NOTHING IN THE YEARS AHEAD.

THOUGH MY LORD JUDAS WAS DISTRAUGHT OVER THESE OBSCENE UNTRUTHS, HE HELD NO RESENTMENTS TOWARDS HIS ONETIME COMPANIONS WHO OBVIOUSLY HAD SPREAD THESE STORIES IN A SELFISH GESTURE TO GAIN SOME POWER FOR THEMSELVES. IN FACT, TIL THE DAY HE DIED MY LORD CONTINUED TO PRAY FOR THEM AND WISH THEM WELL, WHILE HE HIMSELF REFUSED TO PUT FORTH ANY EFFORT TO EXONERATE HIMSELF OR REVEAL THE TRUTH OF HIS DEAD MASTER. IT WOULD BE AS CASTING PEARLS BEFORE SWINE, HE ONCE TOLD ME, WHERE THE TRUTH WOULD BE TRAMPLED INTO THE MUD BY HERETICS.

WHILE SERVING OUT HIS SELF-EXILE HERE ON THE ISLAND OF PHAROS JUDAS ISCARIOT, THOUGH LONGING TO SEE HIS HOMELAND AGAIN, SPENT THE REMAINDER OF HIS DAYS MINISTERING TO THE SICK AND POOR, ACCEPTING NOTHING FOR HIMSELF EXCEPT THE BAREST MINIMUM ON WHICH TO LIVE. HIS GENEROSITY, LOVE AND COMPASSION WERE UNEQUALLED AND HIS FORGIVENESS KNEW NO BOUNDS. TO THOSE WHO KNEW HIM HERE DURING HIS FINAL YEARS, HIS MEMORY WILL CONTINUE TO SHINE LIKE THE BEACON OF PHAROS THAT IS A LIGHT FOR ALL TO SEE. MY VERY HEART ACHES AT THE PASSING OF A MAN WHOM I SHALL EVER REGARD AS THE BRAVEST, WISEST AND KINDEST MAN I OR THIS WORLD HAVE EVER KNOWN.

AS I RELATE THIS STORY TO MY SCRIBE, IT IS MY DYING WISH THAT THE TRUTH OF MY MASTER, JUDAS ISCARIOT, AND HIS MASTER, JESUS OF NAZARETH BE MADE KNOWN TO THE WORLD SO THAT THEY BOTH MAY BE GRANTED PROPER AND

EQUAL REVERENCE. FOR NEITHER WAS A GOD, BUT MEN OF GOD, AND THE WORLD DESERVES TO KNOW THE TRUTH AND LEARN FROM THEIR EXAMPLE.

Ten

Thomas and Nicholas sat upon the log staring straight ahead, saying nothing. Neither of them could speak. They were afraid to say anything.

Nicholas felt his insides churn, and thought he might vomit. Though he could barely believe what he had just read, the thought of it gave him great anxiety. He had been raised to believe in sacred Scriptures, and his faith—indeed the entire Christian world's faith—hinged on the Gospels and their unquestionable veracity. Never before had Nicholas questioned the Bible and what it contained. He had accepted it with unwavering faith and trust, yet now, here was something refuting the divinity of Jesus Christ. Nicholas wondered how strong his faith was if this document could disturb him so.

"It cannot be authentic," Brother Nicholas said weakly, unaware that his voice wavered.

Thomas barely heard him. He was preoccupied with what this codex could mean to the world, and the repercussions it might cause. Thomas could think of it only as an incredible find, and that his name would be linked to it. Scholars from all over the world would wish to study it. Both Thomas and the monastery would garner instant fame and recognition. Here, as fantastic as it sounded, was a true Gospel written by someone who had known and served one of Jesus Christ's own disciples closely. It was an unknown story, never suspected or imagined. It might possibly be the greatest find in all the world.

"Brother Thomas," Nicholas broke in on the other's musing, "I asked if you believe this to be authentic."

Thomas paused in his thoughts. "There is only one way for us to find out," he said.

Wrapping the codex up in its cloth, Thomas of Worms tucked the volume up beneath his habit, and with Brother Nicholas headed back to the monastery.

In the scriptorium they found Brother Gregori diligently at work, copying from an exemplar of an eighth-century French manuscript. Thomas and Nicholas stood beside Brother Gregori's desk, until the other paused in his work and looked up.

"Brother Thomas," Gregori asked, in a friendly but authoritative manner, "why are you not at your work station?"

"Brother Gregori—" Thomas ignored the question—"with the death of Brother Bartholomew, you are now the chief *armarius* in the monastery."

"Yes. That is correct."

"Which means that in this entire monastery, indeed, in the entire region, you are the foremost expert on rare and ancient books."

Gregori nodded, not knowing to what Thomas was alluding.

"Brother Nicholas," Thomas said turning to the young monk, "did you know Brother Gregori here has travelled extensively, studying and researching sacred documents? I would venture to say he knows more about scripts and scrolls, vellum and *membrana* than any man in Christendom."

"Mox non in rem," Brother Gregori said, tiring of this idle talk. "What is it you wish, Brother Thomas?"

"Do you recall, Brother Gregori, when you offered me your

services?" Thomas asked, lowering his voice and taking on an earnest tone.

"If I recall correctly, Brother Thomas, I offered you my assistance while you were in the scriptorium."

"We are in the scriptorium now," Thomas said. "And I am in need of your assistance."

"You need not go around the cloister if you can cut across the courtyard, Brother Thomas," Gregori stated. "If you are in need of assistance, you have but to ask."

"What I am about to ask is much," Thomas said, still speaking low. "I must swear you to secrecy."

"That is highly unusual, Brother Thomas."

"So it is, yet if you knew why I needed your total discretion, I am certain you would understand."

"So, you are asking me to swear an oath of secrecy to something I know nothing about, but I cannot know what it is until I am sworn."

"Rem acu tetigisti" Thomas exclaimed. "You touched the thing with a needle."

"You do indeed ask much."

"I would not ask if it were not important."

Brother Gregori studied the two monks who stood before him. "I will swear your oath."

Thomas smiled, and motioned to Nicholas who then walked over to Thomas's table, and picked up the Spanish book he was copying. Nicholas brought the book to Brother Gregori who placed both hands upon it.

Thomas recited the oath which Gregori repeated. "I swear before this humble assembly, and before God, that I will not disclose to anyone what I am about to see here today."

It was a simple oath, but sufficient.

"Now," said Brother Gregori letting out an exasperated breath, "what is it you have that warrants such secrecy?"

Thomas drew the book from beneath his habit and placed it

on Brother Gregori's table. The *armarius* removed the wrapping, looked at the item briefly, then at his companions questioningly.

"We would like you to study this codex, Brother Gregori," Thomas said softly. "Study the ink, the writing, the pages—everything. We need to know its date and place of origin. We need to know beyond all doubt if this codex is authentic."

Gregori stared at them mutely. He nodded slowly and opened the codex.

Thomas and Nicholas left the scriptorium to allow Brother Gregori to examine the codex in private. The two monks found themselves walking the cloister, contemplating their latest find.

They walked for some time, not speaking, before Brother Nicholas broke the silence.

"Brother Thomas, if we discover that the codex is authentic, what do we do then?"

"What do you mean?" Thomas asked. "If it is authentic then *nihil obstat*—nothing hinders it from being published."

"Yes," Nicholas said, but he sounded doubtful.

Thomas intuited his distress and asked, "Exactly what is it that troubles you, Brother?"

Nicholas donned a thoughtful countenance, and spoke with care. "Perhaps we have not thought this out to its inevitable conclusion. What if it does more harm than good?"

"What are you saying, Brother Nicholas? That we should suppress it? My young friend, you must learn that in all things *quaere verum*—seek the truth!"

"*Ruat caelum?*" Nicholas came back.

"*Fiat iustitia ruat caelum!*" Thomas expounded. "Let justice be done though the heavens fall!"

Thomas and Nicholas spoke little to each other for the remainder of the day, and the next. Neither disturbed Brother Gregori in the scriptorium. Though Nicholas highly respected Thomas as a learned man, he could not wholeheartedly agree with the German monk about the Judas codex. Nicholas could not describe exactly what he felt towards the book, yet he knew nothing good would come of it. He suspected there was an evil presence at work here—that the codex itself was evil. He could not tell Brother Thomas this, of course. Thomas of Worms had little regard for feelings or intuition or anything that could not be proved. Yet Nicholas knew in his heart that something was wrong. It consumed his waking days, and kept him from sleeping at night. He would lie awake upon his cot and fret, tossing and turning in between bouts of prayer, at odds over what to do.

Nicholas thought back to how the entire mystery had begun, and cursed the day he had told Thomas of his discovery of the book in the library. Brother Gregori had returned the book for Brother Bartholomew, and Nicholas had examined the book and had discovered the hidden writing. It had started so simply, but it had led to weeks of intrigue, from secret rooms and cyphered messages to dark and mysterious crypts. The end of the mystery could very possibly lead to years of theological debates, and in the end might tear Christianity apart. Were not the East and West churches already on the brink of a schism over relatively minor points? The Judas codex could possibly bring about the end of Christianity. Nicholas felt sick to his stomach that he had played a part in the affair.

Thomas of Worms did not sleep well either. His sleep was warded off by his excitement that their discovery might be the most important find in Christendom, even surpassing the time an original volume of Origen's Hexapla was found in Alexandria.

Two days later, Thomas was busy at work in the scriptorium, along with several others, including Brother Gregori, when the latter approached him.

"And how is your work progressing today, Brother?" Gregori asked, in his pragmatic fashion.

Thomas stared at him briefly, then replied; "Very well, thank you, Brother Gregori. That ink you gave me was much better than my own mixture."

"That ink is a special blend I have recently developed," Gregori said. "The special ingredient is extracted from oak galls—you know, those nutlike growths on the leaves and branches of oak trees. They are actually gall wasp cocoons."

"Why, Brother Gregori, that is astounding!" Thomas said, sincerely impressed.

"Thank you. If you like, come the spring I will show you how I collect the galls, crush them and soak them in warm rain water."

"Thank you," Thomas said, awestruck by the man's knowledge. "That sounds fascinating. I would enjoy that very much. How do you come up with such things?"

"My father," Gregori said simply. "He was a very intelligent man."

"And your father was . . . ?"

"Philip of Corsica."

"I believe I have heard of him," Thomas said. "It has been said in some circles that he was brilliant."

"Yes," Gregori said. Thomas could see sadness in the other's face. Though Thomas was not so insensitive as to mention it, Gregori's sadness must have come from the fact that his father had been excommunicated from the Church for his many brilliant, yet radical ideas. It was not a story with which Thomas of Worms was wholly unfamiliar.

Brother Gregori turned away with a dour face, but before he did, the master scribe deftly slipped a small slip of parchment onto Thomas's table in such a way that even if they were being watched closely, no one would notice.

Thomas, himself, barely saw it. He picked up the small piece of parchment and concealed it in his hand. After several minutes he carefully placed it on his work so he might read it. There was tiny writing on the parchment, but Thomas could read it clearly: MEET ME ATOP THE TOWER.

Thomas casually looked about the scriptorium. There were several of his brothers hard at work copying out sacred text, but he did not see Brother Gregori. If Gregori had slipped out of the room without Thomas's seeing him, then Thomas was certain no one else had observed his leaving either. Thomas waited several minutes before he slowly stood up from his table, stretched his arms and shoulders, rubbed his eyes, and walked out of the scriptorium.

Thomas of Worms ascended the steps leading up to the tower. He trod carefully, remembering Brother Ryan and his fateful fall. Thomas still did not believe Brother Ryan's death had been an accident, yet neither had he found a solution to the matter.

Thomas found Brother Gregori waiting for him on the roof of the tower. It was a cool, early-December day. The clouds that passed overhead hung so low that from atop the tower it appeared that one could reach up and touch them. Snow had not yet fallen on the monastery, but undoubtedly it would come soon. A stiff breeze gusted, as if reluctant to pass over the mountain. It seemed to carry a sense of foreboding. Standing at the south wall of the tower that rose to chest-height was Brother Gregori, whose sober expression reflected that foreboding. He leaned against the wall and stared off at the horizon as if he wished to be where his gaze rested, as if he wished to be anywhere but here. Both monks had their hoods turned up against the north wind. Thomas approached the other and stood beside him, following Gregori's gaze.

"I sometimes come up here to pray when I am troubled," Gregori said, still staring off into the distance.

"Are you troubled now?" Thomas asked.

"Sorely troubled," the other said.

"Does your trouble have anything to do with the codex I gave you?"

Gregori nodded.

"It has been my experience that shared trouble lessens the load," Thomas said. "Perhaps you had best tell me the results of your study of the book."

Brother Gregori nodded again at Thomas's suggestion.

"As you obviously noted, the work is a codex," Gregori began, his gaze still resting on the horizon. "Codices originated in Rome two hundred years before the birth of our Lord. Most written works that have survived from the second century are codices, and the majority of those are Christian texts. Of the codex you gave me, I found the pages very interesting. They are, as I am certain you noticed, made of papyrus. Now papyrus was originally used on scrolls but ceased to be used in copying six hundred years ago, for by then they were being made from parchment. Papyrus scrolls originated thousands of years ago in Egypt, where papyrus grew in abundance on the Nile delta. As you most likely observed, the papyrus is old. It is difficult to know for certain how old it is, yet I would estimate anywhere from seven hundred to one thousand years old. So if we were to disregard what is written in the text, we could assume the codex's point of origin and time of origin."

"Somewhere in Egypt in the second century," Thomas said, trying to suppress his excitement.

"That fact is further supported by the writing style," Gregori continued. "The manuscript was written in a Greek dialect. Not classical Greek, but rather a koine that was common in Egypt. The writing was not done in columns, which began sometime later, but rather ran across the entire page. The ink and the writing style are similar to those originating around Egypt in the second century.

"I also examined the leather cover and the hemp thread used to bind the gatherings. It all seems consistent with other codices I have studied of that period. The text states that it was written during the reign of Trajan whom we know ruled the Roman Empire early in the second century."

Gregori stopped speaking. When Thomas was certain the other monk had nothing else to say, he asked, "So, are you saying the book is authentic?"

"Judge not according to the appearance," Brother Gregori said, quoting James. "If it were not for the contents, I would say the book was authentic and would require further study by the Church."

Thomas drew back and said; "The contents? What have the contents to do with it? From everything you said the book is authentic and should be taken to Rome to verify its authenticity for publication."

Gregori turned and faced Thomas with a look of incredulity.

"Brother Thomas, have you lost your reason?!" he exclaimed. "The very contents of the codex prove it to be false. We cannot take it as a true statement."

"Why not?" Thomas came back just as strongly.

"Because what we believe—the New Testament of the Holy Bible—refutes everything it says."

"Let us look at this a little more dispassionately, shall we?" Thomas said, trying to stay calm and rational. "Let us suppose for a moment that the Book of Judas is correct." Gregori motioned to object but Thomas stayed him. "For a moment we shall put aside our steadfast beliefs, and allow our minds to be open to other possibilities. Now, if the Book of Judas is correct and Jesus was a mere prophet, does it not seem possible—even highly likely— that the apostles would have concocted stories to make him more than what he was, and also to discredit the only man who insisted on speaking the truth?

"We know that the testaments of Jesus began as oral tradition. Nothing was put down in writing until long after Jesus's crucifixion. That would give anyone plenty of time to change a story to suit his own ends. With Judas Iscariot portrayed as the most evil, despicable, and traitorous person who ever lived, who would listen to him? Indeed, who would wish to be he? If we were put in his place, we would, in all probability, run away from Jerusalem, wander around, and finding that wherever we went our name was besmirched, we would in all likelihood take refuge upon an island to live out our days in peace, confiding in perhaps only one other person—a faithful and trusted servant.

"Now tell me, Brother Gregori, when you read the Book of Judas, did it seem more or less believable than the stories in the Bible? Is there not a rational sense in the Book of Judas? Is there not something in your heart and mind that shouts out to believe it to be true?"

Gregori looked at Thomas suspiciously, and with a hint of fear. "Brother Thomas, are you an advocate of the devil?"

Thomas almost smiled. He said, "I am merely a man, one who seeks the truth in all things. Now the Gnostics who treasured this book as their most sacred text were a knowledgeable order. They would never have accepted it at face value, but undoubtedly studied it closely to know if it was true. They did not believe Jesus of Nazareth was the son of God, and the Judas codex verifies this."

Gregori shook his head. "But if the book is true, then all Christianity is based on a lie."

"Whether it is or is not, people deserve to know the truth," Thomas said.

"I cannot believe it."

"Then tell me this, Brother, why would anyone go to such lengths to write this book?"

Gregori turned away. He gazed once again at the horizon and said, "I do not know why."

"Neither do I," Thomas said. "But if we are followers of a faith, then we must know what we are following. If we are to defend a belief that we trust is true, then surely it must be capable of standing against anything. Believe me, Brother Gregori, I am not intent on tearing down a thousand-year-old institution. I only wish to make it what it is meant to be in God's eyes."

"Brother Thomas, have you thoroughly thought this through?" Gregori asked more sombrely than usual. "Think of your reputation. If you pursue this line, your character will surely suffer shipwreck. You are purposely putting yourself in a very precarious position, from which your renown may not survive. You may very well be putting your life in danger."

Thomas of Worms looked out over the surrounding countryside as he considered this.

"In a letter to St. Jerome, Innocent I once wrote: *A man will gladly face misrepresentation or even personal danger on behalf of the truth.*"

"If he is looking for the blessedness that is to come," Gregori finished. "Are you looking for the blessedness, Brother Thomas?"

Thomas of Worms did not respond. In all honesty, Thomas knew in his heart he was not looking for a blessedness. He was reluctant to consider his motives, so he did not think of them.

Gregori saw that Brother Thomas would not answer. "Do you intend to show the Judas codex to the abbot?" the *armarius* then asked.

"No, I think not. The abbot and I have never seen eye to eye on anything. I am afraid he would disregard the book on principle alone without considering the evidence, and like Benedict of Nursia, the abbot would order the book destroyed. No, I think I shall have to take it to Rome for their consideration."

"And if they disregard the codex, what then?"

Thomas considered this. "Then I will have done my sacred duty, and if nothing else, it will undoubtedly lead to some fascinating discussions. The Church will be stronger for it, believe me, Brother Gregori. It is this very kind of situation that has helped promote the faith over the centuries."

"I pray that you are right."

Thomas studied the man before him. Though Gregori could be overly sullen and quite maudlin at times, Thomas respected him. The man had proved to have a strong intellect and a rational mind. Also, it was evident the man had honour. "Brother Nicholas told me how you saved him from the clutches of Brother Sebastian," Thomas said.

Gregori only nodded. "It was nothing," he said.

"Do not be modest. It does not befit you," Thomas said, and

Gregori almost grinned. "I wish to thank you for that. I am doubly in your debt."

"You owe me nothing," Gregori said. "You are very fond of Brother Nicholas, aren't you?"

Never one to be timid, Thomas answered; "Yes, I am very fond of him."

"And I can see Brother Nicholas loves you very much."

Not wishing to dwell too deeply on that possibility, Thomas merely nodded.

Eleven

Thomas of Worms now felt he could trust Brother Gregori completely. He gave the brother both the Benedictine journal and the Gnostic codex to study, pressing upon him the importance of utter discretion regarding these texts. Brother Thomas had now brought two brothers into his machinations, but he felt no regret or remorse over contributing to their trespasses. Brother Gregori accepted the books eagerly, as a child receiving a gift.

Brother Nicholas had felt extremely unsettled since reading the Judas codex. He spoke little with Thomas of Worms after they had given the book to Brother Gregori to study. Nicholas did not know the results of Brother Gregori's findings, nor did he care. The young monk occupied his time with his work in the library and preparing for the *Missa solemnis* at Christmas. The precentor, Brother Bagnus, had arranged a special selection of hymns, canticles, Scripture, responses, and prayers to be sung, and Nicholas spent all of his free time rehearsing his patterns. The pitch and tone of melodies changed in accordance with the liturgy. Intensities and inflections were ever so subtle in the calm ordered progression of a single symbolic pattern.

"On this line you must begin with the *podatus,* two short notes ascending, then the *tractulus* until you reach the end and finish with the *clevis,* two long notes descending. That is to be followed by the *porrectus,* two short notes and a long in a high—low—high pattern, then a *torculus,* two short notes and a long in a low—high—low pattern. Is that clear?"

"Yes, Brother Bagnus."

"Is there something bothering you, Brother?" the precentor asked Nicholas. "Your mind does not appear to be on your work. *Age quod agis,"* Brother Bagnus said, sternly but softly. "Do what you are doing. You must concentrate and attune your voice to God's ear. Remember that the gift you were given comes from God, and it must be returned in kind. You are the one who sets the rhythm and pace. Everyone will follow your lead, yet you must lead them correctly. If you stray, then the entire body will go astray. Everyone is dependent on what you do."

Nicholas was momentarily taken aback. These words held a deeper meaning for the young monk. They struck a chord in his heart that spoke of duty, responsibility, and obedience. He had always been a follower. Did he have the courage and wisdom to be a leader? To be someone like Thomas, or Gregori, or the abbot? If he did stray, could he possibly lead others astray? His life was not his own; he knew that now. With life came the responsibility to every other living being. It was not enough to know what was right, but rather to do what was right. More than that—to do what was best. Brother Bagnus was right. If Nicholas led, he would have to lead whoever followed him correctly. He would have to do the right thing.

"Yes, Brother Bagnus," Nicholas said humbly. "I am sorry. I suppose my mind is preoccupied. I will endeavour to do better."

"If you feel you must speak to someone—"

"Thank you, Brother Bagnus, I was hoping you and I might—"

"I was going to suggest you talk to the abbot about what is

troubling you."

"Oh . . . Do you really think so?"

"The abbot is a good man," the precentor said. "If there is one man in this monastery you can trust, it is the abbot."

Thomas of Worms carefully wrote the letter J. He paused with quill in hand, and looked down at the parchment that sat upon his table in the scriptorium. The letter caused him to think of the Judas codex.

Then again, almost everything did. He could think of little else. The manuscript had given him little peace since he had read it, and he was anxious about where it would all lead. He decided not to speak with Brother Nicholas about the codex, since the younger monk displayed misgivings about the book. Even with Brother Gregori there now existed an uncomfortable relationship. Though they did speak—not of the codex, of course—more often than not things went unsaid. Thomas would often catch the *armarius* staring at him during the day. Thomas began to feel there was no longer anyone he could trust in the monastery. The early Benedictine book and the Gnostic journal were well hidden in the library, but Thomas kept the Judas codex hidden in his cot. He slept easier knowing the book lay at his fingertips. During the day, though, he often wondered if the book was safe.

He had considered leaving the monastery soon after he had learned from Brother Gregori that the codex was authentic. He had planned to set off immediately and take the book to Rome, yet in the end had thought better of it, and decided to wait. Yes, Thomas reasoned, he would wait until the spring thaw, when travelling would be easier. This would be his last Christmas at the monastery. Besides, he wished to finish copying out The Revelation to John, and leave it so the brothers here would have something by which to remember him.

After *compline* one evening, Thomas entered the dormitory and went directly to bed. As had become his custom, he felt around to be certain the book was still there. When Thomas did not feel the book in its usual spot, his body went hot and his skin broke out in a cold sweat. Outwardly calm, he felt around the whole bed, not wishing to draw attention to his actions. It was not there. Thomas's mind raced. Where could it be? Who could have taken it? Thomas concluded it could only have been Brother Nicholas or Brother Gregori.

Thomas left the dormitory and went to the library. If Nicholas had taken the book, Thomas was certain he would hide it here. Finding the library empty, he systematically began to search the entire room, yet to no end. He grew even more agitated when he could not find the Benedictine and Gnostic texts he and Brother Nicholas had secreted there. Next, Thomas went to the scriptorium, where he assumed Gregori would have hidden the codex, if he had taken it.

By the time Thomas had given up on his search for the codex, it was almost morning. That day, before Thomas had a chance to question Nicholas or Gregori, he was approached by the prior.

"The abbot wishes to speak with you in his chamber, Brother Thomas," Brother Vittorio said in his usual zealous manner.

"I will see him shortly," Thomas told the prior. Secretly, Thomas did not like Brother Vittorio. He had prayed much about it and tried to like the man, yet he found he could not.

"The abbot wishes to see you now," the prior said sternly.

With reluctance, Thomas followed the prior to the abbot's chamber.

Thomas entered the abbot's chamber with Brother Vittorio right behind him. The prior closed the door and stood sentry by it. The abbot was sitting at a table. Upon the table sat the book containing the palimpsest pages of the early Benedictine journal, the Gnostic codex, and the Judas codex. Thomas's heart sank when he saw them, yet he tried not to show it.

Thomas took up his position across from the abbot, with his clasped hands hidden beneath the large sleeves of his black habit, and his head bowed.

The abbot did not look directly at Thomas, but allowed his gaze to rest on the three objects upon his table. The room remained quiet for many moments. The quiet seemed to last longer than it actually did, yet as uncomfortable as it was, Thomas of Worms stood perfectly still. He tried not to anticipate what the abbot would say, and what his own response would be. Instead, Thomas practised something he had learned long ago from a Coptic monk in northern Africa while on his sojourn in the Egyptian desert. He emptied his mind of everything. He had learned many sayings of the Desert Fathers, and the one Thomas called upon in times of struggles now came to mind. The axiom was attributed to Arsenius, whose sage counsel instructed: *Be solitary, be silent, and be at peace.* Thomas embraced the last two counsels, and emptied himself of all thoughts and strife. He did not think of the Judas codex, or of his predicament with the abbot, or of anything else. He simply allowed God to enter his heart and mind, for when he did, Thomas knew an indescribable peace would follow that would allow him to deal with any eventuality.

"I see you have been very busy of late," Thomas heard the abbot say to him. The words stirred him, and he was once again aware of his surroundings.

"Tell me, Brother Thomas," the abbot continued, "have you considered nothing we spoke of regarding your conduct? Was everything I said *vox et praeterea nihil*—a voice and nothing more? Your conduct gives me great distress, Brother Thomas."

"I am grieved that I have given you any distress."

"Are you truly?" the abbot said. "You have gone against my orders. Have you nothing to say about that?"

"Forgive me, Abbot," Thomas said sincerely. *"Video meliora proboque, deteriora sequor*—I see the better way and approve of it, yet I follow the worse way."

"I believe the latter but not the former," the abbot said sternly. "Just exactly when did you plan on telling me about these books,

Brother Thomas?"

Thomas did not answer, but rather asked, "What will you do with them?"

The abbot paused to consider the question, then said, "They will remain here in my chamber for further study."

"Abbot, I believe you already have studied them," Thomas said.

Surprisingly this did not garner a rebuke from the abbot. Instead, he asked quite calmly, "What do you think should be done with these texts, Brother Thomas?"

Thomas was startled by this wholly unexpected question. "They should be forwarded to Rome to be studied," he responded slowly, as if it were a trap.

The abbot sat back in his chair and shook his head. "No. I think not."

"Why not?" Thomas asked, careful not to sound demanding.

"It is not right that you question my decision, Brother Thomas."

"At least allow me to put forth an *argumentum.*"

"No, Brother Thomas, there will be no *argumentum.*"

"Perhaps," Thomas said in his most amiable manner, "we should contact the Bishop and see what he thinks."

Though he said it pleasantly, the abbot caught the threatening hint in Thomas's words. Much to the abbot's chagrin, Thomas of Worms had consistently displayed an unwavering intractability not generally found in the brothers. The abbot knew the monk who stood before him was an intelligent and resourceful man. Brother Thomas could very likely make this matter quite disagreeable, even embarrassing. The abbot had no intention of being embarrassed.

"Very well, Brother Thomas," the abbot finally said. "You will be given the opportunity to present an *argumentum.* I and two other brothers will make up a tribunal. I will also choose a brother to act as an opponent."

"When?" Thomas asked.

"The day after tomorrow," the abbot said. "You are dismissed, Brother Thomas."

Thomas turned to leave, but was called back by the abbot.

"One other thing," the abbot said, "you are not to speak with Brother Nicholas or contact him in any way."

"Why?" Thomas wanted to know. "Why may I not speak with Brother Nicholas?"

"Brother Thomas, you will not take that tone with me!" the abbot spoke harshly. "It is my decision that you are not to speak with Brother Nicholas, and you are not to question it. Is that understood?"

Thomas did not answer, which the abbot took to be a sign of insolence or disobedience.

"Brother Thomas, your behaviour leads me to conclude that you continue to transgress in the Rule which we have all taken an oath to obey. I believe you know what the Rule says about transgressions, especially since we spoke of it just the other day. Brother Thomas, I hereby decree that you are to receive a public reproof for your persistent transgressions, namely disobedience to your abbot, and directly afterwards you will receive a scourging. I trust this will cure you of this behaviour that you continue to exhibit."

Thomas of Worms stood speechless. He had always known the obstinacy of his nature would one day lead him into direct opposition with his superiors, but he had never considered the possibility that he would push the limits so far as to receive a scourging.

The abbot could interpret Brother Thomas's distress, and he sought a solution that would suit his purposes.

"Brother Thomas," the abbot said, with a trace of kindness, "if you wish to avoid the public rebuke and the scourging, you may freely leave this monastery now, this very minute."

"Abbot, do I have permission to ask a question?" Thomas asked meekly.

The abbot paused to consider what Thomas would say next. "You may ask a question, Brother Thomas."

"If I were to leave now to avoid this punishment, what would become of the books I discovered?"

"The books would, of course, remain here in this monastery under my care."

"And my opportunity to present an *argumentum?*" Thomas asked.

"If you choose to leave now, there naturally cannot be an *argumentum,*" the abbot pronounced.

It took Thomas only a brief moment to decide.

"Then I choose the scourging," Thomas said, "and I will stay to present an *argumentum* as you agreed."

"Very well, Brother Thomas," the abbot said reluctantly, "you will have your *argumentum* as agreed. As for now, you will await your rebuke and scourging in the courtyard."

Thomas of Worms stood in the courtyard alone. It was a cold December day, and he brought up his cowl and tucked his hands into his large sleeves for warmth. The sun was blocked by layers of grey clouds. A stiff wind blew steadily and carried with it a strange foreboding that transcended the scourging that was to come. In his entire life as a monk, he had only once seen a public scourging. That was at an Eastern monastery in Constantinople. An older monk by the name of Brother Marco could not control his penchant for giving himself sexual pleasure in his bed at night, and he had received a scourging that had led to his death three days later.

Thomas did not believe this scourging would kill him, or even injure him permanently, but neither did he welcome it or think it would improve his character with regard to obedience to the abbot. It was not that he did not wish to change, to conform, to become more amenable, it was simply that Brother Thomas did not believe he could. At times he experienced an almost unnatural contrariness that he could neither control nor explain. He had often prayed about it, but not always earnestly.

While he stood alone in the courtyard awaiting his punishment, Thomas of Worms prayed to God for guidance and strength and courage.

A short time later the bell tolled for all the brothers to gather in the courtyard. They arrived by ones and twos and threes, and gathered around Brother Thomas, who stood with head bowed and his hands clasped in front of him. The last to arrive was Abbot Michael accompanied by the prior, Brother Vittorio, who made no attempt to conceal the short whip he carried. At a signal from the abbot, Thomas removed his habit, and bared his back and chest. He stood thus with head bowed and hands clasped before him while the stiff chill of the day caused his skin to break out in gooseflesh.

The abbot entered the circle created by the black monks and paced around Brother Thomas as he spoke.

"My brothers," the abbot began, "what brings us together is not of my choosing but the choosing of another. It gives me no pleasure to see what is to take place here today, yet neither am I reluctant to carry it out, as it is for the benefit of this entire monastery. For if even one of us should transgress, let there be no doubt, it surely affects us all.

"Brother Thomas of Worms came here two years ago, and though he has been a Benedictine brother much longer than that, Brother Thomas has transgressed from the Rule which he took an oath to follow before his brothers and God. Brother Thomas has allowed the desire for personal glory to blind him to his vows. He has constantly opposed your Lord Abbot by knowingly and willfully disobeying me. He has been dishonest in his actions, and has even stooped to entice one of our young brothers into his machinations with no regard for that young monk's soul.

"Brother Thomas has been warned that his transgressions would have consequences. He was given a penance to carry out in the scriptorium. He has received a private rebuke—more than once. He was put on a ration of bread and water. Yet, still he persisted. Now we come to this public rebuke where all the brothers of this monastery can look upon him with shame and ridicule.

"But in our hearts we wish for Brother Thomas to return to us with humility and contriteness. And so, along with this public rebuke, in order to impress upon Brother Thomas the seriousness of this matter, he will now receive, before this holy assemblage, a scourging."

The abbot motioned to Brother Vittorio, who circled around the bare-backed monk and took up a position behind him. The prior swung the whip back and forth, then finally laid it across Thomas's back with force.

Thomas winced in pain, but he did not cry out. Silently, he prayed to God, as he was lashed over and over again. He did not count the blows, but concentrated on his prayer. Thomas imagined Christ Jesus accepting his punishment at the hands of a Roman soldier, and he drew strength from that. He felt his knees buckle, and he fought to regain control over his body. Suddenly, he was aware of two brothers, one on either side of him. The scourging had ceased, and the brothers were leading Thomas to the infirmary, where his wounds were treated. Then he was dressed and taken to his cot where he lay face down and forced himself to sleep.

Thomas of Worms slept until called for *vigils*. He moved stiffly, wincing at the pain. To remove his mind from the soreness, he thought of what lay ahead.

He did not know why the abbot had ordered him not to contact Nicholas, yet he would deal with that in his own way. Even in his present state, Thomas had no doubt that he could make a good *argumentum* for the Judas codex regardless of who opposed him. After all, hadn't he excelled in his studies of logic and rhetoric? He had appreciated all of the liberal arts taught in the monasteries, yet these two he prized most, and they had long ago become his field of study. After *lauds*, Thomas went directly to the scriptorium where he found Brother Gregori and informed him of the latest development.

"Do you know whom the abbot will choose to oppose you?" Gregori asked.

"No, he did not say, and I would not presume to guess. Perhaps it will be you, Brother."

"That would prove interesting," Gregori responded convivially, then resumed his usual grave demeanor. "Why did you do it, Brother Thomas? Why did you accept the scourging?"

Thomas paused thoughtfully, as if he were not certain. "If I had fled," he said, "then everything we had accomplished—finding the clues that led to the books, solving the riddle in the cloister, everything—would have been for nothing. These discoveries are important, I know it. God would not have led me this far only to have me forsake my mission. I must be allowed to bring these works to Christendom and lend credence to these writings."

"You feel that strongly about it?"

Thomas nodded. "I wish I knew how the abbot discovered I had found those books." With a wry hint of suspicion he added, "You did not happen to mention the Judas codex to anyone, did you, Brother?"

"How could you suspect me, Brother Thomas?" Gregori asked, insulted. "Especially after you went to the trouble of asking me to swear an oath."

"My apologies, Brother Gregori," Thomas said, smiling and clapping the other on the back. "I know you are to be trusted, just as I trust Brother Nicholas. You haven't seen him, have you?"

"No, I cannot say I have."

Thomas asked Brother Gregori for a spare sheet of parchment. The *armarius* found him a large clean folio. Thomas took it to his table and started to organize his thoughts on paper to aid him in his *argumentum*.

The next day, Thomas went to the library to find the references he planned to use tomorrow. He also hoped to find Brother Nicholas, so he might inform him of what had transpired, yet Nicholas was not there. Later, he entered the library, but when Thomas attempted to engage him, he found the young monk was uncommunicative and refrained from looking him in the eye.

Thomas explained to Nicholas everything that had occurred. The young monk listened inattentively.

"Did you understand everything I said?" Thomas asked Brother Nicholas.

"Yes, I understand," he replied.

"You do not seem surprised by any of it." When Nicholas said nothing, Thomas pressed the matter. "Brother Nicholas, is there something you wish to tell me? Is there something you know about this?"

Nicholas appeared pensive. Twice he started to say something, and stopped. Finally, he said, "I do know something of the matter."

Thomas looked at him suspiciously.

"I have just now come from the abbot's chambers," Nicholas continued. "The abbot is aware that I know about the books."

Thomas did not ask him how the abbot knew of Nicholas's involvement, but now Thomas suspected the reason.

"Do you know that the abbot ordered me not to speak with you, or contact you in any way?"

Nicholas nodded, and said, "Yes. He also told me not to speak with you."

"Why?"

Nicholas turned away, unable to face Thomas. "Please, Brother Thomas, do not ask me."

Despite his inquisitive nature, Thomas decided to respect the young monk's request.

"The abbot also informed me of the *argumentum* scheduled for tomorrow," Nicholas said, reluctantly.

"He did, did he?" Thomas did not like how the abbot was showing a special interest in Nicholas. "I am expecting opposition," Thomas said stiffly. "Did the abbot tell you that?"

"Yes, he did."

"It would appear Abbot Michael has taken you completely into his confidence." Thomas made no attempt to hide his resentment. "And has the abbot told you who the opposition will be?"

"Yes, he has."

Thomas asked arrogantly, "And which of my esteemed brothers will oppose me?"

Nicholas turned and faced Thomas. "I will."

Twelve

The *argumentum* was derived from ancient Roman days when a man was judged on his public speaking skills, especially in the areas of structure, cadence, and style. If a man was so eloquent and entertaining that it was a pleasure simply to listen to him, he might also be persuasive enough to influence his listeners to adopt his own reasoning. Originally, the *argumentum* was not an argument or disagreement between two or more opponents, but rather a display of proof to help in illuminating or clarifying a point of view or opinion.

The *argumentum* was to take place in the meeting room immediately after dinner. Heading the proceeding was the abbot, with Brother Vittorio on his left, and on his right Brother Antonio, the sacrist, who was in charge of the monastery's maintenance. Most of the brothers were allowed to attend the *argumentum*. The only ones who did not attend were those whose work kept them away, or those who did not wish to attend.

Brother Thomas was permitted to make his appeal first, and he decided to begin with a statement. He stood as he spoke, then slowly paced back and forth in front of the assembly, meeting the gaze of all who were present and speaking with expressiveness and conviction.

"Brothers, our beliefs are based on sacred writings that began as an oral tradition of stories being passed down and around until these stories were finally recorded for future generations. The first Christian codices were written early in the second century. In 325, the Emperor Constantine commanded the highest authorities in Christendom to Nicaea, in order that certain controversies might be settled and agreed upon to establish a universally accepted canon of the New Testament. All writings to that date were considered on merit and likelihood. Some were accepted, and some were rejected. What we are doing here today is not deciding whether or not to accept this newfound text, rather only whether it should be considered by men more knowledgeable and wiser than we.

"What I am about to tell you is a tale so remarkable it will echo Tertullian's words: *certum est quia impossibile est*—it is certain because it is impossible. What started as a fantastic find of a forgotten text among some palimpsests, led to the incredible discovery of a manuscript, which, had it been known of during the Nicaean Council, surely would have been considered, if not accepted. What we will hear here today is how this manuscript and others were discovered, and of their validity. These are not common editions, yet *editio princeps*—first written editions of ancient texts. What I pray for most is that everyone present will keep an open mind while they listen to everything presented here today."

Thomas of Worms proceeded to tell in his well-refined manner how Brother Nicholas had found the palimpsest pages in an obscure library volume, which were actually early accounts of the first Benedictines who had come to their monastery. That book in turn had led them to the Gnostic text, which was a remarkable historic find in itself. Yet, what was even more remarkable, by using both books, Thomas and Nicholas had found the dubitable Judas codex.

To prove the authenticity of the texts, Brother Thomas questioned Brother Gregori in front of the assembly. Brother Gregori gave excellent testimony and stated that in his expert opinion all the texts in question were genuine.

"My brothers," Thomas of Worms again addressed the assembly, "during the Council of Nicaea, which I referred to previously, there were certain theologians—Arius, and Eusebius of Caesarea, and Eusebius of Nicomedia —who, for very good reasons, argued against the divinity of Christ. Now, I know the council's final decision, and the Church's opposition to Arianism. I know, as everyone in this room knows, that the council banished Arius to Illyria for his views. Yet, what most forget, or choose to overlook, was that Arius was reinstated to his position, and would have been welcomed back into the fellowship of the Church in a formal ceremony, had he not died before this could take place. We may ask ourselves why the Church did have a change of heart if it disagreed with Arius on the question of Christ's divinity. And, as surely as the world is flat, my dear brothers, we must conclude that even the Church had its doubts."

Many in the room murmured at Thomas's statement, yet none was willing to voice opposition to his views.

At this point it was time for *none,* and the abbot thought it best to adjourn the *argumentum.* After *none,* they reassembled in the meeting room, where Brother Nicholas was permitted to express an opposing view.

While everyone waited for him to begin, Nicholas sat in his seat and prayed silently, so that God would put the right words into his mouth to present the best case he possibly could. When he was ready, he took up a position where he could be seen by the assembly, the abbot, and Brother Thomas. As Nicholas stood before them, he folded his hands in front of him while he spoke.

"Brothers, as Brother Thomas stated earlier, we do have a long history—a long and painful history. Many of the apostles of our Lord Jesus Christ died because of what they believed. Up until

the time of Constantine, Christians were persecuted to the point
of death, and many of their books were burned. What did survive
was the good news that we live by today, which can be summed
up in lines from a creed derived from that same council Brother
Thomas spoke of earlier: *We believe in one Lord, Jesus Christ, the
only Son of God, eternally begotten of the Father, God from God,
true God from true God, begotten, not made, one in Being with the
Father. Through him all things were made. For us men and for our
salvation he came down from heaven: by the power of the Holy Spirit
he was born of the Virgin Mary, and became man. For our sake he
was crucified under Pontius Pilate; he suffered, died, and was buried.
On the third day he rose again in fulfillment of the Scriptures; he
ascended into heaven and is seated at the right hand of the Father.
He will come again in glory to judge the living and the dead, and his
kingdom will have no end.*

"My brothers in Christ, this is what we believe. These are the
beliefs we base our entire lives upon, and are the very beliefs we
would give up our lives to defend, as did saintly martyrs who
lived before us. We hold the New Testament as sacred, and it is
sacred not only to us, for these writings are divinely inspired, so
they are sacred regardless of who believes them. Late in the sixth
century, St. Gregory I, the Great, once said, Sacred Scripture is
set up as a kind of lantern for us in the night of this life. We use
this light to guide us in this world and it will lead us to the next.
Without it, we lose our way and are damned.

"Our esteemed Brother Thomas is a knowledgeable man. In
all of Christendom there is perhaps no man who exceeds Brother
Thomas in logic and reason. He could, in all likelihood, by sheer
reason, convince you the world is round and revolves around the
sun. But what is the total virtue of reason. St. Gregory I the Great
said; If the work of God could be comprehended by reason, it
would no longer be wonderful, and faith would have no merit
provided proof.

"In regards to the books that bring us here today, and especially one book in particular, the Judas codex—which I have read—refutes everything we believe, everything we hold sacred. How then can there be any relevance in it? I do not dispute Brother Gregori's expert opinion that all the books in question are authentic, as to where and when they were written. What I do dispute is that the Judas codex is accurate. Why it was written, I do not know. It may have been written by a Jew in Alexandria in order to undermine Christianity, which was, at the time, only beginning to spread.

"My brothers, I proclaim that this book is dangerous. Nothing good can come from it being made known to the world. Even the Gnostic codex has the potential for danger to anyone who reads it. The Gnostics themselves grew corrupt through their own practices. Even our esteemed Brother Thomas was drawn into the glamour of its appeal. Only by the grace of God was he delivered from his own obsessions.

"Brother Thomas has brought forth the point—and rather brilliantly, I might add—regarding Arius and his views on the divinity of our Lord, Jesus Christ. What Brother Thomas of Worms failed to mention, however, was that Arius did not dispute Christ's entire divinity, only that he did not believe it was equal to the divinity of God the Father Almighty. If Brother Thomas believed that the Judas codex had any validity, I am certain he would not have failed to mention that point.

"My brothers in Christ, I find I must dispute Brother Thomas's claim that all knowledge is good knowledge. There is such a thing as dangerous knowledge, and, brothers, I tell you this: the Gnostic codex and the Judas codex are dangerous. Let us consider, brothers, that if all our words and deeds, thoughts and actions are *ad maiorem Dei gloriam*—for the greater glory of God—then our decision here today must reflect that. So we must ask ourselves: how does lending credence to these books, particularly the Judas codex, glorify God?"

Brother Nicholas gave a slight bow, and took his seat.

The room remained silent for several moments. The majority of the monks present had nodded in assent at Nicholas's statement. Thomas of Worms was impressed. Even though Nicholas was speaking against him, Thomas could not help feeling proud of his young friend. Nicholas had spoken eloquently, succinctly, and with a deep conviction of faith. Brother Nicholas had made several good points, and in this stagnant age he might even have swayed some of the assembly. Yet Thomas was confident that what he was asking was not beyond the grasp of simple minds, for he believed *magna est veritas et praevelet*—great is truth and it prevails.

"Brother Thomas," the abbot spoke, "you may make a final plea to this assembly."

Thomas rose, but remained where he stood. He knew that what he said here could sway the minds of his brothers. Even if he did not convince the abbot, he would take consolation if the general opinion of the monastery was on his side, and that might sway the abbot. He determined it was time to use every one of his oratory skills, even the harsh ones.

"Brothers, as I sat here and listened to Brother Nicholas, I was pleased and surprised at the eloquence of one so young. I trust that many years from now Brother Nicholas will be a fine member of this order. As for now, he is still young and inexperienced, and his youth has not given way to wisdom. He is *vox et praeterea nihil*—a voice and nothing more. No one is asking that we turn aside our beliefs, and immediately accept something else. Brother Nicholas stated that there exists dangerous knowledge—*e contrario*—there is no such thing as dangerous knowledge! The only dangerous thing about knowledge is to turn a blind eye to it out of fear and superstition, as Brother Nicholas suggests. Our Apostolic Fathers gave their lives to preserve what they believed, and we should honour their devotion, yet what they did not die for was our lack of faith, and the inability for that faith to grow. Our faith must grow, brothers. It must be able to stand up against anything—an idea, a book, anything. For if our faith cannot stand up against challenges, what good is it? It would be a faith such as Brother Nicholas demonstrated in his remarks here today, *telum imbelle sine ictu*—a feeble weapon without a thrust. I fear the day is coming when our faith will be put to the test, and we will find ourselves in spiritual battle for the souls of all mankind. When that time comes, my brothers, we must equip ourselves with the full armour of God, as St. Paul instructs, so that we may be prepared for battle. We cannot be prepared for battle if we have not sought out and examined every aspect of our faith. What I am asking for today, brothers, is not that these books be accepted on faith, but that they be forwarded to Rome for examination. That is all."

Thomas took his seat, and was met with many consenting faces. The abbot's expression was not agreeable though. The abbot asked Brother Nicholas if he had any final words, but Nicholas only shook his head.

"Then we will adjourn these proceedings, and resume tomorrow after this council has had time to deliberate, and our decision will be made known."

Everyone stood and left the room as the call to vespers sounded.

After the evening meal, Thomas searched for Brother Nicholas and found him in the library. Nicholas received him coldly.

"You spoke very well today," Thomas told him.

"For one so young and inexperienced," Nicholas added sarcastically.

"I had to say those things," Thomas said. "You do not know how important this is to me."

"I fully realize it is more important than our friendship."

"I am not the only one who betrayed our friendship."

"I am sure I do not know what you mean," Nicholas stated.

"You spoke to the abbot."

"Yes."

"Regarding the books?"

"Yes."

"So you admit it!"

"Admit what?"

"That you told the abbot about the books."

"You think I told the abbot about the books?" Nicholas asked incredulously.

"Didn't you?" Thomas said.

"How could you think that of me?" Nicholas said, truly hurt.

"But you just said you spoke to the abbot about the books."

"When the abbot questioned me about the books, he already had them in his possession."

Thomas saw the pained look on the other's face, and realized the truth.

"Well," Thomas said, "if it was not you, who was it?"

"Brother Thomas, we have both been told by the abbot not to speak to each other," and without saying another word, Nicholas walked out of the library, leaving Thomas to himself.

The next day the monks of the monastery assembled once again in the meeting room to hear the council's decision. It was a cold December day, yet Thomas felt a chill in the room that had nothing to do with the weather.

"My brothers," the abbot began, "we have listened carefully to what Brother Thomas and Brother Nicholas had to say. Both have made fine points. Before I render the decision of this council, I wish to make it clear that this decision is final, and there will be no further discussion."

Thomas anticipated the worst.

"It is virtually impossible," the abbot continued, "to separate our belief and faith from what some might refer to as a purely logical and rational motive. If our lives are steeped in faith, then we must ask: what is faith? Scripture tells us that faith is the assurance of things hoped for, the conviction of things not seen.

We may then plainly say that faith is believing without seeing, without proof. One might think the apostle Thomas had little faith when he demanded to have irrefutable proof of our Lord's resurrection. The apostle Thomas was not unlike our Brother Thomas of Worms who also needs, it would seem, to put his hand in the wounds of our Saviour, so his beliefs might rest easier. Yet as Brother Nicholas stated earlier, if we were to have irrefutable proof of our beliefs, something tangible that we could see and examine and show to others, then what would be the need for faith?"

Thomas gave up all hope.

"It is the decision of this council that the Benedictine book be put into our library and may be copied. Both the Gnostic codex and the so-called Judas codex are to be restricted to my chamber until a more permanent solution can be reached. Brothers, these proceedings are over."

Thomas did not rise with his brothers. Even when the other black monks had left the room, he remained sitting. Thomas of Worms was not used to failure. It did not sit well with him. He did not like it. Of course, he was disappointed, but he was not one to let disappointment be an obstacle. Thomas did not even consider dwelling on his disappointment very long, for since the beginning of the *argumentum,* he had decided he would be in *utrumque paratus*—prepared for either alternative. He sat there in the meeting room, calculating his next course of action. It would prove to be an act of desperation.

Nicholas walked the cloister with his head bowed, deep in thought. He seemed to pray so often that he never allowed himself the opportunity to think, yet now his mind was plagued with thoughts. Brother Nicholas thought of his life, and the lie he lived. He thought of Brother Thomas, and his love for a man who had humiliated him in front of everyone. Nicholas wondered how he might ever hold up his head in this monastery again. What was it that drove men to do the things they did, he wondered? Surely, if angels did God's work, then in the same vein there were demons who served Satan. Nicholas knew this to be true, for did he not have demons of his own? After all these years in the monastery, he had not purged himself of them. They dwelt in him, corrupting his mind and senses. He felt his very soul was in peril, and there appeared no way to save it. He had hoped to tell Thomas one day—almost had, in fact, the night they were lost in the crypt. Of all the people he knew, he believed Thomas would understand. If Nicholas confessed to Thomas that he loved him, would Thomas love him in return? Nicholas was uncertain, and the uncertainty of it all consumed him.

"Five hundred years ago some monks chose to live their lives atop pillars, and came to be known as 'Stylites.'"

Nicholas looked up, startled to see Brother Thomas standing beside him.

"These Stylites believed that living atop a pillar would separate them from the world. Simeon the Elder of Syria spent the latter half of his life atop a sixty-foot pillar where food had to be sent up to him in a basket. Simeon inspired followers, such as Daniel of Constantinople, who in the fifth century perched atop a column at the age of fifty-one. Daniel suffered the blazing summer sun, and freezing winter nights. When he died thirty-three years later, he was emaciated, disease ridden, baked and burned from sun and cold, and his hair was infested with lice. What he and the other Stylites failed to understand was that we must live in the world. Try as we might, we should not separate ourselves from it. Even here, living within these walls is not natural. Our Saviour would venture into the wilderness alone, yet most of his time was spent with people, speaking with them, ministering to their needs. That is what we should be doing."

"Why are you here, Brother Thomas?" Nicholas asked unconcerned by everything Thomas had just said.

"I need your help."

"No, I mean why are you here in this monastery? If you believe what you just said, why are you here?"

Thomas looked thoughtful. He forced a grin and said, "I believe I started out the same as all of our brothers. *Domino optimo maximo*—to the Lord, best and greatest. I once believed that personal salvation could only be obtained *in vacuo,* yet nothing can grow isolated from the rest of the world. I will be leaving this monastery soon, never to return."

"What do you want of me?" Nicholas queried curtly, in an attempt to cover his sorrow and pain.

"As I have said, I am in need of your assistance."

"To do what?"

"I intend to retrieve the Judas codex from the abbot's chamber and take it to Rome. I need your help to do that."

Nicholas shook his head. "You have chosen a road for yourself that I do not wish to share. I cannot help you steal that book."

"Then I shall do it alone," Thomas spoke defiantly.

"I have no doubt," Nicholas responded in melancholy. "If you are intent on your course, and if we are to part here, may I offer you one last advice: *quidquid agas prudenter agas*—whatever you do, do with caution."

The abbot's chamber was sparsely furnished. Brother Thomas believed he would have no problem locating the Judas codex. Thomas waited until he knew the abbot had left the room before entering it. The room contained a desk, two chairs, a cupboard, and a stand that supported a very large Bible, which lay closed. Behind a curtain was a sleeping cot and a small table upon which sat a clay basin and water jar. The room was not difficult to search, and Thomas made a systematic inspection, yet he did not find the codex. His eyes rested upon the closed Bible.

In every case when he had been summoned to the abbot's chambers, Thomas had never seen the Bible open. He walked over to it and, laying his hand upon it, tapped it with his fingertips. He was mildly astonished to discover it was made of wood. Thomas ran his hands along the edges of the wooden Bible feeling for a catch or a hinge. Finding neither, Thomas pulled and pried the cover until it came loose and opened it like a book. He gave an audible intake of breath. Inside the wooden box, carved to look like a Bible, sat the Judas codex, still wrapped in the worn, heavy cloth. Thomas lifted the codex out of the box.

"So, Brother Thomas, you have been reduced to this."

Startled, Thomas turned to see the abbot standing by the door of the room with a dour look upon his face.

The abbot stepped into the room, and went behind his desk. His face remained grim as he studied Brother Thomas who clutched the wrapped codex to his bosom.

"It would appear that no matter what I do to curb your flagrantly disobedient nature, you resist and fight any attempt to change." The abbot said sadly, "Did not even the scourging have an effect on you? Was it only your flesh that was changed by it? Brother Thomas, do you not see how Satan has a hold over your humility? I truly believe you would prefer death rather than submit to the will of another."

Thomas of Worms stood staring at the abbot. A secret fear welled up inside him. He feared the abbot was right, and the idea that Satan was influencing his decisions revolted him. But he could not let it go. He had started on a course of action, and he had to see it through.

"Exactly what do you propose to do now, Brother Thomas?" asked the abbot.

Thomas thrust out his jaw and said, "I am going to Rome, and I am taking this book with me."

"You are a very stubborn man," the abbot observed.

"Some have said so," Thomas remarked, and added, "Please do not attempt to dissuade me or in any way try to prevent my departure. I have made up my mind."

"I am sure you have," the abbot said. "No one will try to stop you, Brother Thomas, nor will I demand that you return the book in your hands, which is the property of this monastery."

"This book belongs to all of Christendom," Thomas countered.

"I will not argue the point with you, Brother Thomas. I ask only that you leave this monastery immediately."

"Will tomorrow be satisfactory?"

"Please be gone before *prime.*"

As Thomas moved towards the door, the abbot added, "We will pray for you, Brother."

Thomas stopped at the door, and looked back towards the abbot.

"You are being too complacent," Thomas told him. "Why?"

"I am not certain what you mean."

"I find it difficult to believe you are simply going to let me walk out of here with the book."

"I have no intention of wresting it from you, Brother Thomas, if that is what you mean. Besides, your journey will prove a difficult one."

"What do you mean by that?"

"When I first confronted you with the Judas codex, I wrote several letters that very day immediately after our discussion. One was a very special letter to his Holiness with regard to you. I also wrote several letters to all the monasteries between here and Rome. I sent out some of the brothers to deliver the letters. You will find no monastery between here and Rome that will allow you within its walls. And on the chance that you do get to Rome, you will not be received."

"That is why you permitted the *argumentum,*" Thomas said. "You needed time for your letters to precede me, on the chance I would take the book and leave. You never intended to find in my favour. All that you did was *mala fide*—in bad faith."

"I did what I thought was best for the Church," the abbot said.

"To suppress important historical information?"

"It is heretical!" the abbot shouted.

"Then let it be proved!" Thomas shouted back. "Let it be put in the light instead of left hidden in the darkness. Let it be as the deeds of men, that when exposed to light we may see it for what it is."

The abbot took in a deep breath through his mouth, as if to respond, yet he did not. He did not bother to look at Thomas when he said, "You have my decision, Brother Thomas."

Thomas nodded, moved to leave, then turned back to the abbot. He studied the man with a suspicious eye.

"You are still too accommodating."

"Perhaps it would be best if you left the monastery immediately, Brother Thomas!"

Staring at the abbot, Thomas experienced a sinking feeling. "You are too anxious to be rid of me. Even more anxious than usual." He looked at the book in his arms, and then at the abbot. Thomas unwrapped the cloth to discover that it was not the Judas codex inside, but rather an obscure psalter. He walked over, placed the psalter upon the desk, and said to the abbot, "It appears you are not above a bit of chicanery yourself. Where is the Judas codex?"

The abbot stared at him, before saying, "Good day, Brother Thomas, and goodbye."

Thomas arose early the next morning. He had slept little that night, yet it was not a hardship to rise before everyone else. Thomas was eager to honour the abbot's request and depart from the monastery secretly. Though ownership was discouraged, Thomas packed his few precious possessions and left the dormitory. Stopping by the kitchen he packed a meagre meal and a goatskin of wine for his journey. He did not know how far it would take him, but he trusted God would provide. He then went to the church and prayed. That done, he began to walk out of the church, when a voice caused him to stop.

"*Quo vadis?*"

Thomas looked up to see Brother Nicholas, standing by the door of the church. His eyes were red from lack of sleep, and Thomas saw traces of tears on his face.

"I am leaving for Rome," Thomas said, in answer to the young monk's question.

"Let me come with you," Nicholas said weakly.

"No, you were right. It is a road I have chosen for myself. Your place is here. I do not belong in this monastery. I have never been at peace in any monastery."

"Still, why can I not come with you?" Nicholas pleaded.

"I cannot ask you to forsake your vow."

"Is it that you do not wish me to come with you?"

"It would not be right or fair that I ask you to come."

"Yet, I wish to come."

Thomas shook his head, and said, "Stay here, and be at peace with God."

"I will never see you again," Nicholas spoke, as if admitting a painful truth.

Thomas approached the young monk, and quite unexpectedly Nicholas threw his arms around Thomas and hugged him tightly.

"I love you, Brother Thomas," Nicholas said, choking back his tears.

"And I love you, Brother Nicholas."

Thomas pulled back to look Nicholas in the face. It was a pitiful face, contorted with anguish and with tears running freely. There was something in that face that Thomas had not seen before, though he was at a loss to know what it was.

"I must go now," Thomas said, pulling himself free of the other's grip. "Goodbye."

Thomas walked away to the heartrending sobs of Brother Nicholas.

Thirteen

Thomas of Worms walked down the familiar mountain path. He tried to feel unambivalent over his departure—best not to be tied to the things of this earth—but he could not. This had been his home for the past two years, and though in his heart he had known there would come a day when he must leave the monastery of St. Benedict, he did not wish to depart in this manner. He found it difficult to turn his back on it.

Halfway down, he stopped and turned to look back at the monastery one last time. Though he tried to regard it fondly, Thomas could not help feeling that there was some malevolence at work *intra muros*. To Brother Thomas, it was evident that some evil existed here on this mountaintop, and he was tempted to stay and uncover what it was. There were still the three murders that remained unsolved, and he felt a reluctance to leave, yet the abbot had made that decision for him.

Thomas reached the base of the mountain, and a quesiton presented itself: should he travel by foot through the mountains to Rome, or travel to the coast and board a ship bound for the South? Thomas did not have to make the choice. He was standing at the crossroads when he heard a voice calling his name. He knew it was not God, for it came from the direction of the mountain. He turned to look behind him and saw that he was being hailed by Brother Nicholas. Thomas had no desire to repeat their scene and was prepared to wave the other back, when something caused him to pause. From the frenetic sound of the young monk's voice, and the manner in which he ran down the road with arms and legs flailing beneath his black habit, Thomas knew that something was desperately wrong.

"Brother Thomas! Brother Thomas!" the frantic monk screamed. *"Laus Deo! Laus Deo!* I feared I would not find you!"

"What is it, Brother Nicholas?" Thomas asked quickly. "What has happened?"

"Oh, you must come back to the monastery, Brother Thomas! Tell me you will come!"

Brother Thomas was reluctant. He started to refuse, when Nicholas violently grabbed two handfuls of Thomas's habit and with a wild-eyed look reiterated, "Tell me you will come!"

"I will if I must, but what has happened?"

"Immediately after you left, we found him! Oh, it is *horribile dictu, horribile dictu!*"

"What is so horrible to relate?"

"The abbot did not wish me to fetch you, but I knew. I knew you were the only one who could help. What was it you once told me? *Felix qui potiut rerum cognoscere causas*—fortunate is he who has been able to learn the causes of things. That is what I told the abbot; we are fortunate that Brother Thomas is able to learn the cause of things. And you will learn the cause of this new tragedy, I know it. I know it!"

Thomas gripped the young monk tightly by the shoulders. "Brother Nicholas, what is it?"

The young monk's eyes stared blankly, and his mouth hung open as he searched for the words. Finally, Nicholas crossed himself and said, "It is Brother Vittorio, the prior. He is dead! I do not know for certain, but he may have been murdered!"

The two monks trudged hastily up the mountain, praying as they went. Thomas assumed it would be pointless to question Brother Nicholas further, given his disturbed state. Better to wait and observe the scene for himself.

Upon entering the monastery Thomas detected a sense of doom that seemed to emanate from the very walls of the structure. Nicholas led Thomas to the library—the scene of the recent tragedy—where outside the room many of the monks had gathered, yet none would dare venture inside. They had been standing about in silence, but some broke into nervous whispers at Brother Thomas's arrival.

"Where is the abbot?" Brother Thomas asked Nicholas.

"The abbot is in his chamber. I do not believe he wished to be here when you arrived. He was not entirely sanguine about your coming back, but I insisted."

Thomas looked at Brother Nicholas, surprised at his uncharacteristic assertiveness.

Their brother monks parted like the Red Sea and allowed Thomas and Nicholas to pass into the room. Thomas did not know what to expect, but he was not prepared for the sight that met his eyes.

In the middle of the room, suspended from a low crossbeam, Brother Vittorio hung by the neck, the tips of his toes barely touching the floor. The cord he had worn around his habit had been looped over the crossbeam, while its ends were tied around his throat. Brother Vittorio's face was bloated and contorted in anguish. His eyes bulged from their sockets.

Thomas circled the body twice, taking in every detail. He looked towards the door and saw Brother Nicholas, standing timidly away from the scene.

"Come closer, Brother," Thomas urged him. *"Mortui non mordent*—dead men do not bite. Come closer, and tell me what you hear from this."

"Hear?" Nicholas asked, as he took a few furtive steps closer to the corpse. "He is dead. How can I hear anything?"

"*Res ipsa loquitor*—the thing itself speaks." Thomas indicated the entire scene. "It is evident that Brother Vittorio did not hang himself."

"How do you know that?"

"Look at the way the cord is tied. It is knotted around his throat, then over the beam, then back and tied to the first knot. No man could or would hang himself in that fashion."

"Could he not have tied the rope while standing upon a stool, then stepped off the stool?" Nicholas proposed.

"There is no stool or anything else to be seen. All the tables and chairs are over on the sides of the room." Thomas examined the dead man's hands. "He was dead or unconscious when his body was hoisted up."

"How do you know that?"

"Brother Vittorio was not one to do manual labour; *ergo,* his hands were soft and tender. If he had been conscious while being hanged, he would have clutched at the cord to pull himself up, yet there are no cord marks on his hands."

"Perhaps the murderer tied his hands," Nicholas proposed.

"His hands are not now, nor were they ever tied, as there would be marks on his wrists."

"Yes, I see," Nicholas said.

"Let us take our dear, dead brother down and examine him. I venture to say he will reveal more to us in death than he ever did in life."

Thomas lifted the body so Nicholas could untie the knot of the cord that suspended it. They laid the body gently upon the floor. Thomas examined the cord and the mark it had made on the dead monk's throat.

"Do you see?" Thomas said. "There, on his throat."

"There is the mark of the cord," Nicholas said, bending to get a closer look.

"Yes, but see those marks there? They are the marks left by a man's fingers. Brother Vittorio was strangled first, then hanged. The evidence forces me to suspect that Brother Vittorio's death was not planned. He was murdered for some unknown reason. Then his killer, also for reasons unknown, wished to create an obvious and gruesome scene to attract everyone's attention. That the killer used Brother Vittorio's own cord confirms the spontaneity of the act."

"But why?" Nicholas asked.

"That is yet to be determined," said Thomas, rising up. "For now, we must make a report to the abbot."

The abbot was in his chamber, sitting at his desk with his hands folded in front of him, praying silently. Thomas and Nicholas entered, and waited patiently until the abbot was finished.

"I did not expect to see you again, Brother Thomas," the abbot said sullenly, without raising his eyes to the other two monks.

"Deus vult," Thomas said.

"Perhaps," the abbot responded. "Yet, was it also God's will that Brother Vittorio die in the manner he did?"

"No," Thomas said curtly. "Brother Vittorio was murdered, and I believe it to be the same murderer who took the lives of Brother Ryan, Brother Gedeon, and Brother Bartholomew."

"Why do you say that?"

"Although the first three killings were all made to look like accidents, this last one was elaborately staged so it would not appear to be an accident. Still, I feel it was done by the same hand as the first three. There is something very sinister afoot here."

"Yes," the abbot said. "I now find myself forced to agree with you. Since the discovery of Brother Vittorio's body, there has been another incident. It may seem minor compared to the death of the prior, and I do not know if it has any significance, yet it appears we cannot locate Brother Domitian."

"Brother Domitian is missing?" Thomas said. "Since when?"

"Since sometime this morning."

"Could the two incidents be related?" Nicholas asked.

"Perhaps." Thomas stroked his hairy chin deep in thought. After a moment he paused with a look of recollection, then asked the abbot, "Before I forget, where is the Judas codex?"

"It is in a very safe place".

"If I find the monk who did these killings, I want the codex," Thomas told him.

"If you find the man who killed our brothers, I will give it to you, but I do not think that is to be."

"Why not?" Thomas asked.

When the abbot did not answer, Nicholas asked, "This last murder was elaborately staged, you say. Why?"

Before Thomas could answer, the abbot said ominously, "Because I do not believe these murders were committed by a man."

The two monks regarded the abbot curiously, as he tapped his lips with his finger in a contemplative pose.

"Brother Thomas, you should have thought of this yourself," the abbot said. "After all, these past many weeks you have been copying John's Revelation—the Apocalypse. I am surprised that that remarkable mind of yours has not hit upon the solution."

"I do not understand to what you refer."

"On the eve of 24 March, we reach the end of the year 999," the abbot explained. "In the months to come, we will enter a new millennium. Revelation speaks of our Lord's thousand year reign after defeating Satan and throwing him into a bottomless pit. Now our Lord's thousand-year reign is nearing its end. It is written that Satan and his evil forces will rise again."

Brother Nicholas crossed himself and said, *"Ora pro nobis!"*

"Are you saying we are at the end of our Lord's thousand-year reign, and the Prince of Darkness is now in our midst?" Thomas asked, not entirely serious.

The abbot picked up on his skepticism, and said, "Scoff if you must, Brother Thomas, yet I am speaking of Holy Scripture."

"I did not mean to offend, my Lord Abbot. Yet, even if we

were to take Revelation literally, this would not occur until the end of our Lord's thousand-year reign, which would not be until the end of the year 1000, not the beginning of 1000."

"Brother Thomas," the abbot said, "I am certain you must have heard of Brother Dionysius, the Roman monk who, in 532, created our current dating system. Perhaps he did not begin counting until the end of the first year after our Saviour's death and resurrection. That would mean the thousand-year reign would end at the beginning of the year 1000."

"It is possible, but very unlikely," said Thomas.

"You are familiar, I am sure, with Revelation. *One who understands can calculate the number of the beast. His number is six hundred and sixty-six.*"

Thomas and Nicholas exchanged confused looks, and the abbot tried to illuminate.

"We are in the year 999," the abbot said, desperately trying to make his point. "By using the Arabic numbering system, which has only lately come to the Holy Roman Empire, if you take the Arabic number 999 and turn it upside down you have 666. We are nearing the end times my brothers! The thousand-year reign is at an end, and the Devil is free! Revelation: *Then I saw an angel come down from heaven, holding in his hand the key to the abyss and a heavy chain. He seized the dragon, the ancient serpent which is the Devil or Satan, and tied it up for a thousand years and threw it into the abyss, which he locked over it and sealed, so that it could no longer lead the nations astray until the thousand years are completed. After this, it is to be released for a short time.*"

Brother Nicholas crossed himself again and uttered, *"Ora pro nobis!"*

"Yet if we are to trust Revelation, Christ will defeat Satan and throw the devil into a lake of fire to suffer eternal torment," Thomas said.

"Yes," the abbot almost hissed. "And then will take place the last judgement when God will resurrect all the people and judge them according to their beliefs and actions. It is the last days, my brothers, the end times, the end of the world!"

The room remained uncomfortably silent. No one dared say anything.

Finally, Thomas said, "What do you propose we do?"

"Our *Cristes maesse* is in three days," the abbot said, speaking nervously, yet with conviction. "Exactly three months from then we will usher in the first day of the new year, and we will hold a special mass at midnight to prepare. Between now and then we must fortify our souls, and strengthen our resolve. We must all make a true and final confession. We must fast and purge ourselves of all sinful deeds and thoughts. The battle that is to come will be mighty, and though we have no doubt that our Lord will be victorious, many may fall before it is over."

Nicholas stepped towards the abbot. The young monk's face was distraught, and his eyes tearful. "I am frightened. I do not know what to do."

"*Vigilate et orate,*" the abbot said. "Watch and pray."

Thomas and Nicholas left the abbot's chamber, and walked in silence for some time—Thomas because he was thinking about what the abbot had said, Nicholas because he was afraid of what the abbot had said.

"What are we to do, Brother Thomas?" Nicholas said, breaking the silence.

Thomas thought a moment. "The abbot's advice was not bad advice, but instead of *vigilate et orate,* I would suggest *ora et labora.*"

"Pray and work?" Nicholas repeated, confused. "What work did you have in mind?"

"The abbot believes the evil perpetrated in the monastery originated *ab extra*—from the outside, yet I believe it is *ab intra*—from within. Our only hope is to find the killer, and it must be soon. The abbot believes something of cataclysmic proportions will happen by the end of this year. I have a feeling that our killer believes it, too, and he very well may be taking steps to see that this monastery is at the centre of it."

"How can we stop him?" Nicholas asked, with simple trust.

Thomas of Worms smiled with pride at his friend. He cupped Nicholas's soft cheeks with both hands. "We must start where this all began."

For the next several days, Thomas and Nicholas questioned their fellow Benedictines concerning Brother Ryan. The only one who appeared to know anything about the dead Celtic monk was Brother Marco, who was elderly and infirm.

"Did you ever speak with Brother Ryan?" Thomas asked him.

"Yes, we spoke. He was from an island called Ireland. He spoke of it often. It sounded like a very miserable place."

"Of what else did he speak?"

"He spoke that he had a fear of high places," Brother Marco responded.

"Of what else did he speak?"

Brother Marco brought up a trembling hand to the side of his head, as if to aid him in his recollection. After a moment he said, "Brother Ryan was a fair scribe. He sometimes spoke of that."

"Brother Ryan was a scribe?" Thomas said, surprised.

"Yes," Nicholas confirmed. "I told you that."

"So you did. I must have had a *lapsus memoriae.*"

"I am certain you had something else on your mind," Nicholas said.

"Did you not also say that while he was here Brother Ryan worked on a manuscript?"

"Yes, that is so. It is in the library."

"Then we shall seek out this book." Thomas turned to Brother Marco and said, "Thank you Brother, you have been most helpful."

It did not take Nicholas long to find the book in question. It was not a large book. Brother Ryan had hand-tooled a leather cover with several designs from his homeland, and in the centre was a Celtic cross. The book itself was a series of studies on early writings by different Christian apologists such as Justin Martyr, Tertullian, Tatian, and Augustine. Thomas of Worms was familiar with some of the writings, yet he decided to read the entire manuscript in hopes of finding a clue Brother Ryan might inadvertently or purposely have left behind. It was not unusual for scribes to leave short notes in the margins or even between lines. By the time he was half-finished, Brother Nicholas had grown weary, then sleepy. Before long, the sound of Thomas's steady, unwavering voice had lulled him to sleep, and he dreamed.

Nicholas's dream was a nightmare. Talk of the Apocalypse had played upon his young mind, which conjured up images of Satan in the guise of a gigantic black serpent. The serpent ravaged the countryside eating the souls of Christians, before it slithered its way to the monastery of St. Benedict, where it scaled the walls and crossed the courtyard.

It came across an unsuspecting Nicholas and chased the young monk through the monastery, snapping at his heels. Terrified to the point of madness, Nicholas ran and ran down the corridors and up the stairs of the tower. He reached the top of the tower panting and whimpering with fright. The awful head of the serpent appeared in the opening and coiled itself on the top of the tower. Nicholas stared at the Satan snake as it reared its head and bared its long, venomous fangs. The serpent's long, forked tongue lashed out like a whip and Nicholas backed away until he found himself up against the wall of the tower. He cast a fearsome glance over the wall and saw the bottomless cliff edge of the mountain below. The serpent's eyes glowed like red coals and it lunged at Nicholas—

"Ha!"

The exclamation roused Nicholas from his sleep. He raised his head from the table and looked about him. His heart pounded, and cold drops of perspiration stood out on his forehead. He tried to clear his mind of the frightening images. He looked up at

Thomas, who sat opposite him with the book open before him.

"What is it?" Nicholas asked of Thomas, who sat there grinning.

"I have just now read the end of Brother Ryan's manuscript," Thomas replied, still smiling. "Listen to what he wrote at the end: *Nunc scripsi totum pro Christo da mihi potum*—Now that I have written so much for Christ, give me a drink."

"That sounds like Brother Ryan," Nicholas noted.

"Indeed," Thomas agreed, but his attention was soon arrested. He turned to the page from which he had just read. He held the book up at different angles to the light as if trying to detect something that lay hidden.

"What are you looking for?" Nicholas asked.

"There appears to be indentations upon the page, as if someone wrote upon it with no ink in their quill."

"Why would anyone do that?"

"The book would have to be checked closely by Brother Bartholomew," Thomas said. "If Brother Ryan wished to add something of his own, he knew the *armarius* would never allow it. So he wrote it in a way that could not easily be detected, yet would remain part of the manuscript."

"How are we to reveal the writing?"

"That is simple enough," Thomas said. He proceeded to obtain some ash and after moistening the page with water, he sprinkled the page with the ash. Carefully, Thomas wiped down the page. The ash adhered to the indentations, and the writing was made clear enough to read. Nicholas listened as Thomas read aloud.

EXTREME CARE MUST BE GIVEN WHEN ONE ACCEPTS SACRED WRITINGS. EVEN THE MOST AUTHENTIC MANUSCRIPTS MUST PASS RIGOROUS SCRUTINY BY NUMEROUS AUTHORITIES AND YEARS OF INTENSE STUDY. MORE THAN ONCE EXPERTS HAVE BEEN DECEIVED BY MANUSCRIPTS

THAT WERE CREATED TO APPEAR AUTHENTIC. IN MY OLD MONASTERY I MADE THE ACQUAINTANCE OF A MONK WHO WAS SO ADEPT AS A SCRIBE HE COULD COPY ANY MANUSCRIPT AND IT WAS VIRTUALLY IMPOSSIBLE TO DISTINGUISH THE COPY FROM THE ORIGINAL.

"What does it mean?" Brother Nicholas asked.

Thomas sat staring down at the page deep in thought. Finally, he said, "I do not believe this is any help to us. That is unfortunate. I was hoping we would find a clue as to why Brother Ryan was murdered."

"What do we do now?"

"Perhaps we are approaching this all wrong," Thomas told Nicholas. "Perhaps we should be trying to see what all the victims—most particularly the first three—had in common."

"What could Brother Ryan have in common with Brothers Bartholomew and Gedeon?" Nicholas asked. "Brother Ryan was younger and did not even come from this monastery. Brother Bartholomew was the *armarius* and Brother Gedeon was the *percamenarius*—what could they have had in common?"

"Books," Thomas said simply. "Brother Ryan had worked as a scribe. That hypothesis is also consistent with the disappearance of Brother Domitian, our missing chancellor."

"Yet Brother Vittorio was the prior. He had nothing to do with books or scribes or parchment. Why was he murdered?"

Thomas thought a moment and said, "Since Brother Vittorio was killed in a more blatant manner than the other three, we cannot place him in the same category as the rest. His death must stand apart, and not be grouped with the others."

"The Christmas celebration is tomorrow," Nicholas said with urgency. "Brother Bagnus has already informed me that the abbot has ordered that the precentor arrange a very special mass for the last night of the year in preparation for the coming of Christ. The end is coming, Brother Thomas!"

"Something is coming," Thomas stated ominously, "but I fear it is not that."

Fourteen

The abbot's announcement of the approaching Last Judgement put many of the monks in a state of near panic. Some of the brothers began all-night vigils, during which they would pray on their knees for hours, going without sleep in anticipation of the Second Coming. Some took to total fasting and subsisted strictly on the word of God, while others took a vow of absolute silence so they might hear God's voice. No one wished to meet his Maker lacking, and so to make up for any spiritual deficiency there was a veritable outbreak of good will. The monastery beheld a plethora of noble deeds, generosity, and kind words, yet beneath it all was an inescapable premonition of impending doom. Some held their breaths as the end of the world drew nigh.

Despite this, the *Missa solemnis* Christmas day was one of the high points of the year. It began with Nicholas singing the *Indroit: Puer natus est nobis, et filius datus est nobis: cuius imperium super humerum eius*—A child is born to us, a son who is given to us, his shoulders shall bear princely power.

Brother Nicholas was in excellent voice. Everyone present seemed captivated by his singing. Brother Bagnus had outdone himself with the arrangements, and Nicholas wondered how the

New Year's mass could possibly surpass it.

After Christmas, tension in the monastery increased day by day. Nicholas spent most of his time rehearsing and preparing for the year-end mass. Brother Bagnus had developed some new and innovative arrangements for Nicholas that both suited his voice and tested his range.

Normally, Thomas felt elated during Christmas. It was a celebration of Christ's birth, an event that bespoke new life, a changed world, and the beginning of a new age. Yet Thomas could not find it in himself to be festive. This holy season had been marred by the mysterious deaths in the monastery, and Thomas's own failure to come any closer to a solution was discouraging. At the eight Divine Offices during the day, Thomas prayed for guidance and illumination into the mystery. When he was not praying, he put all his mental energy into trying to solve the problem. With Nicholas busy preparing for the year-end mass, Thomas was left alone to contemplate the murders.

Whatever the reason for Brother Ryan's murder, Thomas suspected that his death was purposely made to resemble the death of the Benedictine monk who had met his end more than four hundred years ago in this very monastery. Why would anyone do that, he wondered? Suddenly an idea came into his mind. It had to do with Brother Bartholomew's death in the cloister. Thomas began to suspect that Brother Bartholomew had been purposely killed beneath the wood-carved riddle which was the key to the crypt.

Of course! A pattern was forming here. In two instances the locations of the deaths had to do with the newfound manuscripts. In one case it copied a death in the old Benedictine history of the monastery, and in the second case the location of the death had led to the Judas codex.

"What could it mean?" Thomas asked Brother Gregori one day in the scriptorium.

Gregori contemplated the question and said, "One might

consider that events are being enacted for a deliberate purpose."

"Yes," Thomas agreed, "yet for what purpose?"

"I cannot guess," Gregori admitted, "but it sounds simply evil."

"It is strange that you should say that. Brother Nicholas also told me that he believed there was some malevolence at work. He thought it remarkable how the Gnostic monks who once lived in this monastery started out with godly intentions, yet transgressed to a point where some of them conspired to poison Benedict of Nursia. I must confess that I, too, have felt an evil presence here of late."

"The abbot believes it is the work of Satan unbound," Gregori said.

"Yes, his thoughts on the matter have been made known to everyone."

"You do not share the abbot's thoughts?" Gregori asked.

"If Satan is at work in this monastery, he is using a man to do his bidding."

"Why do you say that?"

"Because, my dear Brother Gregori, in every case there are clues that lead me to believe a monk from this very monastery is behind these mysteries. In the case of Brother Gedeon's death, I saw traces that he struggled with and was killed by a man. Brother Vittorio's death bears that out as well. There were marks upon the floor in the scriptorium near the cupboard to the secret room which led me to believe that someone had opened that door before I did, and the marks were fairly recent. When Brother Nicholas and I were lost in the crypt, I was a bit confused finding our way out because I believed we had gone over our own footsteps in the dust, yet I suspect now that there was an extra set of footprints down there, which leads me to conclude that someone had been down there before us."

"So you think someone else was on the trail of those books?"

"Whoever killed Brother Ryan had read that Benedictine

journal; I am certain of it. Things are coming to a climax. I feel I am close to a solution. *De pilo pendet*—it hangs by a hair."

"What of Brother Domitian?" Gregori asked. "Do you think his body will ever be found?"

"What do you mean, his body?"

"I simply meant, what do you think ever happened to him?"

"Brother Gregori, do you believe Brother Domitian's disappearance is part of this affair?"

"It would lead one to suspect so."

"Yes, I, too, had reached that conclusion. Where do you think Brother Domitian is?"

Gregori shook his head. "Only the good Lord knows," he said.

As the year drew to a close, the winter passed without incident. It had been unseasonably mild and everyone longed for spring, as if the Easter season would chase away the evil. The weather seemed to reflect the dark foreboding sensed by the monks. But now, towards the latter half of March, the temperature turned colder, and thunderous clouds hung low and menacing. A wicked wind hammered incessantly on the monastery walls, threatening to beat them down. The wind breached the walls and tore across the courtyard, finding its way into every doorway, every crevice. No room escaped its incursion. Its chilly presence was made known by the awful, eerie sounds it generated. No one felt safe from the looming onslaught.

The last day of the year found the monastery filled with anticipation. By then, all the monks knew of the abbot's thoughts concerning the impending millennium, and most shared his belief of the end times. All were anxious about the midnight mass scheduled for that evening. It would be the most spectacular event of the year, surpassing even Easter. Yet, after midnight, what would the new year bring? some wondered. Would it be a glorious revelation, or the release of unspeakable evil?

CLEAN

FINAL

Thomas did not share in any of these ideas and speculations. A fierce winter storm had forced him inside, and he walked the corridors of the monastery with his head bowed in deep deliberation. He thought of Brother Domitian's mysterious disappearance. The abbot had everyone search the monastery, still there was no trace of Brother Domitian. Thomas concluded that the chancellor was no longer in the monastery—yet where could he have fled? Could Brother Domitian have murdered his fellow monks? After all, Thomas had concluded that the murders were in some way connected with books, and Brother Domitian was the chancellor in charge of the library. Could it have been Brother Domitian who preceded them into the crypt and the secret room in the scriptorium?

Who better than the old chancellor to know there was a secret room in the scriptorium, which had at one time been part of the library? Quicker than he could say *fiat lux,* an idea came into Thomas's mind. The chancellor was still in the monastery. Of this he was almost certain. And if the chancellor was in the monastery, he was hiding. And, if he was hiding well enough to evade a search of the entire monastery, then Thomas knew where he was.

That evening the scriptorium was empty. Preparations were underway for the mass that was soon to take place. Thomas of Worms entered the scriptorium and went to the cupboard at the back of the room. It was difficult for a single person to manipulate the catches, yet he managed to open the door to the room. Thomas pulled the door open slowly, not knowing exactly what to expect.

What he found was the body of Brother Domitian, lying upon the floor. From the marks upon his throat, Thomas could see that he had been strangled.

Thomas knelt by the body, crossed himself, and said a prayer.

That was the last thing he remembered before something struck him on the head from behind.

Brother Nicholas was nervous with anticipation. He had been the soloist at many masses, yet this one was special. He knew it, he could feel it. Even the forces of nature were working towards a crescendo. The fierce storm was building in conjunction with the climactic event. Nicholas could hear a vicious wind as it whistled unceasingly through the monastery. An unnatural coldness crept in and along the floor to chill him beneath his habit. It was close to midnight, and Nicholas needed to speak with Brother Thomas. Nicholas went up to the scriptorium hoping to find him. There was no one in the room, so he went down the hall to the library. The only one in the library was Brother Gregori, who was looking at a book. He looked up at Nicholas's approach.

"Brother Nicholas," he said, in his usual dispassionate manner, "shouldn't you be rehearsing for the big event?"

"Yes," Nicholas said, while glancing about the library. "I stopped by, hoping to find Brother Thomas. He doesn't appear to be about. Have you seen him?"

"No, I cannot say I have."

"I wanted to speak with Brother Thomas before the mass. He is concerned that the murderer may do something drastic when we usher in the new millennium."

"What does Brother Thomas suspect will happen?" Gregori asked.

"He is not certain," Nicholas replied. "I can barely believe all that has happened. Brother Thomas suspects that the murders have something to do with the Judas codex and the other lost books. It is almost too fantastic to believe that it all started when you returned that Benedictine book written on palimpsest pages to the library. Now that I think of it, I am surprised that you did not discover the hidden book yourself."

"I did not even open the book," Gregori said defensively. "I was returning the book for Brother Bartholomew, who did not wish to raise the ire of Brother Domitian."

"Yes, so you said. Speaking of Brother Domitian, what do you believe became of him? Do you suspect he is somehow involved in all this?"

"I truly do not know."

"You are in good company," Nicholas said. "Brother Thomas does not seem to know either."

"You think very highly of Brother Thomas, don't you?" Gregori looked at Nicholas slyly.

"Yes, I do," Nicholas said proudly. "He is the wisest, most learned and astute man I have ever met or am likely to meet."

"He is quite knowledgeable, but I suspect your feelings for Brother Thomas run deeper than that."

Nicholas blushed deeply. He could not bring himself to look at the other, whose cold, penetrating glint unnerved the young monk. Had there always been something about Brother Gregori he feared for some unknown reason? Did Brother Gregori suspect his secret? Nicholas wondered. He tried to change the subject.

"Brother Thomas tells me you are a very learned man yourself," Nicholas said to Gregori. "He said you have studied every sacred writing in all of Christendom."

"Perhaps not all of Christendom."

"Yet, you have been to Alexandria and the islands of Britain. You studied with the Celtic monks in Ireland. Brother Ryan was from—" Nicholas stopped short.

"Brother Ryan was from where?" Gregori prompted.

"Brother Ryan was from Ireland, wasn't he?" Nicholas said, feeling strangely ill.

"What are you implying, Brother Nicholas?" Gregori asked, as thunder broke outside to punctuate his words.

Starting at the sound, Nicholas said, "Nothing. Only that you are a scribe and Brother Ryan was a scribe."

"And how do you know Brother Ryan was a scribe?"

"Brother Thomas and I found one of his books in the library."

Brother Gregori reached into a cupboard close by and brought out a book. "This one?" he said.

Nicholas discovered he could not answer.

"Tell me," Gregori uttered silkily, "has Brother Thomas begun to suspect the Judas codex is a forgery?"

"A forgery!" Nicholas exclaimed. "How could it be a forgery? You authenticated . . ."

As the truth slowly dawned upon Nicholas, he found himself speechless again. For the first time he realized how Brother Thomas must feel when Divine inspiration descended upon him, yet this was not a pleasant experience. Nicholas did not like the malicious intensity in Brother Gregori's eyes. The monk's face seemed to grow dark, and his demeanor became menacing. Nicholas did not realize it, but his whole body had begun to shake. He could not seem to take his eyes off of Brother Gregori's right hand. In it was something that glittered. In his hand, Gregori held a *lunellum,* a knife used by scribes.

As he opened his eyes, Brother Thomas felt an incredible pain throb inside his head. The pain radiated to the other parts of his body. Every movement was nauseating. He stirred and attempted to rise from his prone position. It was an agonizing effort. He moaned and grunted from pain. Only one word managed to escape his lips: "Gregori." He spoke it with a combination of vehemence, frustration, and certitude.

In an instant, thoughts sped through his mind, and Thomas processed them just as quickly. In his mind he saw the note he had found in Brother Ryan's hand, and the note Gregori had slipped to Thomas to meet him atop the tower. Thomas knew Ryan's note had said the same, only it had been written in Celtic runes. In his head he heard Gregori ask if they would ever find Brother Domitian's body, because Gregori knew he was dead. It was Gregori who had confirmed that the Judas codex was authentic. Thomas recalled Gregori's strong grip, and knew it had been those powerful hands that had left the marks on the throats of Brother

Vittorio and Brother Domitian. Of course, it was Gregori who possessed the knowledge and talent necessary to create the Judas codex. He had admitted travelling to Alexandria, where he could have obtained papyrus, and he had studied ancient codices from the area. It was Brother Gregori's skill as a scribe that had been mentioned in the hidden writing of Brother Ryan's text. All these things and more passed through Thomas's mind in a flash, and he cursed himself for not seeing them sooner.

The room in which Thomas found himself now was dark. As he felt around he came across something that he knew was the body of Brother Domitian. Thomas knelt beside the body and said a brief prayer. Once that was done, he began to search for a way out of the secret room. He felt around until he found the door and pushed on it. It did not open. Thomas knew there had to be a catch that would release the door, and he found it near the floor. Thomas stepped upon the catch and pushed the door open.

The physical exertion increased the pain in his head. The scriptorium was dark and empty. An incredible wind whipped through the high windows of the room, while a fierce storm raged outside. Lightning flashed and thunder roared. Thomas could hear hail beating against the walls. He placed his hand tenderly on the back of his head and felt a sizable bump. On unsteady legs, he made his way to the hall. It was deserted. Thomas strained to make his mind work. It was late. Surely the midnight mass must have begun by now. Thomas went to the church.

When Thomas of Worms entered the church, he knew instantly that something was wrong. He did not hear any singing or praying. All the brothers were huddled near the altar. Standing on the altar were Brother Gregori and Brother Nicholas. Some of the brothers parted at Thomas's approach, and he got a better look at the scene. Off to the side, sitting up on the floor with a brother on either side was the abbot, holding his right forearm with his left hand to staunch the blood that flowed from an open wound. Upon the altar Brother Gregori was holding Nicholas in front of him by the hair, with a knife at the young monk's throat. Nicholas had his hands behind his back, and Thomas suspected they were tied.

"Brother Thomas!" Gregori called out. *"Post festum venisti—* you have arrived after the feast. Come. Come, join us. Yet not too close."

As Thomas stepped closer, there was something about Brother Gregori's face that was different and distant. What was it? Thomas wondered. Then he knew: it was evil. It was as if an evil presence had permeated every aspect of Brother Gregori's being: mind, body, and soul. A dark malevolence cast a shadow across Gregori's face. His eyes were hooded by heavy brows, lending them a sinister appearance. His lips were pulled back to expose an evil grin. At times it did not even look like Gregori, and Thomas suspected the monk was in the grip of some unimaginable, sinful wickedness.

"You do not have to do this," Thomas said to Gregori.

"Oh, yet I do," the other responded sardonically. "If only to show you and your brothers for what you all are."

"And what is that?" Thomas asked.

"A pathetic flock of sheep who bleat and baa in unison, and blindly follow where others lead. You are all a bunch of mindless, unimaginative creatures, so deathly afraid to use the mind God gave you. You are content with living out your lives in this purgatorial wasteland."

"Let Brother Nicholas go and we will talk."

"Oh, no," Gregori said, pulling back on Nicholas's hair and placing the knife closer in a threatening gesture. "I want everyone in the monastery—and Brother Nicholas in particular—to know how the great Thomas of Worms was fooled, outsmarted by me. You were going to take the Judas codex to Rome—why didn't you?"

"Because I knew it was a forgery." Thomas said this to throw him off balance. He had not realized the Judas codex was Gregori's forgery until he had awakened, when all the answers had flooded into his mind.

"You are a clever liar, Thomas, but it is still a lie and a sin. You had not a clue that the Judas codex was a forgery—it was perfect."

"Yes, it was." Thomas decided it was pointless to continue his bluff. He thought it best to try another tack. "It must have taken you many years of hard work, done in secret."

"It was a labour of love," Gregori said, smiling wickedly.

"But why?" Thomas asked. "Why go to all the trouble of giving Brother Nicholas the palimpsest pages of the Benedictine manuscript, knowing that he would show it to me, and thus lead to the Gnostic codex, and then to your Judas codex, knowing that I would take it to Rome?"

"*Mundus vult decipi,*" Gregori exclaimed. "The world wants to be deceived, Thomas. You yourself wanted the Judas codex to be genuine, for the same reason I created it, just to see the look on the cardinals' and bishops' faces. To say, you who wear the robes and think yourselves so high and mighty and clever were wrong! To show them for the sanctimonious hypocrites they all are. To stagger a thousand-year-old belief system and to see it totter and reveal it for the fragile thing it is. The Church was built upon a rock, yet it can be brought down with a word."

"And for revenge," Thomas said.

"Revenge?" Gregori said.

"Yes. Revenge for what the church did to your father. For the anathema."

"He was a broken man after that," Gregori spoke with sadness and hate. "His faith was an important part of his life. All his work, his discoveries, were all for the greater glory of God, he believed. He had hoped the Church would appreciate his work, all his efforts. He did not expect them to laud him or honour him, just to acknowledge him and his work. Yet how did the Church show its understanding? Those shortsighted fools proclaimed my father's work heretical and he was cut off from the Church—excommunicated. None of it would have happened if Sylvester II had been pope. He would have appreciated my father's work, but he came to Rome too late.

"It killed my father in the end. I knew someday they would pay for their actions against my father, and if God did not charge them soon enough, then I would exact payment. I am a patient man, I could wait. I planned it very carefully.

"When I found that psalter contained an old Benedictine journal, I first thought of announcing my discovery, but then thought better of it. I used the clues to find the Gnostic codex and again thought what accolades both these discoveries would garner. Perhaps I would be mentioned in the same breath as Thomas of Worms. Perhaps not. I searched for the lost gospel the Gnostic codex referred to, but it did not exist. Then I pondered: what if it did exist? What would it say? What if someone else were to find it? Someone whose reputation preceded him. I began to work on the Judas codex long before you arrived here, Thomas. I had planned it out to the last detail long before. All I needed was for someone like you to find it."

"So for your own vanity and some twisted concept of justice you murdered Brother Ryan, because he knew you in Ireland and saw first-hand a sample of your work and how you could duplicate ancient texts. You enticed him to the tower with a small note on parchment—like the one you gave me—and pushed him down the stairs to resemble the death of the Benedictine brother mentioned in the old manuscript."

"Yes," Gregori admitted. "I thought a touch of irony was in order."

"It was too coincidental. I suspected the death was purposely staged by someone who had read the Benedictine book. Then you murdered Brother Gedeon—why?"

"He was the *percamenarius*. He knew more about parchment than even I did, and he was also an expert on papyrus. It was

Brother Gedeon who told me, innocently of course, how to give parchment and papyrus the appearance of age."

"I meant to compliment you on that detail," Thomas said. "How did you do it?"

"I baked the pages in the oven. I did it early in the morning, yet once or twice Gedeon, on his usual visits to his smelly animals, observed me aging the papyrus pages. I told him I was only doing it to see how they looked. I suspected he did not believe my purpose was that innocent. Before you were to uncover the Judas codex, both Brother Ryan and Brother Gedeon had to be out of the way, or they would suspect the truth."

"And Brother Bartholomew, why did he have to die?"

Gregori smiled that wicked smile that made his face so unfamiliar.

"Brother Bartholomew's death served two purposes. First, he was the *armarius*. Though old, he was vastly experienced with ancient text. He might have discovered the Judas codex was a forgery. Then again, perhaps not. With him out of the way, you would assuredly bring the book to me to authenticate it, which you did. You were so easy to fool, Brother Thomas. You so wanted that book to be genuine."

"So you murdered Brother Bartholomew in the cloister near the entrance to the crypt on the chance that I would solve the riddle on the wood-carving."

"I had to lead you to the crypt," Gregori said. "You might never have found it without my help. I knew, if the body was found there, you would discover the stone that killed him, which would, in all likelihood, lead you to the wood carving, which is the clue to the crypt. I led you around by the nose, Thomas, and you followed where I wished you to go. When I found out you were leaving for Rome without the Judas codex, I had to find a way to get you back."

"And so you murdered Brother Vittorio, and left his body hanging for all to see."

"He was a weasel of a man, always scurrying around and telling the abbot everything. It was Vittorio who followed you on your nightly excursions. Not every time, though—I was keeping an eye on you myself making sure you stayed on the right path."

"It was your light we saw in the scriptorium that night weeks ago," Thomas said. "It was also you who followed us to the scriptorium when we entered the secret room. That is where you were the night Nicholas and I saw the light. That is why we did not pass anyone in the corridor, and why you seemed to disappear so quickly from the room—you never left it. And all the time I suspected it was Brother Lazarus, or Brother Vittorio following us around."

"Sometimes it was Vittorio. Once on his nightly episodes, the prior saw me following you; however, he was not intelligent enough to know why I was doing it. He suspected I was there for the same reason as he, and that I was encroaching upon his duty—the fool. On the morning you were to leave for Rome I was alone in the library, and the prior came in and told me you were leaving without the Judas codex. When he recalled that he had seen me following you, he questioned me about it. It was then I decided what I must do. It was Brother Vittorio, also, who reported to the abbot that you and your young friend here had been spending too much time together. It was he who searched your cot and found the books and turned them over to the abbot. I did not like that man. He was ruining everything."

"And so you killed him," Thomas said, in a detached manner.

"I needed a way to get you back to the monastery," Gregori said, as if it were obvious. "When they discovered the prior dead, I knew they would go after you, and they did. How does it feel, Thomas of Worms, to have been used and outsmarted by someone else?"

Thomas endeavoured to keep his pride in check, for there were greater issues at stake.

"Since first we met, I believed you were very intelligent and resourceful, Brother Gregori."

"Do not patronize me," Gregori said, his face twisting in contempt.

Thomas thought it best not to provoke him, so he asked, "What of Brother Domitian? Why did you kill him and leave him in the secret room in the scriptorium?"

"He saw me kill Brother Vittorio in the library that morning. The old fool. His presence interfered with my plan."

Thomas had to pause and consider the magnitude of the entire affair. He was certain Brother Gregori was in the grip of some unspeakable evil. It had long been a point of contention in the Church whether men were *mala in se*—bad in themselves. Did evil originate *ab extra* or *ab intra?* Was there an outside influence working upon Brother Gregori? The old Benedictine text did refer to some evil presence in the monastery. Could evil be more prevalent in a certain place, and only emerge at certain points in time? Thomas could not say. The only thing he knew for certain was that *nemo malus felix*—no bad man is happy. Thomas would have to be very careful.

"What do we do now?" he asked evenly.

"I want you to admit to everyone present how you were fooled and outwitted, and that in intellect and reason I am your superior."

Thomas felt something rise in his throat, yet he choked it back and said, "I admit that freely. Now release Brother Nicholas."

"Oh, no, not yet," Gregori said, the wicked smile returning. *"Finis coronat opus*—the end crowns the work."

"I do not believe you truly wish to harm Brother Nicholas," Thomas spoke in a soothing tone. "You were the one who saved him from Brother Sebastian in the woods."

"You blind fool, Thomas!" Gregori spat. "I was following our young friend here to see how the two of you were progressing in the game. I did not want anyone to hurt him. It might have taken your mind off the prize. Besides, if I let that pig Sebastian have his way, he would have learned our young friend's secret, and I was not willing to let that happen either."

"What do you mean?" Thomas asked. He suspected that Gregori's mind was wholly deranged, and he encouraged the man's rambling. Thomas needed to keep the man talking as long as possible so he would not harm Brother Nicholas.

"You still do not know, do you?" Gregori chided. "Oh, this is sweet. What an opportunity! I want you to see, Brother Thomas—I want everyone to see—what blind dolts you have been all these years. Tell me, Brother Thomas, did you even know that Nicholas was in love with you?"

Thomas hesitated. He looked uncomfortably about the assemblage. He suspected something highly immoral in Gregori's words. He tried not to let it disturb him and attempted to draw Brother Gregori away from any accusation of perversion on Brother Nicholas's part, lest it cause Nicholas irreparable harm in the eyes of the abbot and every member of the monastery.

"Brother Nicholas and I love each other as brothers in Christ. There is no need to make anything more out of it."

"Oh, yes, there is," Gregori chided. "You never suspected, did you? It was obvious to me the first time I saw Nicholas. Tell me, Thomas, do you believe in *vultus est index animi?*"

"It is very often true," Thomas said. "The expression of one's face is a sign of the soul. That is quite evident before me now."

"Very good," Gregori said, picking up on the other's meaning. "Yet, what of our young friend here?" Gregori caressed the face of his captive with his blade. "What do you deduce from the smooth skin, the bright green eyes, the delicate features? It is quite a comely face, is it not? Have you ever seen such a pretty young man?"

Thomas suspected what Gregori was saying. He was versed well enough in the ways of the world that he had heard of men who had, deep inside themselves, the predilection to behave as women. Though he once or twice suspected Nicholas might possess that tendency, Thomas could not—would not—bring himself to believe it. It was unsettling that Brother Nicholas might have such an unnatural proclivity.

"You still do not know, do you?" Gregori said incredulously, and he posed the *lunellum* threateningly at Nicholas's throat.

"No, Gregori, don't!" Thomas shouted taking a step forward as he feared for Nicholas's life.

With his knife Gregori cut Nicholas's garment at the throat and ripped open his habit, tunic and scapular beneath. The entire assembly gasped. Nicholas cried out and broke into sobs. Thomas stared in disbelief, trying to assimilate the unveiling.

Gregori blurted out a sinister laugh that was accentuated by a clap of thunder. "So, Brother Thomas," he said, "don't you feel foolish?"

Foolish was the last thing Thomas felt, for before him, stripped almost naked with his monk's habit barely hanging from his shoulders was Brother Nicholas. Yet, it was not Brother Nicholas. The body before them was as hairless and unblemished as the face Thomas knew so well. A long thin neck led down from that anguished face to delicate round shoulders, and beneath that, two not overly large yet very round breasts. A flat smooth belly led to a triangular patch of pubic hair, where no male genitals hung. There was nothing masculine about the body at all.

Nicholas continued to sob. Thomas's shock was replaced with pity for the young woman who stood naked in front of him.

"So, Brother Thomas, what do you think of your young monk now?" Gregori mocked. "Did you know she was in love with you? I doubt it. You were too busy displaying your intellect and acting superior."

"Gregori, what are you going to do?" Thomas feared the answer.

"We all came to this mass expecting something to happen," Gregori said menacingly. "I believe something is going to happen. No one appears to know if the new millennium is to usher in

Christ or Satan. I think we should have an old-fashioned sacrifice, and find out which will show up."

Gregori brought the knife up to his captive's throat. The storm raged outside, threatening the integrity of the very walls. Thomas of Worms took another step closer.

Over the wind that beat against the monastery, he shouted, "Gregori, stop!"

A deafening clap of thunder crashed overhead. It was not only heard, but felt, as a tremor ran through the walls and floor. All eyes turned up to the high ceiling above the altar as lightning and wind collapsed the roof, sending stone and timber hurtling down from the ceiling and walls. Screams and cries filled the church. In an instant a terrible crash of stone drowned out the screams. The dust was soon washed away as a heavy rain fell through the hole in the roof.

Thomas had been knocked to the floor and momentarily stunned. He struggled to pull himself free of a wooden support-beam that pinned him. His body ached, and he had suffered several cuts. From all around he heard the moans of the survivors. Thomas stood on trembling legs. Pulling himself free, he found he had lost a sandal, and his habit was torn. He looked around at the carnage and made his way to the altar.

He threw aside stone and timber while calling out hoarsely for Nicholas. Through the rubble Thomas saw a monk's habit, and he dug desperately through the debris. As he threw aside rock and timber to expose the face, he found the cold, dead countenance of Brother Gregori staring up at him. The image was startling, one that would normally inspire compassion, yet such anger gripped Thomas's heart that he felt nothing for the man. Then Thomas was startled. He was certain Gregori was dead, but, if so, why did the body move? It shifted ever so slightly. With great physical effort Thomas pulled the body out of the rubble, and there beneath it lay Nicholas's crushed and injured body.

The rain mixed with the blood and dirt upon her gentle

features. With a compassionate hand Thomas tenderly wiped her face clean. As she moaned softly, he knelt beside her and cradled her head. She had not yet opened her eyes. Thomas spoke to her in gentle, soothing tones.

Over and over she muttered something so weakly that Thomas had to bend his ear to her mouth so he might hear.

"Mea culpa. Mea culpa. Mea culpa. Mea culpa."

"No, no, no," Thomas repeated to her. "You are not to blame. You are not responsible for this. You are not to blame."

Nicholas finally opened her eyes and stared up at Thomas, whose own eyes filled with tears.

"Deus vobiscum," she said tenderly.

"And with you," Thomas managed to say.

"Gloria in Excelsis Deo," she said, and she died.

EPILOGUE

The church was not the only part of the monastery to sustain damage. Due to the intensity of the storm, many of the other buildings had sustained severe wreckage The tower itself had collapsed, and in so doing, fell upon adjoining sections of the monastery. The task to clean up the rubble and rebuild would be monumental. Besides Brother Gregori and Brother Nicholas, six other monks had been killed when the roof had collapsed on the church, which brought the total loss of life since the entire drama had begun to twelve.

Twelve more apostles for Christ, someone commented.

Due to these deaths and the damage to the monastery, many of the surviving monks fled to escape the evil that resided on that mountain. After the disaster, Thomas stayed for two days to help bury the bodies and see that they were properly cared for. The sky was clear and the weather mild. Except for the debris, one could not imagine a storm had only recently wreaked havoc upon the monastery. The sun shone more brightly than it had in many months. The sky held few clouds, and none of them seemed threatening.

Thomas and the abbot stood in the courtyard of the monastery, which should have stood for thousands of years. Neither a building nor a room seemed untouched by the disaster. Though they had never been friends, Thomas and the abbot spoke kindly to each other, as would any two people who had lived together through a horrendous catastrophe.

"You are determined to leave us?" the abbot asked sadly.

"I cannot stay," Thomas responded, equally sad. "I cannot stay after all this . . ."

"Surely the bitterness of death will pass."

"I do not believe it will ever pass. I imagine I shall carry the pain of this until my dying day. I fear my sleep will forever be plagued by these images that have been pressed upon my memory."

"You would be most welcome to stay," the abbot said sincerely. "Many of the brothers have left, and I fear more will leave. A monastery cannot function with so few. What shall we do?"

"Leave this place," Thomas advised. "Begin anew. Choose a town or a hamlet where people are in need of spiritual guidance. Minister to the people. It is what our Saviour would want."

"And what of you, Brother Thomas, what will you do?"

"I will go to Rome. I will let them know what happened here."

"And then what?"

Thomas paused and looked about. "I believe I will devote the remainder of my life to a scholastic and philosophical study that can prove the doctrines of faith by reason."

The abbot rolled his eyes and shook his head. "You are a stubborn man, Brother Thomas."

"Some have said so," he responded.

"Only the good Lord knows what you may come up with."

The two men chuckled.

"Before you leave I shall give you a letter so you shall be graciously received," the abbot said, to which Thomas nodded thankfully.

A sober look came over the abbot's face. "Why do you believe he did it?" he asked Thomas.

"Brother Gregori, you mean? It was obvious he was bitter over his father's anathema. When Gregori joined the order, he might have had good intentions, yet he still held onto old resentments. The entire conception of the Judas codex might have started only as a theory, yet it grew into an idea that festered until he had to put it to the test."

"Surely the devil guided poor Brother Gregori's hand," the abbot stated.

"As he guided my own," Thomas admitted. "It is because I was blinded by ambition and my own secret desire for notoriety that I fell into the pit Gregori dug. I blame myself as much as Gregori."

"Yet, it was the devil, my son," the abbot said, attempting to ease Thomas's guilt.

"Then Gregori and I both should have been more vigilant, more mindful of Satan's traps. If we had, Brother Nicholas would still be alive. I shall always carry the guilt of her death upon my conscience."

After a moment the abbot said, "I do not believe I shall ever understand the mind of Brother Nicholas. If she wished to join an order, why not simply join a convent? Why disguise herself as a man?"

A cool breeze had picked up, and Thomas was forced to bring his cowl upon his head.

"She tried to explain it to me once," he said, "when we were alone in the crypt. I took it for something else, yet now it makes some sense. As a child, she was abused by her father. She did not have the strength, physically or emotionally, to fend him off. She believed if she were stronger, like a man, she could avoid such abuse. For her own protection, I believe, she imagined herself as a man, and as a man she entered this monastery. I was so blind I could not see what she was trying to say. She desperately wanted to tell me the truth, but I did not let her. I had the power to help her, yet I could not."

"Do not rebuke yourself too harshly, Brother Thomas. She came to me a short time ago and confided to me that she possessed emotional feelings for you. I believed these feelings were immoral and corrupt. I told her to stay away from you. That is when I also told you to stay away from Brother Nicholas."

"She came to both of us for help, and we denied her," Thomas spoke weakly. "How are we to live with that?"

"By admitting that we are not perfect, as much as we wish we were. We are human beings, Brother Thomas, created imperfect by a perfect God. We should not question His plan."

Thus ended the Benedictine presence in the mountaintop monastery in northern Italy. When the monks finally deserted the monastery, it slowly fell into disrepair. Though the building remained a recognizable structure, it finally met its end in the Second World War when an Allied air corps accidentally bombed the old monastery in 1945. No historical evidence exists that anyone else occupied the structure after the Benedictine monks abandoned it early in the year 1000. For centuries the ruins were shunned like a place accursed. And if evil does exist in this world, and can be confined to a specific location, then it might very well be found on that isolated mountaintop that has witnessed so much human death and suffering.

Author's Note

This book was inspired in part from another book. It was a book my wife bought me (God bless her), which traced the history of the Bible through the ages, from oral tradition to the time it was developed as a written text and evolved to what we have today. One night while reading the book, I turned the page and was instantly struck by two illuminations from late medieval manuscripts, each showing a group of black-robed monks with tonsures. One page not only proclaimed that these monks were guardians of the Scriptures, but went on to describe life in medieval monasteries. With my eyes fixed on the page I said aloud (my wife was beside me, but even if she hadn't been, I still would have spoken the words.), "This would be a good setting for a mystery story."

This story is, of course, a work of fiction, though much research was conducted prior to writing the first word. The historical elements and customs of the Benedictine order are true to my research, but the monastery itself—the Monastery of St. Benedict—and the characters in the monastery are fictitious. Though the *argumentum* has its roots in historical fact, I could not say if it was ever employed in a Benedictine monastery. The

Gnostic, Brother Alamar, and the Benedictines who encounter him are also fictitious. The customs and beliefs of the Gnostics are as accurate as I can discover.

I have endeavoured to be faithful to all historical figures I mention in the story. The details of Benedict of Nursia's life are either historical fact or based on legend, such as the attempt on his life in a northern monastery in Italy. The historical figures that I quote and mention, such as Tertullian, Augustine of Hippo, and Simeon the Elder, were true-to-life people.

The ancient texts that play a large part in the story, such as the Judas codex, the Gnostic codex and the Benedictine journal are works of fiction, but other ancient texts, such as the Book of Kells and the Lindisfarne Gospels are real. The manner in which books were made and written is portrayed as accurately as could be.

Though the monastery in the book was fictional, in the last paragraph I referred to the destruction of the monastery as a parallel to the bombing of Monte Cassino during World War II.